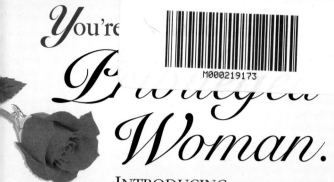

You're a *Privileged Woman.*

INTRODUCING
PAGES & PRIVILEGES™.

It's our way of thanking you for buying
our books at your favorite retail store.

— *GET ALL THIS FREE* —
WITH JUST ONE PROOF OF PURCHASE:

◆ Hotel Discounts up to 60% at home and abroad

◆ Travel Service - Guaranteed lowest published
airfares plus 5% cash back on tickets

◆ $25 Travel Voucher

◆ Sensuous Petite Parfumerie collection ($50 value)

◆ Insider Tips Letter with sneak previews of
upcoming books

◆ Mystery Gift (if you enroll before 6/15/95)

*You'll get a FREE personal card, too.
It's your passport to all these benefits– and to
even more great gifts & benefits to come!*
There's no club to join. No purchase commitment. No obligation.

As a Privileged Woman,
you'll be entitled to all these Free Benefits.
And Free Gifts, too.

To thank you for buying our books, we've designed an exclusive FREE program called *PAGES & PRIVILEGES*™. You can enroll with just one Proof of Purchase, and get the kind of luxuries that, until now, you could only read about.

BIG HOTEL DISCOUNTS

A privileged woman stays in the finest hotels. And so can you—at up to 60% off! Imagine standing in a hotel check-in line and watching as the guest in front of you pays $150 for the same room that's only costing you $60. Your *Pages & Privileges* discounts are good at Sheraton, Marriott, Best Western, Hyatt and thousands of other fine hotels all over the U.S., Canada and Europe.

FREE DISCOUNT TRAVEL SERVICE

A privileged woman is always jetting to romantic places. When you fly, just make one phone call for the lowest published airfare at time of booking—or double the difference back! PLUS

you'll get a $25 voucher to use the first time you book a flight AND 5% cash back on every ticket you buy thereafter through the travel service!

FREE GIFTS!

A privileged woman is always getting wonderful gifts.
Luxuriate in rich fragrances that will stir your senses (and his). This gift-boxed assortment of fine perfumes includes three popular scents, each in a beautiful designer bottle. <u>Truly Lace</u>...This luxurious fragrance unveils your sensuous side. <u>L'Effleur</u>...discover the romance of the Victorian era with this soft floral. <u>Muguet des bois</u>...a single note floral of singular beauty. This $50 value is yours—FREE when you enroll in *Pages & Privileges*! And it's just the beginning of the gifts and benefits that will be coming your way!

FREE INSIDER TIPS LETTER

A privileged woman is always informed. And you'll be, too, with our free letter full of fascinating information and sneak previews of upcoming books.

MORE GREAT GIFTS & BENEFITS TO COME

A privileged woman always has a lot to look forward to.
And so will you. You get all these wonderful FREE gifts and benefits now with only one purchase...and there are no additional purchases required. However, each additional retail purchase of Harlequin and Silhouette books brings you a step closer to even more great FREE benefits like half-price movie tickets...and even more FREE gifts like these beautiful fragrance gift baskets:

L'Effleur ...This basketful of romance lets you discover L'Effleur from head to toe, heart to home.

Truly Lace ...A basket spun with the sensuous luxuries of Truly Lace, including Dusting Powder in a reusable satin and lace covered box.

ENROLL NOW!
Complete the Enrollment Form on the back of this card and become a Privileged Woman today!

Enroll Today in *PAGES & PRIVILEGES*™, the program that gives you Great Gifts and Benefits with just one purchase!

Enrollment Form

☐ *Yes!* I WANT TO BE A *PRIVILEGED WOMAN.*

Enclosed is one *PAGES & PRIVILEGES*™ Proof of Purchase from any Harlequin or Silhouette book currently for sale in stores (Proofs of Purchase are found on the back pages of books) and the store cash register receipt. Please enroll me in *PAGES & PRIVILEGES*™. Send my Welcome Kit and FREE Gifts -- and activate my FREE benefits -- immediately.

_____

NAME (please print)

_____

ADDRESS   **APT. NO**

_____

CITY   **STATE**   **ZIP/POSTAL CODE**

PROOF OF PURCHASE   *SAMPLE ONLY*

Please allow 6-8 weeks for delivery. Quantities are limited. We reserve the right to substitute items. Enroll before October 31, 1995 and receive one full year of benefits.

**NO CLUB!
NO COMMITMENT!**
*Just one purchase brings you great **Free Gifts** and **Benefits**!*
(See inside for details.)

Name of store where this book was purchased_____

Date of purchase_____

Type of store:

☐ Bookstore ☐ Supermarket ☐ Drugstore

☐ Dept. or discount store (e.g. K-Mart or Walmart)

☐ Other (specify)_____

Which Harlequin or Silhouette series do you usually read?

_____

Complete and mail with one Proof of Purchase and store receipt to:

U.S.: *PAGES & PRIVILEGES*™, P.O. Box 1960, Danbury, CT 06813-1960

Canada: *PAGES & PRIVILEGES*™, 49-6A The Donway West, P.O. 813, North York, ON M3C 2E8   PRINTED IN U.S.A

"I warned you they would say things."

Kyle laughed harshly, then continued, "So what exactly is it you want me to tell you? Do you want me to confirm that I'm a murderer?"

"No!" Hallie cried. "I don't believe that! It's just—"

He looked at her and shook his head. "They've really done a number on you, haven't they? A little word here, a little word there. Spread their poison...and it worked!"

"That's not true!"

"What is it, then?"

"It's you," she finally whispered.

"I'm the same person I've always been, Hallie. I haven't changed." Left unspoken was the question: Have *you*?

Hallie held his gaze for only a moment before looking away. She couldn't answer him.

ABOUT THE AUTHOR

Ginger Chambers claims that one of the joys of writing is deciding where to set her stories. In *Father Takes a Wife*, Ginger chose to revisit, in spirit, her uncle Robbie's ranch in central Texas, where "a wonderfully fat pinto horse named Tony was always ready to set off on adventures with a wide-eyed child of the city. And where mornings broke to the smell of fresh coffee, homemade biscuits and good-natured laughter."

Although *Father Takes a Wife* is only the second book Ginger has written for Superromance, this talented author has long been a favorite with readers of American Romance novels and the Tyler series.

Ginger Chambers
Father Takes a Wife

Harlequin Books

TORONTO • NEW YORK • LONDON
AMSTERDAM • PARIS • SYDNEY • HAMBURG
STOCKHOLM • ATHENS • TOKYO • MILAN
MADRID • WARSAW • BUDAPEST • AUCKLAND

ISBN 0-373-70647-2

FATHER TAKES A WIFE

Father Takes a Wife

CHAPTER ONE

THE COUPLE WAITING on the front porch of the isolated two-story farm house looked as harsh and forbidding as the bleak winter landscape. Their shoulders set, their faces carved as if from stone, they might have been two soldiers stationed in grim defense of a vital position.

Remnants of a recent rainstorm dripped from the naked branches of an overhanging tree onto the porch roof and from there to the saturated ground. A chill wind swooped from the north, rattling a window shutter and shaking the car.

Hallie couldn't help it—she shivered, though the car's interior remained unnaturally warm. Kyle had warned her of what to expect, but that didn't make the moment easier. She glanced at the man by her side.

Without her saying a word he turned to look at her, and the familiar tingling sensation started to spread. It had been like this since their first encounter. All it took was the slightest touch of his pale green eyes, and every nerve ending in her body became inflamed.

"Are you all right?" he asked. His voice was low, naturally husky.

Hallie gave a short nod.

The leather seat creaked as he leaned closer. The crowded quarters and his bulky coat of rough suede made movement difficult, but still he reached over and caressed her cheek.

He looked so handsome—his thick reddish brown hair almost the same deep shade of rust as his coat, worn a little long but always well-groomed; his features, freckled beneath his tan, sensitively drawn yet alive with the devil-may-care virility known to millions of television news viewers around the world.

"You look like a frightened puppy," he murmured, smiling slightly. "Maybe we should have waited a little longer before coming here."

Hallie captured his hand and pressed it to her lips. "No," she said. "You shouldn't have to wait. If Sharon wants to be with you, that's all that matters."

He glanced toward the people on the porch, then back at her. "This isn't going to be easy," he warned again.

"I know."

His smile deepened. "I certainly knew what I was doing when I found you."

"I found you, remember?" Memories of the day they first met would be forever etched on Hallie's heart. How, on one of his flights into Atlanta, his luggage had gone missing and he'd come to the VIP lounge to ask assistance. And how, when the receptionist helping him was called away on other business, Hallie—new in the position—had been pressed into service. She had found the luggage, then she'd found Kyle.

Their gazes held, and Kyle slowly kissed each of her curled fingers before opening the door to step outside. As he came around the car, Hallie snuggled more deeply into her coat, doing her best to prepare herself for the wind's icy blast, as well as the coming ordeal. Six months ago she never would have imagined herself in such a situation. Or even married. But that was before Kyle. *Before Kyle...after Kyle.* His coming into her life had changed everything.

The door swung open and she accepted her husband's offer of help getting out. Kyle's hand was warm and reassuring as they started up the path. He led the way, slightly ahead of her, his head high, his walk confident. When they stopped in front the porch steps, Hallie chanced a closer look at the white-haired couple.

The man was in his late sixties, his whipcord body encased in a well-worn cattleman's coat. Leathery skin, tanned to a dark mahogany, stretched tightly over the strong bones of his face. His eyes, pale blue chips of ice, stared from beneath jutting brows.

The woman at his side, also in her late sixties, was an inch or two shorter than her husband and made up in poundage all that he lacked. Outlined by a faded blue jacket, comfortably padded hips swelled below an ample waist and breasts. Her blue gray eyes met Hallie's, and Hallie had a hard time not shrinking from their anger.

''McKenna,'' the man said. The clipped greeting might have been a curse.

"Timothy...Florence." Kyle seemed not the least bit intimidated by their hostility. He squeezed Hallie's hand and lifted it. "This is my wife, Hallie."

Both gazes fixed on her. Hallie tried to smile, but found it impossible.

Kyle planted a foot on the first step. "We've come for Sharon," he said.

Almost faster than Hallie could follow, Timothy Lang leapt forward, striking quickly and silently.

Kyle staggered back, struggling to keep his balance. Of necessity, his and Hallie's hands broke apart.

Timothy pressed his advantage, following Kyle into the yard, ready to strike another blow. But this time the younger man prevented it by grabbing hold of his wrist, an action that added to Timothy's fury.

"If you think...you can just waltz in here...and take Sharon—I'll see you dead first, McKenna!"

Florence rushed to her husband's side. "Timothy! Don't!" she cried, tugging on his arm.

"Leave Kyle alone!" Hallie shouted. Breaking free of her initial shock, she, too, went to stand near her husband.

Timothy ignored them. "If you try it, I promise, I'll personally—"

"Sharon is *my* daughter, Timothy, not yours," Kyle cut him off. "She wants to live with *me!*"

"Only after you messed with her mind! It was the same way with Cynthia. One day she was happy and fine with us, then you came along and filled her head with—"

The screen door swung open and a young girl stepped out of the house. She was as beautiful as the picture Hallie had been shown, with the promise of more beauty to come. On the cusp of womanhood, with straight dark hair falling in a thick curtain past her shoulders, her skin flawless and creamy, she had the same pale green eyes as her father. She questioned softly, "Daddy? Granddad?" Uncertainty trembled in her voice.

Tension drained from the two men as she looked from one to the other. Kyle let go of Timothy's wrist and Timothy retreated a step, flexing his shoulders.

Florence hurried back onto the porch to place a protective arm about her granddaughter.

The girl slipped away and ran to her father. Hugging him tightly, she cried, "Oh, Daddy, I was waiting for you!"

"I came as soon as I could, sweetheart." Kyle held his daughter close. On tiptoe, her head reached his shoulder.

Both grandparents witnessed the scene with distaste.

Pulling back, Kyle smiled down at the girl. "There's someone I want you to meet," he said. He motioned for Hallie to come closer. "Sharon, this is Hallie...my new wife. I hope the two of you can be friends."

There was no spark of welcome in the young girl's gaze. Nothing changed in her face as she took in Hallie's neat, well-groomed appearance, her short, blond hair and her hand extended in friendship. The greeting was over in a second.

Sharon's attention immediately returned to her father. "We waited dinner for you," she said, tugging him toward the porch. "Gran made her special roast chicken and a blackberry cobbler for dessert. She used some of the berries we picked last fall. There were so many, we..." If the girl was aware of any lingering animosity between the adults, she gave no sign of it as she guided her father into the house. Her words became fainter as the screen door closed behind them.

Timothy and Florence exchanged a brief glance before looking again at Hallie. Hallie's legs felt like wooden sticks, as did her spine. She didn't know what to say, what to do. Kyle appeared in the doorway and motioned her inside. She felt the Langs' eyes on her as she followed his direction. They trailed silently behind.

The interior of the house was surprising in its warmth and welcoming comfort. A fire burned in a stone-fronted fireplace in the living room, where an overstuffed couch and several chairs were clustered. A brass lamp sat on a highly polished end table that was protected by a white crocheted doily, and a brightly colored quilt hung over the arm of one chair. The look and feel was in stark contrast to the hostility of the owners.

"Sharon," Florence said once they were all inside, "see if your father and his wife would like to wash up before dinner."

"We've put you in the big room down the hall from mine, Daddy."

"We hadn't planned to stay here," Kyle said, resisting.

Florence harrumphed. "I'd like to know where else you thought you'd stay. You know there's not a hotel or motel for miles."

"We don't mind a long drive. In fact, we'd rather—"

"The arrangement was for a week, McKenna," Timothy butted in. "Are you trying to back out of it? Afraid she might change her mind?"

Kyle stiffened. "No!"

"Then it's here you stay. I'd rather know where a skunk is than have to hunt him down!"

"Timothy!" Florence reproved.

"Dinner will be served in fifteen minutes," Timothy continued, undeterred. "If you and your... *wife* aren't here, we'll start without you. We've already wasted enough time waiting for you today."

"We'll be here," Kyle pledged through tightly held lips.

THE ROOM Sharon led them to smelled of potpourri and furniture wax. A candlewick bedspread graced an antique double bed, the sheer white curtains looked freshly laundered, and an old-fashioned rag rug peeked from beneath the bed and covered a gleaming hardwood floor.

"Gran spent a lot of time getting the place ready," Sharon confided. "She was supposed to be in Houston at some kind of big quilting meet, but she changed her plans when she heard you were coming."

"Another mark against my name," Kyle murmured.

The girl bounced on the bed, then leaned back on her braced arms to look at her father. "Granddad's really upset. Gran says he's going to have a stroke if he isn't careful." She paused to consider. "I am going to come live with you, aren't I, Daddy? It's for sure?"

"If you still want to," Kyle said.

A smile broke over the young girl's features. "Of course I still want to!" she exclaimed, and jumped from the bed to wrap her arms around her father's waist. "I've wanted to come live with you forever and ever!" She looked up at him with glowing eyes.

Kyle swallowed, clearing his throat, and smoothed dark strands of hair away from her face. "I'd better get our luggage. Fifteen minutes isn't very long." He glanced at Hallie. "Why don't the two of you get to know each other while I run down to the car?"

Hallie, who'd been feeling decidedly out of place, nodded.

Silence followed his departure. Hallie noted how Sharon's gaze had clung to her father's back and how, for several fleeting seconds, her face had revealed a child's desperate need for a parent's love. It was a look Hallie was intimately familiar with.

She removed her coat, attracting the girl's attention. "Your father showed me a photograph of you with a horse. Is it yours?" She spoke as warmly as she could, hoping to find common ground.

"He never showed me a photo of you." Sharon's tone remained distant.

Hallie laughed. "I'm not sure he even has one."

"That's silly!"

"I don't have one of him, either."

"*I* do! It was my mother's. They loved each other an awful lot!"

"I'm sure they did."

"An *awful* lot! Enough to run off together and get married. I have a letter my mother wrote to my grandma and granddad, telling them what they planned. They don't know I have it, but I do."

In the silence that followed, Hallie searched for something to say. But Sharon removed the necessity when she announced, "I'm going downstairs," and quickly followed through.

Hallie was sitting on the edge of the bed, staring blankly at the wall, when Kyle returned. "Sharon's gone?" he asked.

"I don't think she likes me very much."

"Nonsense. She doesn't know you."

"I don't think any of them like me."

"I told you the Langs wouldn't."

Hallie looked down at her hands. "Yes, you did," she agreed softly.

He set the suitcases beside the bed, shrugged out of his coat and dropped it on top of them, then he came to stand in front of her. Tipping up her chin, he said quietly, "*I* like you."

All the love Hallie felt was there for him to see. She'd never met anyone like him. Forceful, dynamic, intense, fascinating, seductive, loving, sensitive... He hadn't so much come into her life as swept into it. Changing her, changing everything.

He leaned close and took her lips in a kiss that left her breathless. At its end her arms were clasped about his neck and he'd balanced one knee on the bed. He needed only to push forward a little more for them to be lying together on the mattress.

"I think..." he said, his mouth slanting into a smile, "I think maybe we shouldn't get started with this."

Hallie let her fingers play in his hair, enjoying the full license she had to do so and knowing that if she wanted, she could do even more. "Why not?" she whispered, teasing him.

"Because five minutes isn't nearly long enough. And five minutes is all we have."

"Long enough for what?" she teased again. She traced the outline of his ear with the tip of her tongue.

His powerful body shuddered, but he pulled back, drawing her with him to her feet. After smoothing her short hair and adjusting her collar, he bantered in return, "Long enough to *eat* you." Still, his fingers paused to caress her delicate jawline, and the hungry look in his eyes told her that under other circumstances they would forgo dinner.

She smiled as he moved quickly away from her.

"I'd like to wash up," she murmured.

"The bathroom's down the hall. First door on the left."

His answer came from a casual familiarity with the house, a familiarity born during his marriage to Cynthia. Hallie turned away. Reminders of Cynthia were never easy for her.

She started to leave the room, but Kyle stopped her at the door.

"Hallie," he said quietly, looking unusually serious, "I don't want you to be hurt by anything that happens here."

"I won't be."

He wouldn't accept her glib answer. "Their hatred runs deep. They can't forgive me for what happened to Cynthia."

Hallie lifted her chin. "All the more reason to get Sharon away from them. Unreasonable people aren't fit to raise a child. The child suffers."

"Something you know about firsthand," he murmured. "Go ahead. Wash up. I'll wait for you. Just . . . don't believe everything you hear."

Kyle McKenna was a man respected the world over for his bravery under fire, who filed reports from some of the most dangerous hot spots on earth—places where savagery was the norm and even the slightest spark of kindness was looked upon with suspicion. A man whose body was scarred with the wounds he'd received while doing his job. For him to show so openly that his love for her could make him vulnerable filled Hallie with wonder.

"You've told me that before," she said softly, offering a smile she hoped would allay his concern. "Don't worry. Nothing they say or do can ever change the way I feel about you. I love you."

A silence followed her simple statement. Then he, too, smiled. "Come here," he urged her huskily, holding out a hand.

"But we'll be late," she protested.

"This will only take a second."

"What?" she asked, moving closer. Her heart beat faster as she again responded to the force of his masculinity.

"This," he murmured, pulling her to him.

The kiss was short if measured by the actual passage of time, but so sweet and so profound that it wrapped her in a lingering glow.

CHAPTER TWO

THE PROMISED MEAL was a nightmare of tension. Timothy commanded the seat at the head of the dining room table, with his wife to his right. Hallie sat on his left, while Kyle sat next to her and across from Sharon. None of them did more than push the food around on their plates and wait for the ordeal to be over.

Finally Sharon touched her napkin to her lips and offered, "Candy's grown so much since you were here last, Daddy. Would you like to come see her? She's almost sixteen hands now. Can you believe it? And she's so smart!" Her eyes pleaded with her father to accompany her.

Kyle glanced at Hallie, reluctant to leave her alone with the Langs. "Would you like to come with us?" he asked.

Before Hallie could answer Sharon said, "Just you, Daddy. Please? Just you?"

"Go ahead," Hallie murmured. "I—I'll help Florence with the dishes."

"Are you sure?" Kyle seemed prepared to overrule his daughter's request.

"Of course."

Sharon grinned triumphantly as she escorted her father from the room.

Disapproval was a continuing reality as Hallie started to gather the used dessert plates. She felt the Langs' eyes follow her every move as she stacked first one dish, then another. Finally Florence stood up and snatched them away from her.

"I'll take these," the older woman said gruffly, almost jealously.

Startled by her action, Hallie froze. "But I'd like to help. Please—"

"You've *helped* all you're going to, missy," Timothy said, also rising.

"But—" Hallie tried again.

Florence thumped the plates back onto the table, disregarding the clatter. "All right!" she said, her face tight with anger. "If you insist on doing something to help us, why don't you get Kyle to see that what he's doing here is *wrong!* Sharon belongs on the farm with us, not in some godforsaken place on the other side of the globe with bullets and bombs and..." She choked on the last word.

"But we live in Atlanta!" Hallie objected. "We've just bought a house there!"

"And how long do you think that's going to last?" Florence demanded, recovering quickly. "That man can't stay still. He gets 'restless'—that's his word!"

"Kyle's job is in the city now," Hallie said defending him. "At the network. He's not going to work in the field anymore. There won't be any more bombs or bullets or—"

"If you believe that, you'll believe anything!" Timothy jeered.

Florence braced her hands on the table and leaned closer. "If you're smart, you'll get away from him before you end up like our Cynthia."

As prepared as she was for their deep dislike of Kyle, Hallie was still shocked by the intimation. "What happened to your daughter was an accident!" she cried.

Timothy snorted. "He's told you that, too, has he? Well, I wouldn't be so sure of that, either. Kyle McKenna will tell a woman anything if he thinks it will get him what he wants. He's no good. Never has been, never will be."

Hallie's heart hammered in her ears, her body demanded that she flee, but she remained steadfastly in place. "I know what you're trying to do, and it's not going to work. Kyle is one of the finest, most admirable people I know."

"He's a murderer!" Timothy snarled.

"That's not true!"

"Then why is our daughter dead?"

That question was impossible to answer.

Timothy continued, "We see him on TV all the time—such a big hero. But we know better. We know him for what he really is."

"You're wrong!" Hallie shook her head. This unrestrained display of hatred was beginning to unnerve her. Tears were dangerously close to falling, but she wasn't about to give this pair the satisfaction of seeing her cry.

Florence straightened. "How long have you known him?" she demanded.

"Long enough!" Hallie shot back.

"He's using you. Using you to get Sharon. Once he has her, he won't need you anymore. You'll find yourself completely out of the picture. Alone. Forgotten. He's only taking Sharon to hurt us. He doesn't love her any more than he loved our Cynthia. The man's incapable of loving anyone. Including you. We *know* what we're talking about."

"You hate him! You'll say anything!"

"You're darned right we hate him!" Timothy exploded. "And with good reason!"

Florence suddenly looked very tired. She placed a hand on her husband's arm and shook her head. "It's not going to do any good, Timothy. She won't listen."

"For the sake of the girl if for no one else..." Moisture glistened in the old man's blue eyes.

"No. *No!*" Hallie repeated more strongly. These people would do anything to keep custody of their granddaughter! "I won't listen, and I won't help you. Sharon should be with her father!"

The vehemence of her denial brought the encounter to an end. Timothy turned his face away, Florence looked down at the table, and Hallie at last escaped from the room, hurrying to the only sanctuary in the house that she knew.

KYLE ENTERED the bedroom just as Hallie finished unpacking. After what she'd been through downstairs, she found that she couldn't sit still. She'd unpacked their things, putting them in closets and drawers and all the while thinking about what had happened. When Kyle had warned her that the Langs hated him, she'd thought he was exaggerating. Now she knew it to be an understatement. She was just closing the fastenings on the last empty case when she looked up to see him. His expression was thunderous.

"Florence and Timothy want to meet with us after Sharon goes to bed tonight. They want to see proof that we're married."

"Kyle, couldn't we just take her? Call the police if we have to and have them come help us?"

Kyle laughed shortly. "Timothy and the sheriff out here are like brothers. They grew up together. Since the agreement our lawyers worked out says we have to wait a week after giving personal notification, we have to wait. No one's going to lift a finger to make the situation easier for us. Particularly the sheriff."

"So we'll have to stay?"

"I'm afraid so."

His green eyes moved over her, and noting the way she stood—her body tense, her arms hugging each other protectively—he allowed his expression to soften. "This is a lot to ask of a new wife, isn't it? We're barely back from our honeymoon and I spring this on you. It isn't what I planned." He came to stand next to her and, pulling her close, wrapped his arms about her delicate frame as he nuzzled her fine golden hair with his cheek.

Hallie relaxed against him, surrendering herself to his strength. She felt so safe when she was with him. "You couldn't help it," she whispered huskily.

She felt his deep sigh. "No," he agreed. "But to bring you here, expose you to all this..."

Hallie hesitated, then said, "They think you killed Cynthia on purpose."

He broke contact, moving to stand at the window that overlooked the yard at the rear of the house. A windmill stood just inside the low picket fence, a cistern nearby. Outbuildings of various sizes, shapes and purposes were scattered on the land beyond, as well as, incongruously, a satellite dish. Hallie knew the view laid out before him because she'd spent time at that window herself earlier.

"It's ludicrous, of course," she hurried on when he continued to stare broodingly outside. "There's no way that you could... that you would... I told them they were wrong. That what happened to Cynthia was an accident. How could they blame you? You were almost killed, too!" She hurried over to bury her face against his back, hugging Kyle, willing him to reject the hold she sometimes sensed Cynthia still had on him. "If you had died, I don't know what would have become of me! Or if any of the other times you've been hurt on your job were more serious. You aren't going to change your mind and go back to field reporting, are you? You won't get bored with me? With our life together?"

Kyle turned to face her, his finely cut features angry. "They said that to you? Damn them! But I should have known. I shouldn't have left you alone with them!"

"I'm not trying to hold you back, you know that," Hallie continued. Once the dam had burst, she couldn't contain her worry. "It's just...I couldn't stand the thought of you being shot again, or stepping on a mine, or—"

Kyle gripped her shoulders. "I've told you I want a change, haven't I? I mean it. I've had enough! I want to settle down. Make a home for you, for Sharon."

Hallie kept her chin low as she tried to wipe the tears from her eyes. She didn't want Kyle to see evidence of her weakness any more than she'd wanted the Langs to, but for a very different reason.

"Look at me," he commanded.

She slowly lifted her gaze. Her light brown eyes were large and round and flecked with tiny streaks of gold. With her eyes damp with tears, the golden streaks were greatly intensified.

"You have the most amazing eyes," he said, then took a deep breath. "Hallie, this is going to be a week like none you've ever spent before. No holds will be barred. I tried to warn you before we got here, but I suppose you had to see it for yourself. Cynthia was their darling daughter. To them, she could do no wrong. It didn't matter that she treated them like dirt." He broke off, shaking his head. "All we should be doing right now is focusing on the future. We're going to take Sharon back to Atlanta, make a good life for ourselves and be happy. That's the vision we have to hold on to. It's what we both want, isn't it?"

"More than anything," Hallie whispered. She wanted whatever he wanted. She loved him that much.

Kyle released her shoulders, and for the first time since he'd come into the room he smiled. "She's quite a girl, isn't she?"

"She looks like you."

"She has her mother's coloring—the same dark hair."

"But your eyes, your mouth, your chin."

"I can't believe she's almost fourteen."

"She was six when Cynthia died?"

"Six years, two weeks and three days."

"And she's lived here ever since?"

"In the beginning there was nowhere else for her to go! I couldn't—"

"Of course not!" Hallie interrupted him. She didn't want him to think that she was in any way criticizing an action he'd taken in the past. "You'd have been crazy to have brought her with you. No, what I meant was, if she's lived here for most of her life, don't you think she's going to miss it, miss her grandparents?" She hurried on as his frown deepened, "I know she says she wants to come live with us, but do you think she's...ready?"

"The longer she stays here, the longer she's exposed to her grandparents' poison," Kyle replied, a coolness entering his voice. "It's only by some kind of miracle that they haven't turned her against me up to now. I don't know how much longer that can last." He looked at her intently. "I thought you understood."

"Oh, I do!" Hallie was quick to assure him. That little touch of frost in his tone had triggered memories of other times—when, as a child, she'd frequently had difficulty making her parents understand what she was trying to say. Now, as then, she forced herself to try harder, sure that *she* was the one at fault. "It's just... she's going to have to make some huge adjustments. Going from this to a suburb. She'll have to leave her horse. Has she thought of that?"

"I've promised her we'll send for Candy. We'll board her at a stable not far from our house. I've already checked."

"Oh, good. Kyle, I'm not trying to set up roadblocks. Didn't you hear what I said earlier? I'd like to take her away now. Tonight. I'm in this all the way with you. All the way!"

Gradually the rigidity of his body lessened and his expression grew softer. When he reached out to run his fingers through the short blond hair at the back of her neck, Hallie felt an almost overwhelming wave of love for him rise up and wash over her, erasing any fears.

"I know you are," he said huskily, then sighed. "This damn situation. I should have come for her years ago."

"Hush," Hallie whispered, closing her eyes as she drew his head down to rest against hers. That she, Hallie Wyndham McKenna, loved and was loved by such a man.

They stayed in that position for some time, until Kyle lifted his head. "I love you, Mrs. McKenna," he murmured.

"And I love you, Mr. McKenna," she responded softly.

"I love the way the dimples come and go in your cheeks when you smile."

"I love the way your mouth moves when you talk."

"My mouth can do much better things than merely move when I talk." His pale eyes twinkled as his arms tightened about her slight form.

"Prove it," she retorted, the dimples deepening.

"We don't have to be anywhere for the next hour and a half."

"Will Sharon stop by to say good-night?"

"I told her I'd come to her room at nine-thirty to tuck her into bed."

"Oh, my, whatever will we do with all that spare time?"

"I think I have an idea," Kyle said, and without further comment he scooped her up into his arms and strode across the room to the waiting bed.

TIMOTHY GAZED at the wedding certificate. Unable to make the wording change, he carefully refolded the paper and handed it back to Kyle.

"Three months isn't a very long time," he said gruffly.

"Would it make any difference if it was three years?" Kyle demanded.

"Might mean the marriage was more stable."

"Thirty years wouldn't be enough time to convince you."

Timothy shifted in his leather recliner. His attention moved to Hallie. "Where did you find her, Kyle? In one of those singles' bars? How much are you paying her?"

Kyle's hand paused, then he slipped the certificate back into the folder he'd carried downstairs with them. "I'm paying her nothing," he said, his tone level. "And Hallie's never been in a singles' bar in her life."

"The street, then." Timothy continued his provocation.

"Timothy..." Florence cautioned.

A muscle jumped in Kyle's jaw. "You wouldn't get away with that if you were a younger man."

Timothy struggled forward in his chair. "Just forget there's an age difference, okay? It doesn't make any difference to me!"

"Timothy!" Florence again cut in. "I will not have you fighting in this house. Not even if it's for a good cause."

Timothy sputtered as he settled back against the leather cushion.

"Hallie is due an apology," Kyle insisted, remaining tense.

"Kyle, it's all right," Hallie said softly.

"No, it's not all right. And Timothy knows it."

"Just let it go, Kyle," Florence advised him.

"The insult is hanging in the air, Timothy." Kyle would not back down.

Timothy muttered something to himself, then he burst out, "Oh, all right! I apologize! Maybe she's not a whore. Maybe she just hooked up with you by accident. Maybe she doesn't have the slightest idea about the kind of man she married!''

"Language, Timothy!" Florence scolded her husband.

"Whose side are you on?" he demanded, turning on her.

Kyle remained braced in his chair, ready to continue the fray once Timothy's attention returned to him. Hallie touched his sleeve, and only after reading the plea for peace in her eyes did he relent.

Unknown to the two men, Hallie's and Florence's gazes met and held, before quickly moving away.

"Whatever you might think," Kyle said, still of an uncompromising mind-set, "Hallie is my legal wife. She's been my wife since last October. You can't change that."

Timothy's response was to grind his teeth.

"Kyle," Florence said carefully, lacing her fingers in her lap. It was obvious she'd decided to try another tack. "Have you thought about the interruption this move will cause to Sharon's education? She's doing so well now. She's in accelerated classes in science and math. Next year she starts high school. We may be a small community, but our high school has an excellent program in both subjects. She's already spoken with her teachers, arranged her schedule."

"I'm sure the schools in Atlanta have excellent programs in science and math."

Florence continued as if he hadn't spoken. "This is such a delicate time in a young girl's life. She has so many friends..."

"She'll make friends in Atlanta."

Florence glared at him. "What if she doesn't?"

Kyle's mouth slanted in a caustic smile. "For someone who's supposed to have so much faith in Sharon, you certainly don't seem to have much confidence in her ability to adapt."

"If we were going with her, she'd do just fine," Florence snapped. "But with you?"

"Change is good for a person. It broadens their horizons."

"You broadened Cynthia's horizons, all right," Timothy snarled, "and look where she ended up!"

"It's not the same thing and you know it!"

"It *is* the same thing!" Timothy exited the recliner so fast that it continued to rock long after he started to pace the room. "Cynthia was a blessing to us. A blessing! Everyone loved her. Everyone thought she was special. And she *was* special! We tried for years to have a child, then when Mother and I had given up hope, Cynthia came along to give us something to live for. We would have done anything for our little girl. Anything! The only thing I didn't do was what was needed most—cut the head off the snake that slithered into our lives." He glared at Kyle. "Now he's back. Out from under his rock to steal from us again. All legal-like—with his lawyer and his nice crispy new wedding certificate and his nice fresh-faced wife. And I'm supposed to just sit back and take it like I'm some kind of cowering dog afraid of my own shadow— afraid of him! Well, you may be a big shot in the news business, McKenna, but as far as I'm concerned, you're not one whit better than a—''

Timothy's face had turned an alarming shade of red, causing Florence to prompt, "Timothy, remember what the doctor said."

"I don't give a rat's a—" He didn't complete the word, thinking better of it upon meeting his wife's quelling gaze. "I don't care what the doctor said," he said, instead, dropping back into his chair. His face retained its ruddy hue and his body twitched, causing Florence to call a halt to the proceedings.

"This is enough for one day," she said. "You may not care what the doctor says, Timothy, but *I* do. Kyle, you and your wife...just leave the room, all right? Go upstairs, go outside, it doesn't make any difference. Just leave."

Kyle offered no protest. Without a word he stood up, drawing Hallie with him.

At the door to the hall Hallie hung back. She watched as Florence slid to her plump knees on the rug beside her husband's chair and wrapped him protectively in her arms, white head meeting bowed white head in a tableau strikingly similar to the stance that she and Kyle had so recently shared.

THE STRIDENT CRY of a rooster announced the dawn of a new day. Hallie slipped quietly from the bed to go to the window that overlooked the farmyard. Early-morning sunshine had replaced the dark clouds of the day before, lending a new warmth to the bucolic view. Sheep drifted from around the corner of one outbuilding, pausing now and then to nibble shoots of grass. A pair of horses jostled each other good-naturedly in a corral. Chickens scratched the ground inside their pen, though a few escaped to assemble near the rooster, who stood arrogantly on a fence post preparing to give the world another wake-up call.

A smile tugged at Hallie's lips. City girl that she was, she'd always wondered what life on a farm was like. The rooster crowed and her smile widened. This was exactly as she'd imagined it.

There was movement in the bed behind her. Kyle's arm stretched out across the spot she'd so recently vacated. When it found nothing, it moved again, still trying to locate her. A second later Kyle sat up, his russet hair tousled from sleep, a night's growth of beard covering his jaw.

"Good morning," Hallie called softly.

His expression cleared when he saw her. In the three months they'd lived together Hallie had learned that he awoke quickly but not always easily.

"What are you doing over there?" he asked.

"Enjoying the morning. Come look."

He groaned and collapsed back against the mattress. "I'm not ready to enjoy morning."

"The sun's out. I don't think it's going to rain today."

"Bully!" was his unenthusiastic response.

Hallie turned back to the window and shivered in her light cotton gown. The sun might be shining, but the day still had a bite to it. The animals seemed content enough, though. She watched as the sheep moved off in an untidy group up the side of a low hill, still pausing to munch as they covered ground. The horses continued to play in the corral—one black, one white and another, a brown one, coming to join them. Suddenly they stopped, their ears pricked, their great bodies poised, waiting, their attention centered on the nearest outbuilding. One of the horses whinnied and stamped its feet. When Timothy emerged and slipped between the wooden fence railings, they all promptly followed him into what must be their stable. Breakfast was about to be served.

Hallie's own stomach rumbled, reminding her that yesterday she'd been too nervous to eat before they arrived and that dinner last night had been impossible.

She shivered again, this time not from cold. It had taken her hours to get to sleep last night, thinking about what had happened—wondering how she and Kyle could possibly spend a week in a place where their presence was so deeply resented, wondering at the deep hatred the Langs felt for him.

She looked back over her shoulder at Kyle. She couldn't imagine anyone hating him. He had charmed everyone she knew, making the transition from the television screen to actually sitting in their living rooms with seeming ease. At first the situation had seemed unreal. His celebrity had intimidated her friends. Then gradually they'd accepted him as a person and listened with absorbed interest to stories he had to tell about the many places he'd been. Some of his stories were hair-raising, some intensely sad, some funny.

Hallie moved back to the bed, slipped beneath the covers and molded her body to his. After wrapping an arm across his ribs, she let her hand come to rest on the curling hair that covered his chest.

"You're cold," he murmured sleepily.

"And you're so very, very warm," she murmured in return, her fingers finding the scar that ran across his left pectoral muscle. He'd told her he'd gotten it when caught between opposing sniper fire. He'd been in the hospital for two weeks that time, then gone immediately back to the spot where he'd been hit, the fight still raging. He'd made his report for the network with his chest wrapped, his arm held securely against his side by a sling and one eye trained on the bordering mountain slopes.

Hallie snuggled closer and received an immediate response. He turned over, bringing her into the circle of his arms.

"See if this helps," he offered softly.

His left hand slowly started to roam, trailing along her narrow waist to the slight flare of her hip and then to the length of thigh beyond.

"Your skin is as smooth as silk," he purred, causing Hallie to lift her mouth, searching for his.

Their lips had just met, warmth touching warmth, when someone knocked at their door.

"Daddy?" Sharon called in hushed tones. "Are you awake?"

Hallie and Kyle looked at each other. Then Kyle pulled away from her and sat up, careful to arrange the covers around his naked hips.

"Sharon? Come in," he said.

The door opened and the girl entered the room. Today she wore her long dark hair in a single plait, which she tossed over her shoulder after her gaze made a quick sweep of the bed. She ignored Hallie completely, speaking only to her father.

"I thought maybe we could go for an early-morning ride. You always used to like that, remember?"

"I'd love to," Kyle said, smiling.

"Great. I'll saddle Henry for you." She started for the door.

"Sharon," Kyle called after her, stopping her, "are you going to saddle a horse for Hallie, too?"

The girl turned slowly to face them, her expression blank. "I didn't know she rode."

Hallie sat up straighter. "Kyle, I don't ride. I've never been on a horse in my life."

"We'll teach you," he said.

"No. You two go without me. I—I don't want to go."

"She's afraid of horses, Daddy," Sharon jeered.

Hallie shook her head. "It's not that. I just—"

"Go saddle Henry," Kyle instructed his daughter, "I'll be along in a few minutes, after I dress."

"Whatever you say, Daddy," Sharon agreed, but the look she sent Hallie wasn't placating.

Once they were alone, Kyle murmured, "She'll soon come around," an assurance that seemed directed more to himself than to Hallie. "We should be back inside an hour. Why don't you stay in bed and get some more sleep? After that we'll go down and see about breakfast.''

"But what about Florence and Timothy? Won't they expect us sooner?"

"I doubt they'll be holding their breath," Kyle said wryly as he collected his watch from the bedside table and checked the time. "Anyway, it's early yet."

He leaned close and gave her a quick kiss. Then, grinning, he gave her another. When he leaned forward yet again, Hallie raised a hand to stop him.

"Sharon's waiting," she said.

"Are you really afraid of horses?" He changed the subject in the blink of an eye.

"I have no idea."

"They're very nice animals."

Hallie folded her arms and lifted an eyebrow with mock severity. "Sharon," she repeated.

Kyle laughed and stole another kiss. Then he got up and, with a fluid masculine grace that never failed to stir her, started to dress. His actions were completely uninhibited. But if everyone had a body as nicely put together as his, there would be no need for inhibition. Hallie lay back on her pillow and feasted her eyes. Long, lean muscles were sculpted over a perfect frame—broad shoulders, slim hips, powerful legs.

He caught her appraisal and winked. "Be careful, Mrs. McKenna. The big bad wolf has very sharp teeth."

"I wasn't doing anything," she claimed innocently.

"Uh-huh," he teased. He buttoned his shirt and stuffed it into his jeans, then he went to the closet to retrieve the boots she'd placed there yesterday.

"I wondered why you brought those," Hallie murmured.

"Now you know my deepest darkest secret—I never outgrew my cowboy fantasy." After pulling on the boots, he reached into the closet once again for his coat.

"Did you learn to ride after you married Cynthia? I mean, did you learn to ride here?"

He stopped, one arm partway into a sleeve. "I thought I'd told you. I grew up on a ranch."

"You did?"

"Just outside San Antonio." He finished shrugging into his jacket.

"San Antonio isn't far from here, is it? Would you like to stop by? Since we're so close..."

"There's nothing to stop by for."

"Not even an old friend?"

"Nope, no one. Now listen." He again changed the subject with lightning speed. "Are you sure you're going to be okay while I do this? I'd hate to disappoint Sharon, but if you feel in any way uneasy..."

"I'm fine," Hallie assured him. "Go for your ride. Enjoy yourself. You and Sharon have a lot to talk about."

"Will you go back to sleep?"

"Possibly. But I'll be fine. Now, go! I promise I won't get into any trouble."

His pale green eyes moved over her, then he gave a quick nod and walked to the door. Before stepping into the hall, though, he paused, looked as if he wanted to say something, but instead, smiled slightly and closed the door behind him.

Hallie frowned. Was he afraid she might have another dustup with the Langs and this time come out a bigger loser? But he needn't have worried. The bed felt wonderful, she was as warm as toast, and her eyelids were growing heavier. Maybe she *would* take a little nap.

CHAPTER THREE

GIRLISH LAUGHTER, excited and free, mixed with the sound of pounding hoofbeats. The horses strained, their muscular legs working to dig in and reach out, a coordinated ballet of power and will. On they raced, one just slightly ahead of the other, until they passed the agreed-upon point.

"I won!" Sharon cried, pulling her horse up and wheeling around in a tight circle. "I beat you, Daddy! Candy and I beat you!" Her face was flushed with pride and triumph, her pale green eyes, exact replicas of her father's eyes, aglow.

Kyle pulled Henry up, as well. Both horses, breathing hard and still elated from the short race, skittered this way and that, wanting to continue. Kyle smiled at his daughter over Henry's bobbing head. "That you did. Fair and square. Henry and I are mortified." He patted the horse's neck.

Sharon's laughter bubbled up again. "You didn't give us a head start, either!"

"Like I said, fair and square."

Soft taps with booted heels and a little direction from the reins soon had both horses walking side by side. The road they were following had been abandoned years ago. All was quiet except for the muted plop-plop of the horses' hooves and the twittering of an occasional bird.

"You've turned into quite a good rider," Kyle said to his daughter.

"I ride every day after school."

"You'll still be able to do that in Atlanta. Not like this, but..."

"What's Atlanta like, Daddy?"

"It's a big city."

"Like Houston?"

"Something like Houston."

"Did you meet *her* in Atlanta?"

"Hallie?"

Sharon nodded.

"As a matter of fact, I did."

"Have you known her a long time?"

"I met her last summer."

"Just last summer?"

Kyle slanted his daughter a look. "You have a problem with that?"

"It's just...why *her?*"

"Why not her?" Kyle asked lightly.

Sharon frowned and stared at Candy's ears.

"I want you to give Hallie a chance, Sharon," Kyle said.

Sharon remained silent.

"You'll like her when you get to know her."

"No, I won't," Sharon muttered.

"She wants to be your friend."

"I don't *want* any more friends."

This time Kyle wisely said nothing.

The horses continued along the deserted road. Saddle leather creaked when Kyle shifted his weight. It had been months since he'd been on a horse. Not since last summer during one of his visits with Sharon. He'd known then that his relationship with the Langs was reaching the breaking point. Their association had always been troubled, but in the last couple of years dislike had evolved into outright hostility. He'd always tried to visit Sharon at least three times a year, sometimes more if he could make the necessary arrangements—arrangements that were often extremely difficult to pull off. Wars and skirmishes had a bad habit of not respecting anyone's plans. But when he could, he traveled back to the States to visit his daughter—only, all too frequently as time wore on, to be met with excuses as to why their visits had to be cut short or delayed.

Kyle glanced at Sharon. "Let's stop for a bit up here," he suggested, giving a short nod toward the narrow wooden bridge that lay ahead of them.

They tied the horses to the rail and clambered down the tree-lined embankment to the narrow creek. The water was crystal clear, bubbling over moss-covered rocks. Sharon dropped to the ground without a care and Kyle followed suit.

"I love this creek," Sharon said, crossing her legs and leaning forward, her elbows balanced on her knees.

Kyle watched as she poked around in the dirt, finding and then worrying a beetle with the tip of her finger. There was so much about his daughter he didn't know. He'd missed out on so much of her life. On the surface she was easy to read. But inside? She had to be aware of her grandparents' dislike for him. Did she ever wonder at the cause? Had she asked? And if she had, what had the Langs told her? Not the truth as they saw it, obviously. Or if they had, she didn't believe them. At least, not yet. Given enough time, though...

"Sharon," he began, drawing her attention. But he couldn't just come out and ask her how much she knew. Instead, he asked, "You aren't worried about coming to live with us in Atlanta, are you?"

"I *want* to live with you."

"Everything will be very different," he warned her.

"I know."

"Your school, your friends... You'll live in a house with lots of other houses around it. There'll be sidewalks and stores and freeways."

"I don't mind."

"I just want you to be prepared. I don't want the strangeness to come as a shock."

She lifted her gaze from the beetle and her chin quivered. "Don't you want me to come live with you, Daddy?"

Immediately Kyle realized how his litany of cautions must have sounded. He reached for Sharon, holding her slim shoulders as he studied her face. As she'd grown older, her physical resemblance to Cynthia had diminished, but her expression held something of the vulnerability that had pulled at his heartstrings the first time he'd met her mother. The realization was both touching and distressing. It sparked old memories, replays of situations he would rather forget. But this wasn't Cynthia sitting so defenselessly across from him. It was her daughter, and she needed reassurance.

"Sharon," he said quietly, "everything I'm doing, I'm doing for you. Getting you back again is the most important thing in the world to me. The worst mistake I ever made was leaving you with your grandparents seven years ago. Afterward, I stayed awake nights wondering if I'd done the right thing. You were my little girl! But I wanted what was best for you, and I thought at the time that letting you stay with your grandparents was the best. Now, well, I think it's best if we become a family again. It's what I want more than anything."

"Oh, Daddy," Sharon whispered, her eyes filling as she threw herself against his chest.

His arms went around her and he held her until her tears dried. Then tipping up her chin, he teased, "At your age, telling you that there will be lots of stores around isn't much of a threat, is it? Do you like to shop?"

"There's a mall in the next town that I go to with my friends," she sniffed, "but the stores aren't all that great."

"Wait until you see the mall near our house in Atlanta— Whoa! What am I doing? Will my credit cards ever cool off?"

"Oh, Daddy!" She giggled, straightening away from him.

"Hallie will be happy to take you there anytime you want," Kyle said.

A little of her brightness dulled. "What about you?" she asked. "Won't you come?"

"If you want me to come, I'll come."

At that, Sharon's smile returned.

Kyle helped her to her feet and they moved up the embankment to the waiting horses. Sharon looked back at him several times, flashing a jubilant smile.

After unhitching Henry's reins, Kyle glanced at his watch. "We'd better get a move on," he said. "I told Hallie we'd be back in less than an hour."

Sharon bounced into the saddle as Kyle took a little longer to get settled. "But I want to show you something! Please, Daddy?" she pleaded. "Just a little longer? It will only take a few minutes."

Kyle checked his watch again. "All right. But then we go back. I'm getting hungry for breakfast, aren't you?"

"I had a piece of toast earlier."

"A few minutes," Kyle stated firmly.

Sharon grinned and urged Candy forward with a touch of her heels.

HALLIE CAME AWAKE with a start. She checked her watch and saw that more than an hour had passed since Kyle's departure. Had he returned and decided not to wake her? She jumped from the bed, dressed, combed her hair and applied a little makeup—all in the space of ten minutes. The Langs already had a bad enough opinion of her, she didn't want to give them grounds for further condemnation.

The smell of freshly brewed coffee teased her as she made her way downstairs. It also helped lead her to the kitchen, a large sunlit room at the back of the house. Obviously remodeled since the house was built, it had all the modern conveniences—a large double door refrigerator/freezer, a dishwasher, a built-in range. The cabinets were painted white, the countertops were laminated butcher block. Bric-a-brac decorated the walls and spilled over to the countertops, cluttering the clean lines yet offering a welcoming homeyness. Off to one side of the room sat a round pedestal table of solid dark wood. It looked old but well loved.

Hallie gathered these impressions in seconds, then her attention was quickly drawn to Florence. The woman stood at the counter, stirring something in a large ceramic bowl.

Hallie's first instinct was to leave. She had no idea where Kyle and Sharon were, but it was apparent they weren't here. Then she reconsidered. If Florence had heard her come in, it wouldn't do to seem as if she was beating a hasty retreat.

"Good morning," she said, her words ringing clearly.

Florence threw a resentful look over her shoulder before continuing with her task.

"I thought Kyle and Sharon might be here," Hallie said.

"Don't seem to be," Florence replied.

"Kyle said... I thought they'd be back by now, but then—" she shrugged "—it's such a beautiful day."

Florence would not respond to her attempt at pleasantness.

Sighing, Hallie glanced at the coffeemaker. "Mind if I have a cup?"

"Help yourself."

There were cups and saucers on the counter. Hallie took one of each, poured coffee and added sugar from a nearby bowl. Instead of seating herself at the table, though, she stayed where she was and watched Florence work. The woman was making bread. She turned the dough out onto a floured board where her strong hands could then knead it to proper elasticity. She worked quickly and efficiently, as if she'd done this task a thousand times before, which she probably had.

"I love the way a house smells when bread is baking—all fresh and yeasty," Hallie remarked. "My aunt loves to make bread. She isn't a particularly good cook, but she can do that. She doesn't bake every day, though. Usually it takes a special occasion. But then she makes it on a grand scale and sends loaves home with her friends. Everyone who knows her looks forward to holidays just because of her bread." She sipped her coffee and smiled. "When I was little and visiting her, she always gave me first taste."

Florence formed the dough into a ball and returned it to the ceramic bowl to rise. "I did the same thing with Cynthia and Sharon," she surprised Hallie by saying.

"Good memories for a child," Hallie agreed.

Florence was about to say something more when Timothy stamped in from outside. He was already scowling, but when he saw Hallie, his scowl deepened.

"The pickup won't start," he announced. "I've done everything I can to get the dang thing going, but it just sits there. Must be something wrong with the ignition again. We'll have to call Walker."

"But he just finished working on it," Florence said, frowning.

Timothy's eyes flashed. "What's the matter? Walker's suddenly not good enough for you?"

"He's not a professional."

"No, and he doesn't charge like one, either!"

They glared at each other, then, remembering Hallie, transferred their gazes to her.

Hallie took her coffee to the table and sat. Glancing surreptitiously at her watch, she wished Kyle and Sharon would return.

"Sharon not back yet?" Timothy asked, echoing her thoughts.

"Not yet," Florence replied. She took another bowl from a lower cabinet and dipped into a canister for more flour.

"It's after nine," Timothy said. He turned on Hallie. "This isn't some kind of plan to get her away from us sooner, is it?"

Hallie blinked. "What?"

"They go for a ride, only they don't come back."

"Kyle wouldn't do that!"

"You can bet your sweet patootie he would!"

"He wouldn't leave *me!*"

"Oh, yeah?"

Hoofbeats sounded in the yard, along with high-pitched laughter. "Candy and I beat you again!" they heard Sharon cry. Kyle's reply was lost to them.

"I'm going to wash up," Timothy said, and left the room.

Sharon and Kyle came through the door, flushed from the cold and their bracing ride. They were laughing at some shared exchange.

Sharon hurried to her grandmother's side and gave her a quick hug. "Will breakfast be ready soon, Gran? I'm starving!"

Florence's expression underwent a miraculous change when she looked at Sharon. Gone were the lines of strain and anger. In their place was unadulterated love. "I'm making the biscuits now," she said. "It won't be long."

"Wonderful!" the girl exclaimed. She shrugged out of her jacket and waited for her father to divest himself of his. "I'll hang these in the hall closet," she said.

Hallie felt the sweep of the girl's gaze as Sharon passed her on her way into the hall, but she might as well have been invisible for all the acknowledgment Sharon gave.

She looked up to meet Kyle's eyes. He crossed to her and bent to kiss her cheek. "Sorry we were late," he apologized.

Hallie mustered a smile. "It's all right."

Sharon breezed back into the room. "Candy and I beat Daddy in two races, Gran! He didn't *let* us win. We really won! He says I'm a very good rider."

Florence wielded the biscuit cutter with a little more ferocity than she had earlier. "That's nice," she said, but it was easy to see she didn't mean it.

"Where's Granddad? Is he going to eat with us?"

"As far as I know," Florence replied.

Sharon giggled. "When I saw him earlier he was fussing because he'd gotten a late start. He said we kept him up too late last night. But *I* didn't! I was in bed!"

The girl chose a place at the table and began to play with the salt and pepper shakers. Hallie watched her, fascinated by her ability to block out unpleasantness.

Kyle touched Hallie's shoulder. "I'm going upstairs for a minute."

"I'll come with you," Sharon said eagerly, and hopped up from the table to hurry after him.

Florence watched her leave. "That girl is headed for a terrible fall. It's just too bad her dad's not..." She didn't finish her thought.

Hallie fiddled with her cup handle. If she rose to Kyle's defense, it would only rekindle yesterday's rancor.

"Is there anything I can do to help?" she asked, instead. "With breakfast?" she added quickly, narrowing Florence's field of choice.

"I'm not doing anything special, just our usual bacon and eggs."

Florence placed the biscuits in the oven and after reaching into the refrigerator, lined strips of bacon in a large skillet. She didn't ask how Hallie liked her eggs cooked. She automatically broke eggs into a bowl and began to whip them. Every movement was made with practiced authority.

"I could set the table," Hallie persisted.

"You don't give up, do you?" Florence demanded, turning. She sighed impatiently. "All right, set the table. The dishes are in that cabinet over there. The flatware is here." She motioned to each location in turn. "It's usually Sharon's job, but since she's otherwise occupied..."

Hallie found the plates and had started to position the knives, forks and spoons when Timothy reentered the kitchen. He seemed startled to see her at work.

"What's this?" he demanded, flashing his wife a questioning look. But before Florence could answer Kyle returned with Sharon. Once again, they were laughing.

Timothy glanced at them sourly as he took his chair.

Sharon stopped to hug his neck. "Don't be so grumpy, Granddad," she chided as she took the chair next to him. "We had a great ride! I showed Daddy that new cave opening I found last week."

"I wish you'd stay away from those things," Florence complained.

"I don't go in very far!"

"You shouldn't go in at *all*."

"I agree," Kyle said, surprising them with his quick concurrence. "They're too dangerous. When I worked at the station in San Antonio, I remember several times when amateur cave explorers came to rather drastic ends." He explained to Hallie, "The land around here has a limestone base. Hundreds of caverns honeycomb underground."

"You wouldn't let the fact that something's a little dangerous stop *you,*" Sharon challenged her father.

"See?" Timothy snapped, seizing the moment. "You're already a bad influence on the girl. Just think how bad it'll be if she lives with you!"

"When she lives with me she won't be near any caves!"

"They'll be other things!"

Hallie watched as the two men's anger grew. Their fuses were short, their tempers primed.

"You don't know the first thing about being a father!" Timothy charged. "All you care about is having your face on TV. Kyle McKenna this, Kyle McKenna that. I get sick of hearing about you!"

"I just do my job," Kyle answered tightly.

"I've seen you with those little kids, visiting those hospitals. You talk to one and then another, making people think you care—when in reality you abandoned your own daughter!"

"I didn't abandon—" Kyle started a vigorous defense when a sob cut into his words.

A single tear rolled down Sharon's cheek as she looked from one man to the other, then uttering a cry, she ran from the room.

"Well," Florence said after a stunned moment, "are you proud of yourselves?" She slid the skillet of partially cooked eggs off the burner and marched away from the stove. She didn't say another word as she went to comfort her granddaughter.

Timothy glared at Kyle and pushed angrily away from the table. He let the screen door slam behind him as he stalked outdoors, leaving Hallie and Kyle alone.

Kyle looked so miserable that Hallie took his hand and squeezed it. Then she went to the stove and continued to cook the eggs. The process took only moments. After spooning them onto the waiting platter, she brought it to the table along with the plate of crisp bacon and the fluffy biscuits just out of the oven.

"I don't know about you," she said briskly as she sat down, "but I have to eat something." She started to serve herself and saw with satisfaction that Kyle slowly did the same.

She expected each bite to taste like sawdust, but it didn't, possibly because it had been so long since she'd eaten. More likely, though, because so many of the ingredients Florence used had been homegrown.

"This is wonderful," she said.

"Florence always was a good cook."

"She's never worked away from the farm?"

"Not that I know of."

"She's a traditionalist," Hallie surmised.

"In more ways than one. It's not something she talks about. It's the way she lives her life. She didn't like it at all when Cynthia went to work after Sharon was born."

"Did you?" Hallie asked. Normally Kyle wasn't forthcoming about his first marriage, other than to describe it as "difficult." She couldn't help but be curious.

"I wanted her to do whatever made her happy," he said flatly.

"Did working make her happy?"

"For a time." He pushed his plate away, his food barely touched. "How did it go between you and the Langs this morning? When Sharon and I came inside you looked...disgruntled."

Hallie debated whether to tell him what Timothy had said and decided to do so. Timothy's opinions weren't new to him. "Timothy thought your ride might be a cover. That you were spiriting Sharon away without letting them say goodbye."

Kyle laughed shortly and shook his head.

"I, of course, told him you wouldn't do such a thing," Hallie said.

"The perfect wife."

Hallie smiled, but something in the way he'd said that made her uncomfortable. She stood. "I wonder what we should do about all this." She indicated the huge amount of food left on the serving platters. "Do you think they'll come back anytime soon?"

"Florence wouldn't be able to live with herself if she let food go to waste."

"So you think we should leave it?"

"I would."

Hallie hesitated, then conceded that he was probably right. She carried their plates and utensils to the sink, while he followed with their cups and saucers.

After giving everything a quick rinse, they loaded the dishwasher.

"Kyle," Hallie said, straightening after adding the last plate. "I've been thinking. What happened earlier—"

"—shouldn't have. I know. I've been thinking about that myself."

He pulled her close and rested his chin on top of her head. Holding her seemed to lend him comfort.

"Whenever you and Timothy argue—" she began.

"—it upsets Sharon."

"Yes," she agreed. "So you should call a truce."

Kyle took a deep breath and expelled it slowly. "I'm willing, but I doubt Timothy is."

Hallie drew far enough away to look at him. "You wouldn't have to respond when he provokes you."

He held her gaze. She could see his mind at work, deeply-held emotions pulled this way and that. "I wouldn't, no," he agreed at last.

"For Sharon's sake."

"Yes."

A pleased smile curved Hallie's lips and she leaned forward to kiss him. His arms, still around her, tightened. The kiss lengthened, deepened—

"Excuse us," Florence said stiffly, but she didn't back out of the doorway. Her hands braced Sharon's shoulders as the girl stood just in front of her. Sharon didn't look any more pleased at witnessing this display of affection than her grandmother did. With their faces pinched in disapproval, they might have been two Puritan judges who had happened upon an act they considered particularly sinful.

Hallie's instinct was to jerk away, to break all contact, as if they *had* been caught doing something sinful. But Kyle wouldn't let her go. He kept her close, an arm curved around her waist. *Get used to it,* seemed to be his unspoken declaration.

"We left everything out for you," Hallie said with some difficulty. Such strong disapproval catapulted her back to a time when it was just her and her parents and she could never seem to satisfy them. "It's probably cooled, but you could—"

"I think I should be able to handle it from this point," Florence said stiffly.

It was obvious their presence was no longer wanted in the kitchen. Hallie looked at Kyle, who gave an almost imperceptible nod.

"We'll be outside," he said. Then he addressed his daughter, his voice warming. "Sharon, when you're finished with breakfast, come join us. I thought we could show Hallie around. She's never been on a farm."

"All right," Sharon said tonelessly.

Hallie's movements felt uncoordinated as she and Kyle walked out of the kitchen and into the hall. Kyle's jacket was nearby, but hers was upstairs. Her sense of awkwardness continued even when, alone in their borrowed room—her mission to retrieve her jacket temporarily on hold—she sank slowly onto the foot of the bed.

Kyle had done his best to warn her, but she'd had no idea how upsetting this week was going to be. Yet beyond the tribulations of the moment, what had ever made her think Sharon would welcome her with open arms? Was it some kind of naive wish left over from that terrible time in her childhood when all she'd had to cling to was the dream that one day she'd be part of a happy family?

Sharon didn't want her in her life, and she didn't want her in her father's life, either, and that wasn't going to change once they returned to Atlanta.

Didn't Kyle see that?

edge on... right as... tain. Trying to be Oh So Nice...

CHAPTER FOUR

SHARON WATCHED HER without revealing that she was
watching her. She knew every move the woman made
as they passed through the barn and the various outbuildings, saw her every reaction. The woman seemed
nervous, laughed a little too much with that funny
edge people unconsciously have when they're uncertain. Trying to be Oh So Nice, listening when she
spoke, asking questions. What rankled most, though,
was the way Dad acted with her. He was always
touching her, on the arm, on the back. He couldn't
seem to keep his hands off her. It was disgusting!

They stood at the corral. Sharon called to Candy,
who responded with a snuffling whicker before trot-
ting over.

Candy was beautiful, Sharon thought with satisfaction. Her brown coat gleamed with copper high-
lights in the bright rays of the sun. Sharon was so
proud of her. She spent hours brushing her, talking to
her, sharing secrets she would never confide to another living being.

Candy thrust her head over the rail and shook it
back and forth, all the while stamping her front feet.
Sharon's father laughed, but the woman backed away,
laughing, too, but at the same time showing fear.

Sharon's lip curled. She didn't like people who were afraid of horses.

"It's all right," her father said. "She won't hurt you. Here—" he caught the horse's head by the leather halter strap "—you can pet her."

The woman tried to cover her cowardice by stepping closer. She reached out, then her hand fell away. "I've never been this close to a horse before," she confessed.

Her father smiled. "Come on. Touch her."

"Candy used to bite," Sharon said helpfully, pleased with her own cleverness, "but she hasn't bitten anyone in a year or two. You'll be safe."

Her father looked at her. "I didn't know she'd ever bitten anyone."

Sharon kept her expression clear. "Oh, yes. She nipped one of my friends. Karen said she almost took her finger off."

Her father's eyes narrowed, then he looked back at his new wife. "She won't bite you," he said. "I won't let it happen."

The woman lifted her hand again and this time made contact with the animal's warm cheek. "Oh!" she cried, startled. Then she said, "Oh!" again, only with surprised delight as she started to use longer petting strokes.

Candy rolled an eye but remained still under Kyle's firm grip. It was all Sharon could do not to jerk the other side of the halter and pull her horse away. The woman already had her father under her spell. Did she want to steal her horse, too?

"See?" Kyle said. "She likes you."

"Do you really think so?" she asked, her face flushed with pleasure.

Candy gave her own answer. She jerked her head away and danced back a few steps, challenging the woman's budding confidence, proving that her fealty wasn't so easily won.

That the woman found the incident amusing irritated Sharon. So did the fact that her father joined in with the woman's laughter, as if Candy's reaction had been hilarious.

Sharon hopped down off the fence rail, turned her back on them and started to walk away. She'd had enough.

Her father called after her. "Sharon?"

"I'm going to help Gran," she answered over her shoulder, not missing a step. "She asked me to come back inside when we were done." That wasn't true, but it was convenient.

"Well...okay. We'll see you later, then," he said.

"Yeah," Sharon muttered sullenly.

As she passed through the farmyard she saw her grandfather sitting inside the pickup truck, while their neighbor Walker Bucannan leaned under the raised hood to do something to the engine. Her grandfather waved at her and she waved back, but she didn't alter her course. She intended to go to her room and hide out for a while, watch some music videos on TV. Maybe that would make her feel better.

She didn't get much farther than a step inside the kitchen door when her grandmother called to her. As usual for a Thursday, the older woman stood at the counter, continuing the long process of making bread. Sharon couldn't understand why Gran went to all this trouble every other day, when it was so easy to buy a loaf at the market. But it was something her grandmother did religiously.

"Yes, Gran?" she said, pausing, but not happy about it.

"Is that Walker out there with your Granddad?"

"Yes, ma'am."

"I thought I heard him drive up."

Sharon started off again, only to be stopped once more by her grandmother.

"What does she think of the farm?"

There was no need to ask who *she* was. Sharon shrugged.

Her grandmother turned back to her bread making.

"I don't think she'd last a minute out here on her own," Sharon volunteered. "She's too...soft."

Sharon was well aware that her grandmother put a premium on hard work. For everyone except her granddaughter, that is. *She* got by with doing very little.

"Figures," Florence snorted, a wealth of meaning contained in the single word.

Sharon finally escaped up the stairs, a little smile pulling at her lips. Candy was on her side and so were her grandparents. None of them liked the woman her father had married. *Your grandparents don't like your father, either,* her mind insisted. But Sharon discarded the thought as soon as it formed. She didn't care to think about that. It was the woman she wanted to be rid of.

CANDY REMAINED ALOOF, observing them from the far side of the corral. But two other horses took her place at the rail, coming over to greet Hallie and Kyle with unabashed curiosity. One was black with a white blaze down its nose, the other white with light gray spots.

"Is one of them Henry?" Hallie asked, remembering the name of the horse Kyle had ridden that morning.

"This one," Kyle said, reaching out to pat the strong black neck.

"What about this one?" Hallie asked. "What's his name?"

"Jill," Kyle said, grinning. "There used to be a Jack, but he died a couple of years ago. They were twins."

"Ohhh," Hallie sympathized, looking into the white horse's gentle brown eyes. "You poor baby," she cooed. Her touch had grown more assured. The horse whickered softly, enjoying the attention. When Hallie stopped stroking her to give Henry a pat, Jill thrust her nose between them, keeping the greeting short.

"I think you've made a conquest," Kyle said.

Hallie chuckled as she went back to petting Jill.

"Rub her ear," Kyle suggested.

Jill pushed against the rail to get closer.

"She's so sweet!" Hallie exclaimed. Her parents had never allowed her to have a pet. Her aunt had had a cat, but he was old and crotchety and didn't like to be handled.

"How would you like to learn to ride her?" Kyle asked.

Without conscious thought Hallie stepped back.

"It might help pass the time," he said. "There isn't much else to do around here."

"I don't know," Hallie said, shrugging. "She's nice, but..."

"Think about it," Kyle advised. He gave Henry a final pat and took Hallie's arm, drawing her away from the corral.

"It's not that I'm afraid," Hallie tried again to excuse herself. As Sharon had implied earlier, Kyle didn't run from danger. "It's just—"

"—not all that important. Don't worry about it."

Still Hallie felt as if she was letting him down, a feeling that dated back to her childhood. She glanced at Kyle, trying to gauge his mood, trying to see if he'd really meant what he said. At twenty-eight, she should be past all this. She'd worked hard to build up her opinion of herself: graduated from college, earned a position of some responsibility at the airline, dealt with famous people on a daily basis, met and married a man like Kyle. She'd thought she'd finally gotten her life in order.

Kyle didn't notice her uneasiness. He looked straight ahead, frowning at something he saw.

Hallie followed his gaze. An old black pickup truck, battered and worn, sat in front of a lean-to at one side of an outbuilding. Two men stood beside it, discussing something. One was Timothy, the other...

The second man looked up, saw them and stopped talking. He was a big man, towering over Timothy. He was big in every sense of the word. Big head, broad shoulders, immense hands, long sturdy legs, huge feet planted firmly on the ground. He looked to be Timothy's age, but his years seemed not to have diminished any of his strength. His hair was steel gray, cut short with military precision.

Timothy looked around and Hallie saw him mutter something under his breath, probably a curse.

The man beside him continued to watch their approach as he wiped his hands on a faded red square of cloth, which he then stuffed into his back jeans pocket. Part of it hung out like a flag.

Hallie hadn't known whether Kyle would deviate from their path to the house or even acknowledge the men's presence. He ended up doing both.

"Walker," Kyle said, extending a hand as he reached him.

The huge man studied Kyle, before letting his gaze move on to Hallie. Prepared for more hostility, she was surprised by the quizzical kindliness in his wide-spaced gray eyes. With no further hesitation, he enveloped Kyle's hand.

"Good to see you, Kyle," he said, his voice a low rumble from his chest.

He towered over Kyle, as well, which meant that he must be nearly seven feet tall. The only other times Hallie had felt so tiny was when she assisted traveling college or professional basketball players.

"This the new wife?" the man asked.

"Yes, this is Hallie," Kyle said, drawing her forward. "Hallie, Walker Bucannan. He's the Langs' nearest neighbor."

"And have been for the past forty-eight years. How do you do, Hallie."

The callused hands smothered Hallie's hand next, but they were surprisingly gentle. Hallie offered a small smile.

Timothy did not look at all happy. "Now that the pleasantries have been attended to," he grumbled, "could we please get back to what we were doing? You say we're going to have to rebuild the carburetor? How much is that going to cost?"

Walker eyed his old friend. "You want the truck running? Or do you want to fill it with dirt and use it as a planter?"

"Running, of course," Timothy answered shortly.

"Then you're going to have to spring for a few bucks. Not a lot, but I have to buy the kit."

"How much?"

"Twenty should cover it, and I'll bring you back the change."

Timothy frowned. "I don't have that much on me," he said, "but hang on, I'll get it." Then he stomped off toward the house.

Walker shook his great head as his friend moved out of earshot. "That man holds on to a nickel so tight the Indian can ride the buffalo."

When Hallie looked mystified, he explained, "The old buffalo nickel—with the image of an Indian on one side and a buffalo on the other. Don't see those much anymore, I suppose." He sighed. "Oh, well. Another sign I'm getting old."

"Not too old to help out Timothy," Kyle remarked.

"Nope. Guess I'll keep doing that till the day I die. We've been friends for too many years."

"Place has gone down a bit," Kyle said, looking around. "Sharon said he's been sick."

"Off and on. High blood pressure, a little trouble with his stomach, and he doesn't like to take his medicine." Walker leaned back against the truck, a boot heel propped against the tire. "This business with Sharon isn't helping."

For the first time since she and Kyle had stopped to talk Hallie sensed Kyle's body stiffening.

"It can't be helped. I want my girl."

"I can understand that, but it's hard on the two of them."

"They make a lot of their own trouble," Kyle said stiffly.

"They say the same of you."

"They say a lot worse than that!"

A moment passed before Walker commented, "I saw those reports you made last summer. Those kids. You did a good job."

"Thanks."

"It must've been hard."

"It wasn't a picnic."

Kyle shifted position. Hallie knew he didn't like to talk about that time. She'd seen the reports, too, and they'd been heartrending. She'd met him for the first time shortly afterward.

Walker spoke to her but nodded toward Kyle. "You must be proud of this new husband of yours."

"I am."

"I was the first person around here to meet him. Came to my place when he was just starting out. A twister had come through and killed several people. I was one of the lucky ones. It only flattened my barn."

Timothy harrumphed behind them. "That twister wasn't the only ill wind to come through that day!" He stepped past Hallie to hand Walker a twenty-dollar bill.

"You mean me," Kyle concluded.

"If the shoe fits!"

Kyle stepped forward, his voice low yet ringing with anger. "You have a big mouth, Timothy. You always have had."

"That's better than being a liar and a cheat!"

"When did I lie, Timothy? You just tell me when I lied."

"Every time you opened your mouth!"

Hallie tugged on Kyle's arm. In the heat of the moment he'd forgotten his earlier resolve not to give in to Timothy's taunts.

Walker pushed away from the truck and, ignoring the two men, spoke to Hallie. "How would you like a ride into town? I'm not going to be long, and maybe when we get back these two will have either settled their differences or killed each other."

"There's no way I'll ever settle my differences with him!" Timothy spat.

"Then why don't you waive the requirement for us to spend the rest of the week here?" Kyle challenged him. "Hallie and I would be gone in an hour. You wouldn't have to worry about differences anymore."

"And let you take Sharon?"

"Sharon's coming with us no matter which day we leave."

"Like hell she is!"

"The law's on my side, Timothy."

"There's such a thing as moral law!"

"*Sharon* wants to come with us."

"Sharon doesn't know what she wants!"

"Like Cynthia didn't know?"

"Exactly like Cynthia!"

Kyle shook his head. "You don't know your granddaughter any better than you knew your daughter."

A faint trembling seized Hallie's body. The strain of listening had become too much for her. She looked from one man to the other before her gaze settled on Walker.

She didn't know him, but the kindness in his craggy face was like a port in a storm. "Yes," she heard herself say. "I would like to go to town with you."

Walker nodded approval. "Kyle, I'll bring your wife back in about an hour. If we're longer, don't send out the rangers. We might decide to stop for a soft drink."

Hallie wanted to go to Kyle. She wanted to press herself against him, to gain comfort and assurance. But she contented herself with a fleeting touch of their hands. "Take care," she said huskily, and to her relief, she saw that he understood what she meant.

BECAUSE OF HIS SIZE, Walker Bucannan overwhelmed the cab of his pickup. The bench seat was pushed all the way back to accommodate his arms and legs. The air smelled faintly of a good cigar.

"Bad blood between those two," he said as he started the engine.

Hallie looked back over her shoulder to where Kyle and Timothy had been standing. They were no longer there. Straining a little more, she saw Timothy disappear into one of the outbuildings. She couldn't see Kyle anywhere. She hoped he wasn't disappointed she'd deserted him.

"Yes," she said softly, a little anxiously. Maybe she shouldn't be doing this. Maybe Kyle needed her. Surely Walker had been joking when he said the men might kill each other, but in this place anything could happen.

The truck bounced over the rocky ground, then turned onto the graded road that led away from the house.

"Relax," Walker advised after glancing her way. "Nothing's going to happen."

"How can you be so sure?"

"Both of them have too much to lose."

"Sharon?"

"Precisely."

"But Timothy and Florence have already lost Sharon."

"They still have visitation rights. Every year she gets to spend a month with them in the summer.

Hallie looked at him in surprise. "She does?"

He glanced away from the road. "You don't know about that?"

Hallie frowned. "No, I don't."

"That's the deal the lawyers worked out. Timothy said Kyle fought them tooth and nail. But since they've raised her for the past seven years, their lawyer argued it would be cruel to cut them out completely."

"Kyle didn't say anything about it." Hallie still frowned. Why wouldn't he have told her?

"He was probably planning to tell you later," Walker said.

Hallie retreated into silence. There were areas of Kyle's life she doubted she'd ever be privy to. Areas he kept to himself. Like the darker aspects of his job or his years spent married to Cynthia. She hadn't felt the need to know everything when she married him. She respected his privacy, just as she was grateful he respected hers. He knew something of her painful past, but he'd never delved too deeply. Yet when it involved the future—their future!—shouldn't they share everything that might affect it?

Hallie waited in the truck while Walker bought the needed auto supplies, passing the time by watching the townspeople. Most of them were middle-aged or older, with strong character lines etched on their faces as befit people who rely on the land. Smiles flashed as greetings between them were exchanged. Others went determinedly about their business.

Walker came out of the store and resettled himself in the driver's seat. His keen gray eyes moved over her. "Well, what do you think?" he asked.

"Of the town? It seems . . . nice."

"Place is dying. Most all the young people have left. Can't make a decent living farming anymore, so they pulled up stakes and moved to the big cities. A few have come back because they find out they can't make a living there, either, but most either stay in the city or keep moving on."

"Do you have children?" Hallie asked.

He started the truck. "A son. Lives out in California. Works for the Department of Transportation as a structural engineer." Walker chuckled. "The way the place keeps shaking, he stays pretty busy."

"Grandchildren?" Hallie asked, adopting his abbreviated speech.

"Boy and a girl. Don't see as much of them as I'd like." He sat in silence for a moment, then said, "How about that soft drink? I could sure use one."

"It isn't necessary. You don't have to."

"Only thing I *have* to do is die and pay taxes!" Walker chuckled at his ancient joke. "This is something I'd *like* to do. It's not every day I get to share a soda with a beautiful young lady.''

Hallie smiled. "I have a feeling you cut quite a swath among the local females when you were a young man.''

Walker lifted an eyebrow and teased, "Still do.''

"Doesn't your wife object?''

"She might if she was around. She got bored with things around here—especially me—about thirty years ago. Took off and hasn't been heard from since.''

He backed the truck out of its slot and started off down the road, waving laconically now and again to people he knew.

Near the end of the street he pulled the truck into another parking slot, this time in front of a small café. When he caught her speculative glance, he grinned and said, "A true Texan never walks when he can ride—a horse, a car. It doesn't matter.''

"Is that left over from your cowboy heritage?''

"You could say that, or you could say that we're just plain lazy.''

They swung out of their seats and met on the sidewalk. "Don't you need to lock it?'' Hallie asked, feeling odd about leaving the open truck as it was.

"Who from?'' Walker asked. He motioned her through the screen door and into the café.

The medium-size room was crowded with tables. Each was set with paper place mats, flatware, paper napkins and short, round coffee cups flipped bottom-side-up on matching ceramic saucers. In the center of each table was a thin white vase sporting a fake cluster of tiny blue flowers. Only a few of the tables were occupied.

"Hey, Walker!" a man called from one of them.

"Long time no see, Pete," Walker drawled in return. But he didn't stop for conversation. Instead, he ushered Hallie, who had immediately become the object of everyone's scrutiny, to a table by the wall.

After seeing her into a chair, he settled his great bulk into the chair opposite her. "Coke all right with you?" he asked. When she nodded he called over his shoulder, "Two Cokes over here, Martha. Then we won't bother you again."

"Coming up!" a disembodied female voice returned from somewhere on the other side of the counter.

Hallie ran her fingers over her slacks, needlessly smoothing away invisible wrinkles. The clothing she'd packed for this trip had not been chosen with country life in mind. Her idea had been to look as sophisticated and stylish as she could, to impress the Langs with her poise and competence. That so far nothing had proceeded along the lines she'd expected was borne out by her present discomfort. She felt like a hothouse flower suddenly sprouted amongst a cluster of buttercups. *She* was in the wrong place, not them. It was their field.

"Things aren't really as bad as they seem, you know." Walker's quiet voice broke into her thoughts.

Hallie met his gaze. "An optimistic view," she murmured.

Walker shrugged.

Two ice-filled glasses appeared at their elbows. A plastic straw stood at attention in each. Hallie leaned forward to remove the straw, and when she looked up, she saw that Walker had done the same thing. Both grinned.

Hallie took a sip of her drink.

"You're a city girl, born and bred," Walker said after a moment.

"Richmond, Virginia," Hallie replied. "Then Atlanta."

"Ever been to Texas before?"

"No."

"And you're only here now because you have to be—correct? No, no need to answer that," he amended before she had time to do so. "I'm just stating the obvious."

"I'm here because Kyle is here," Hallie said softly.

Walker's eyes moved over her. "How long have you two been hitched?"

"Since last October."

The gray eyes narrowed, yet he made no comment. "How are you and Sharon hitting it off?" he asked, instead.

"We're not."

Walker shook his head. "That girl can be a handful sometimes. Knows what she wants and goes after it. A lot like her mother that way."

Hallie's fingers tightened on the glass.

"Cynthia was my godchild, did you know that?" Walker continued. "Prettiest little thing you'd ever want to see. Pretty young woman, too. She walked on water as far as Timothy and Florence were concerned. Nothing was too good for her."

Hallie was growing tired of hearing how perfect Cynthia was and how her parents had doted on her.

"'Course," Walker continued, "that kind of treatment isn't good for a child. At least, not to my way of thinking. If a child gets everything he wants without ever having to stir a hair, he starts to expect it. My boy had to work for what he got. He didn't have a thing handed to him. And he ended up the better for it. Kind of surprised me the way Timothy and Florence behaved. But I guess it does something to people when they have to wait a long time to start a family...." His words trailed off.

Hallie didn't know what to say. Her position was delicate. She didn't know Walker, didn't know if he would run to the Langs with everything she said. He didn't seem the type of person to do that, but she couldn't take the chance.

To her relief, he continued, surprising her even more by what he said, "'Course considering everything, that's why it's so strange to see it happen all over again with Sharon. You'd think they'd've learned. But they spoil her as bad as they did her mother. Timothy worst of all. For my part, it's like watching a terrible train wreck and then having to watch it happen all over again a few years later. The train hasn't run off the tracks yet, but the steam's building and bridge is down up ahead—and there isn't a damn thing I can do about it!"

Hallie proceeded cautiously. "So...you think it's a good idea that Kyle and I—"

"Who's to say?" he interrupted her, shrugging. "The bridge could be down up ahead of you, too."

"But Kyle—"

"Kyle had a blind spot where Cynthia was concerned. It's not hard to imagine him having one for his daughter, too. It's pretty easy for a woman to wrap a man around her little finger, no matter her age."

Hallie took another sip of her Coke and pushed the glass away. Kyle and Sharon. Sharon able to wrap Kyle around her little finger—just like Cynthia. Kyle loving Cynthia so much that he would *let* her manipulate him. Hallie shook her head, denying the unpleasant thought. Then another idea took hold: did he love her, Hallie, as much as that? Would he allow her such privilege? Or did he feel safe because he'd married against type the second time? *She* had never been spoiled by her parents a moment in her life. And by the time she was ten and moved in with her aunt, she'd been too emotionally wounded to demand anything.

"Like I said before," Walker said quietly, "things are never as bad as they may seem at first."

"But what about the train wreck?" Hallie whispered, her throat tight.

"Bridges can be rebuilt," Walker said firmly. "All it takes is the inclination."

CHAPTER FIVE

ALL IT TAKES is the inclination. Walker's words echoed in Hallie's mind as she opened the back door of the farmhouse. She understood clearly what he was trying to say to her: that the situation desperately needed someone to intervene. But if he meant her— that *she* should be that person—how on earth was she supposed to accomplish it? If *he* didn't feel qualified, someone who was such a good friend to the Langs and who also got along with Kyle—he'd known all of them for years!—what could she, a newcomer, do? But then, sometimes, wasn't an outsider able to view a situation much more clearly than someone close to it?

The house was quiet, seemingly empty. A note from Kyle told her that he and Sharon were off somewhere. Timothy, she knew, was with Walker—he'd come out of the barn the moment they'd returned, extending a clipped greeting to his friend while at the same time bestowing her with a dark glower. Only Florence was unaccounted for.

Hallie found her in the living room, sitting in a chair, sewing. With the tip of her left middle finger protected by a thimble, she worked her needle deftly, stitching a pattern of colorful cloth strips onto another, much larger square of cloth.

Hallie walked across the room. "That's very pretty," she said, tilting her head for a better look. "Is it for a quilt?"

"Yes."

Hallie watched as the woman worked, fascinated by her skill.

After a moment Florence looked up, impatience written on her features. "I don't like an audience," she said tightly. "If you have something to say, say it."

"I didn't mean to bother you," Hallie apologized, quickly moving to a seat on the couch.

Florence stared at her. "Are you playing some kind of game?" she demanded.

Hallie frowned, confused. "I don't understand."

Florence's sharp eyes cut over and through her, probing for any sign of deception. "I've made it perfectly clear that I don't trust you. That I'm only suffering your presence in my home because I'm forced to. And yet you—"

"I've come to offer a proposal," Hallie interjected. The idea of soliciting Florence's assistance had occurred to her in a flash, spurred no doubt by Walker's admonition.

Florence anchored the needle in the material and set it aside. "What kind of proposal?" she asked.

"Something that will make the situation easier for Sharon."

"Easier for Sharon—or for you?"

"For Sharon," Hallie repeated.

"I'm all ears," Florence answered mockingly. She removed the thimble and held it in her curled hand.

"I've already talked to Kyle about this—" Hallie began.

"I'll bet you have."

"—and he's agreed. If you would talk to Timothy as well—"

"I thought you said this involves Sharon!"

"—and get him to agree." She took a breath. "It's never easy for a child to watch the people she loves argue. You've seen the way Sharon reacts whenever Timothy and Kyle start to tear at one another. I know! You think it's all Kyle's fault. But to be fair, you have to admit . . . it's both."

"If Kyle wasn't trying to steal her from us there wouldn't be any arguments," Florence countered stubbornly.

"The argument is between the adults. It should stay between the adults."

Florence stood. "This is just another ploy to make us step aside quietly. As if the past seven years don't count for anything!"

"No! It's not a ploy. And if you'd just— I know you love Sharon. I've seen it in your face when you look at her. But you need to open your eyes and see that Kyle loves her just as much."

Florence turned her back, her arms folded, her spine rigid.

"Sharon is the one who counts here," Hallie said quietly after a moment. "What's best for Sharon. And these continual arguments aren't what's best for her. Kyle is willing to call a truce. Unilaterally, if need be.

He's not going to respond in future if Timothy baits him. Not in front of Sharon, at any rate.''

Florence spun around. "What are you getting out of all this? You don't know Sharon. You don't know us."

"I'm Kyle's wife," Hallie said simply.

The woman continued to look at her, then she slowly started to shake her head. "I don't understand what it is about that man that causes women to throw good common sense out the first window they come to. He's handsome, but the devil is said to make himself handsome, too."

"Kyle isn't a devil."

"As I said, good common sense—thrown away."

"For Sharon's sake Kyle is willing to call a truce," Hallie persisted. "Is Timothy?"

The question placed Florence in a difficult position. If she said no, it would seem that the Langs didn't care about their granddaughter's feelings. If she said yes, Hallie had achieved her goal.

"I'll speak with Timothy," Florence answered stiffly. Yet as she continued to look at Hallie, there was a gleam of something different in her eyes. Anger and resentment had been joined, albeit unwillingly, by a first faint inkling of respect.

IN BED THAT NIGHT Kyle held Hallie in his arms, wrapped in the afterglow of lovemaking. It was hard for him to believe that such a passionate spirit could so easily exist within the slightly reserved, poised young woman the rest of the world was familiar with.

She responded to his touch like dry kindling to flame. Giving generously of herself, she hungrily demanded that he do the same. Sometimes he was in awe of the depth of feeling he experienced with her.

She moved, her smooth cheek rubbing against his bare shoulder. By the light of the full moon streaming in through the parted curtains, her short pale hair looked alive with streaks of silver and gold. Her eyes, when she lifted them, glowed with love.

It was enough to make any man catch his breath, to make his heart pound faster, to stir the blood in his loins. Only this time Kyle reacted differently. Instead of rejoicing in the possibilities offered by the moment, memory swooped down like a dark bird of prey. Before marrying again he had often jerked awake at night, his body drenched with sweat, his mind screaming in protest. Faces would storm through his mind. Faces of people he had seen over the years— adults, children, babies—all speaking to some of the worst damage human beings could inflict on fellow human beings. Unbearable pain, unbearable suffering. Faces twisted in agony, begging someone—anyone!—to stop their hurt. And worse, no longer begging, because they'd passed the point of mere physical suffering and moved to the stage where they knew no one could help. People who held their loved ones cradled on their laps as the light of life slowly ebbed away. And—another time, another place— himself holding Cynthia, her body battered and bleeding, as the spark of her life was slowly extinguished....

He bent down to kiss Hallie's parted lips, desperately needing to lose himself in her sweetness, needing to make the nightmarish pictures in his mind disappear. She was like a honeyed elixir, able to ease his troubled spirit.

A moment later, concern in her voice, she whispered, "Kyle... just now, you looked so sad."

Kyle forced the terrible memories into the farthest recesses of his mind. They weren't gone forever; he knew that. But they could be temporarily put away.

He brushed a soft strand of hair from her cheek, his head on the pillow next to hers. "Ghosts," he explained. "You help chase them away."

A frown puckered her brow. "I wish..."

"What do you wish?" he asked lightly, determined to put aside those events he could do nothing to change.

"That I had known you when you were a little boy."

Her answer surprised him. "Why would you want that?"

She smiled in the moonlight. "What's the children's verse? 'Snips and snails and puppy dog tails.' I'd like to see if that's what you were made of."

He laughed. "Of course, you were 'sugar and spice.'"

"Of course."

"I never thought that saying quite fair. Girls are great and boys are rotten."

She tickled his stomach. "Isn't that the way it truly is?"

He fended her off, mock wrestling her into submission. Then as he looked down into her laughing face—her hair tousled, her smooth skin bare—he felt his body immediately respond.

"No, really," she continued, unaware of the tumult taking place within him. "I would like to have seen you as a little boy. Was your hair the same color as it is now? Did you laugh a lot? On the ranch, did you have to do chores?"

He released her wrists and rolled onto his back, the heat of passion dulling. "I did lots of chores," he answered neutrally.

"What kind?" she asked, propping her head on her bent elbow and looking at him with wide eyes.

"Feeding the animals, helping to clean up—that kind of thing."

"Did you enjoy it?"

"No."

"Why not?"

Coming so closely upon his last dark thoughts, Kyle was unable to endure this line of questioning. It conjured up too many other ghosts he would rather not have to deal with right then. "I just didn't, okay?" Then, as he saw her instinctive withdrawal, he repented. He hadn't meant to wound her. "Can't we talk about something else?" he asked.

His impatient request hung in the air. Finally she murmured, "I did something earlier."

"What?" he asked, relieved by her generous willingness to acquiesce. He wanted the atmosphere between them to return to normal, for the last few minutes to be erased.

"I talked to Florence about calling a truce, and she said she'd talk to Timothy."

"How did you get her to do that?"

"I have my ways." She grinned.

Kyle turned back onto his side and reached for her. It was all right. She held no grudge. She let him pull her close.

"As I well know," he teased. "Do you think it'll work?" he asked, becoming serious again.

Hallie shrugged. "Florence might be willing, but Timothy? Timothy is another matter."

"Timothy was always another matter," Kyle muttered.

"But he listens to her. And in this case..."

"It's what's best for Sharon."

Hallie was silent a moment, then she said, "I know you don't believe this, but I really do think they love her, Kyle."

Her body was molded to his from foot to forehead. Kyle kissed her temple, her ear, his lips playing in her hair. He breathed deeply of her sweet fresh scent. "In a sick kind of way, maybe," he murmured, his mouth moving to her throat. "But right now I don't want to think about either one of them. Right now—" his hands were busy "—we have other much more interesting things to think about."

She made a soft sound of pleasure and arched her back... and that was the last they spoke, or even thought, of the Langs for the rest of the night.

BREAKFAST NEXT MORNING was strained. Timothy excused himself as quickly as possible and even Sharon was subdued, picking at her food desultorily. Only the telephone brought her relief. A friend, who was at home from school for the day because of a sprained ankle, had called to ask her to visit.

"You don't mind if I go, do you, Daddy?" she asked Kyle, wrapping her arms around his neck from behind, suddenly as animated as the day before.

Kyle twisted in his chair to look at her. "Do you need a ride?" he asked.

"Are you offering?"

"There and back." Kyle smiled.

"That would be great." She looked at her grandmother. "I won't be long—just a couple of hours."

"Tell Jenny I hope she feels better soon."

"I will. Daddy—" her attention returned to her father "—will you come in to meet my friend? She's watched you on television. Her whole family has."

Kyle frowned. "I thought I met someone named Jenny the last time I was here."

"That was another Jenny. Jenny Foster. This is Jenny Douglas."

"Ah," Kyle murmured.

"Please, Daddy?" Sharon begged.

"Sharon!" Her grandmother tried to hush her.

Sharon wouldn't listen. "Please, Daddy. Please, please, please?"

Kyle glanced at Hallie and laughed. He knew he was being manipulated and he was enjoying it. Hallie thought of what Walker had said yesterday, about the likelihood of his having a blind spot where Sharon was concerned, and she knew it was true. Had he enjoyed Cynthia's manipulation just as much?

"All right, all right—no more!" Kyle said, still laughing. "I'll be more than happy to meet her. Anyway, it's not that big a deal."

"She'll think it is," Sharon assured him. "All my friends think you're special."

"When do you want to go?" Kyle asked.

"Right now?"

Kyle started to push away from the table, then paused.

"I'll stay here," Hallie said, a message of reassurance passing between them.

"Okay, kid," he said to Sharon. "Let's go."

Sharon squealed and grabbed his arm, pulling him from the kitchen.

Without a word Florence began to clear away the dishes. Hallie joined her, and this time Florence made no protest.

They were almost finished loading the dishwasher before Florence spoke. "I talked with Timothy and he agrees," she said. "He won't pick a fight if Kyle doesn't. The man's stubborn as all get-out, but Sharon means the world to him."

Hallie added the last glass and Florence switched on the appliance; the hum of its motor was almost non-existent. Florence was quick to leave, walking down the hall to the living room, where she made herself comfortable in her favorite chair and picked up her needlework. Hallie followed at a discreet distance and settled on the couch, just as she had yesterday.

While Florence concentrated on her work, seemingly absorbed by it, Hallie let her gaze wander about the room. Today, there was no need for a crackling fire. The morning was warm, almost springlike. The windows were even open partway, the gauzy curtains stirring slightly on a playful breeze.

Two days ago she'd been surprised by the apparent contradiction of the place: bitter, angry people versus a warm and welcoming home. Now the contradiction wasn't nearly as puzzling. The house was Florence's domain. It reflected her personality. And even though she and Hallie were still at odds, Hallie sensed that a warm heart beat strongly beneath her rigid exterior.

Her gaze dwelled on the older woman, who was still intent on her work. Florence's round face wore her age with pride, the wrinkles more a badge of honor than something to be hidden. Her nose was short and straight, her mouth—even in repose—set with determination, her white hair a snowy cap of curls.

Hallie decided to break the silence. "There's something I'd like you to know," she said, gaining Florence's attention. "When we go back to Atlanta, Kyle has arranged for two free months before he starts his new duties at the network. Then I'm going to take a month—possibly two months—of leave from my work at the airline. So someone is always going to be at home with Sharon, at least during her first few months of transition."

"You work?" Florence asked sharply.

Too late, Hallie remembered what Kyle had said about Florence's negative attitude toward Cynthia's working after giving birth to Sharon. "Yes," she said, lifting her chin.

"And you're planning to continue with this job even after Sharon comes to live with you?"

"Sharon isn't a baby. My aunt worked the entire time I lived with her. It didn't hurt me."

"A child should have someone at home with them at all times."

"That's the ideal. Yes, I agree—"

"This aunt you keep mentioning," Florence interrupted her, frowning. "You lived with her and not your parents? Did something happen to your parents?"

"They're both very much alive."

Florence waited, but when Hallie said nothing more, she resumed her needlework. Only this time she didn't cut herself off from conversation. "How old were you when you went to live with this aunt?" she asked.

"Ten."

"And you didn't mind her leaving you every day to go to work?"

"Not when she came home and was happy to see me."

"You make it sound as if—" Florence stopped herself. "Sharon isn't accustomed to being on her own."

"She's almost fourteen."

"She's still a baby!"

"At most she'll only be by herself for a couple of hours in the afternoon after school. And in the summer there are all kinds of great programs."

"You don't know what she can get up to in a couple of hours!"

"Is her behavior that bad?"

Florence sputtered. "Yes! No! Oh, you know what I mean. Children are children! They have to be watched or they'll get into trouble."

"Sharon isn't a child," Hallie reminded her softly. "She's almost an adult."

Florence's teeth clamped down on her bottom lip. "I know that. It's just..." She turned her head, unable to continue.

Hallie shifted position, allowing Florence time to recover. "We'll watch her very carefully," she promised. "And if what we planned doesn't work out, we'll do something else. Kyle's schedule isn't set yet, and mine can be changed. We won't let Sharon suffer in any way."

Florence startled her by moaning, "Can't you understand? She'll suffer if she goes off with that man!"

Hallie shook her head sadly. "We always come around to that again, don't we?"

"Because it's true! If only you knew some of the things Cynthia said."

Hallie jerked her hand up, halting further confidences. "No," she said firmly.

"It's for your own good!"

"*No,*" Hallie repeated.

Florence drew a sharp breath. After a moment she confessed tightly, "I want to dislike you. I want to hate everything about you. I want to spit in your eye and call you every name in the book. But I can't do it. You're not what I expected."

Hallie allowed a small wry smile. "You're not exactly what I expected, either."

Florence lifted an eyebrow. "What did you expect?"

"Oh, no. You first."

The corners of Florence's mouth twisted. "A floozy. Someone willing to play house for a week or two and then walk off with a much heavier purse."

Hallie chimed right in, "A mean, nasty couple, self-involved and more than half-crazy, with absolutely no redeeming qualities."

"Did Kyle tell you all that?" Florence demanded.

"No. I came up with it myself."

"Well, I have to say I'm relieved."

"Me, too." Hallie grinned.

There was a tiny stretch of silence before Florence motioned casually toward a rustic-looking chest. "There're some magazines in the bottom drawer."

Hallie went to investigate. She chose a couple from the stack and returned to the couch. Then, while Florence stitched, Hallie thumbed through the glossy pages. The strain between the two women had provisionally eased.

When Timothy found them a half hour later, he stood in the doorway and glowered. "Well, if this doesn't look cozy!"

Florence refused to accept the rebuke. "What do you need, Timothy?"

"I'm going to catch a ride into town with Raymond. The dang truck has something else wrong with it. Needs another part. I'm going to get it myself to save Walker some time. And don't tell me again I should get a professional to look at it."

"I guess it's just old and tired, Timothy, like us."

"Speak for yourself, woman!" he growled. And for a second Hallie thought she saw a spark of mischief come and go in the old man's blue eyes. But any such spark had completely disappeared by the time he spun on his heel to walk back down the hall.

"At least Walker knows something about what he's doing," Florence grumbled. "Raymond likes to think he does, but he only makes matters worse. Raymond is another neighbor who lives farther up the road."

"It sounds like Timothy needs a new truck."

"Ha!" Florence scoffed. "Not so long as he and anyone else he can rope into helping him can keep this one running."

Hallie chuckled.

Florence smiled along with her for a second, then the smile disappeared. She put her work aside and stood up. "I've got to go check on the chickens," she said by way of explanation. "See if they've laid any eggs." Then she left the room.

Hallie stared after her. One moment things were fine—or at least a little more promising—the next they weren't. But she couldn't let herself be discouraged. Timothy had agreed to her proposal, and Florence's staunch antipathy, at least in regard to her, had begun to crack.

Not a bad beginning for a rank amateur bridge builder.

CHAPTER SIX

"I CAN'T BELIEVE that Kyle McKenna is your father! And the way he looks! He's better-looking off TV than on! And he's sure a hunk on!" Jenny Douglas gushed. She and Sharon were sitting on Jenny's bed. "To tell the truth, I didn't really believe you when we first moved here and you told me you were his daughter. I thought you were just making it up. Then the other kids told me it was true, but it still didn't *seem* true, you know what I mean? Then to meet him! Did you see my mother's face? I thought she was going to start drooling all over the carpet. You know, if you'd brought him here before he got married again, we might have become stepsisters. I know that look in my mother's eye!"

"I didn't think of it," Sharon said. "Anyway, I didn't think your mother's divorce had come through yet."

"It hasn't, but she's never let that stop her before. My last stepdad moved in just after my other stepdad moved out."

Sharon was in a funny mood. She'd wanted to come see Jenny, but now that she was here, she wanted to be back at the farm. She'd been in a funny mood all morning. "Do you remember your real father?" she asked.

Jenny adjusted the pillow that cushioned her left foot and ankle. "A bit," she said. "I was three when he left."

"Do you ever miss him?" Sharon started to draw imaginary circles on the bed cover.

"Not really. Mom says he doesn't miss us, so why should we miss him?" Jenny's hair was a riot of blond curls, her eyes huge and blue. She'd been in beauty contests since she'd been a baby, winning most of them. When she tilted her head, she did it with practiced skill. "What do you think of your new step-mom? Is she nice?"

The imaginary drawing stopped. "She's ridiculous."

Jenny smiled encouragement. "Oh?"

Sharon shrugged. "All goody-goody, sweet-sweet. She reminds me of Mrs. Schneider."

"Euuu!" Jenny sounded properly nauseated at the thought of their school counselor.

"Imagine having Mrs. Schneider for a step-mother!"

"Euuu! Euuu!" Jenny cried more loudly and started to giggle.

"My dad's probably going to divorce her as soon as he has me safely in Atlanta."

Jenny leaned closer and lowered her voice. "Do you think they *do* it? Do they sleep in the same bed?"

Sharon thought of all the touching and the passionate kiss she and her grandmother had interrupted in the kitchen. Her lips twisted. "Would Brad Donaldson do it with Kelly Karson?" She named the current teenage heartthrob of their favorite television show, as well as its most reviled villainess.

Jenny dissolved into another gale of giggles and this time Sharon joined in, but only for show. There wasn't the slightest bit of laughter in her heart.

On the way back to the farm, Sharon was quiet. She sat beside her father in the sleek black rental car. The engine purred its power even as her father kept the speed at the local limit.

"Jenny seems to be holding up well," Kyle remarked.

Sharon frowned. "How do you mean?"

"Her ankle. From all the noise you two made upstairs, it doesn't seem to be causing her much pain."

"I told her some jokes to cheer her up."

"How much school will she have to miss?"

"Only a couple of days. Then she gets to go back, but only if she uses crutches."

"Is she your best friend now?"

Sharon shrugged. The idea of her father and his new wife together in bed *not* sleeping had disturbed her. She couldn't erase the thought from her mind. Normally she and her friends enjoyed speculating about the private lives of the adults in their midst—but not her father. Not with Hallie!

Hallie. What a ridiculous name. It wasn't one thing or another. It was just there, like her.

Sharon laced her arm through her father's and leaned close, snuggling her cheek into his sleeve, enjoying the solid feel of him. She didn't want another woman in his life. She wanted to be the only one he thought of. The only one he loved.

Suddenly she found herself crying. Huge tears rolled down her cheeks and there was no possible way she could stop them. She buried her face deeper into his sleeve, hoping to hide what was happening, but he must have heard her muffled sob, because the car instantly slowed and pulled off the highway.

"Sharon? What is it, honey? What's happened? Why are you crying?" The questions were sharp with surprise and concern.

Emotions Sharon was unable to fully comprehend continued to roil within her. All she could do was cling helplessly to her father's arm.

He tried to break away to wrap his arm around her, but she wouldn't release him.

"Sharon!" he said again, only this time more forcefully.

Sharon responded to the note of command in his voice. She sat away from him and rubbed vigorously at her flushed cheeks. She couldn't meet his eyes. She'd totally disgraced herself, acted like a stupid little kid—the same little kid that years ago he hadn't wanted to have tagging along with him because she'd be a nuisance and get in the way.

"I'm sorry," she whispered on a hiccup.

"Don't apologize."

She chanced a quick glance and saw that his face was set. She looked away quickly. She couldn't make herself say anything more.

"Sharon," he said at last, "whose idea was it for you to check out of school early the end of last week?"

Sharon was surprised. "Gran's," she said.

"Why?"

"She said I needed time to get used to the idea that I'm going to move away from here."

"Away from your grandparents, away from school, away from your friends?"

"Yes."

He hesitated. "Have you changed your mind?"

Her head jerked around. She stared at the man whose features were so familiar to her. From the day she was six and he left her with her grandparents, she'd kept his image close to her heart. And whenever one of his reports was on TV and she was alone in the room, she would scoot close to the screen and pretend he was talking just to her. It didn't matter what he said or that he might be half a world away. Sometimes she'd even touch the screen and kiss it. But no one knew that—except Candy. She told Candy everything and Candy understood.

"No," she croaked in answer to her father's question, and looked away when her voice broke.

"Then what was all that about just now? Are you crying because you're going to miss your friends?"

She couldn't tell him the truth: that it was because she loved him so very, very much. So much it almost hurt! And deep inside she was afraid that maybe he didn't love her nearly as much. And that one day he might leave her again. She had to give him some kind of answer, though, so she fell back on the all-purpose shrug.

Her father ran his hand over the back of her head, smoothing her hair. She sensed that he felt relieved by the ambiguity of her answer, because he could take from it what he wanted. She even heard the relief in his voice.

"If that's it," he said quietly, "we can solve the problem very easily. Your friends will have to come to Atlanta and visit us. At spring break, in the summer—whenever you like."

"Gran said I'd be coming back here for a month every summer."

His lips tightened. "That's in the agreement we worked out," he said levelly.

"Do I have to?" she asked, responding to his unspoken reluctance: he didn't want her to come back!

A long moment passed in which her father said nothing, then he answered in a measured tone. "An agreement is an agreement."

"But what if I don't want to come back?" she persisted. Not that she truly felt that way. She didn't want to completely turn her back on her grandparents or the farm, but if the choice was between pleasing her father—which also meant pleasing herself—and pleasing them ... Her conscience niggled for a second but she ignored it.

Kyle restarted the car. "We'll talk about that when the time comes," he said.

Typical adult reaction! Sharon thought, and was surprised by the spurt of anger that followed. She had never felt anger toward her father before. He'd always been so absolutely perfect in her eyes, someone to adore—which she still did! He *was* perfect! Perfectly wonderful! It was just this foul mood she was in that made her irritable.

She forced a bright smile and looked at him. "It's okay, Daddy," she said reassuringly. "I don't care about all that silly stuff now. I'll see my friends again, and I'll make bunches of new ones. What I want most in the whole world is to go to Atlanta with you so I can be your real daughter."

Her father swallowed, and his voice was huskier than usual when he said, "You've always been my real daughter, Sharon."

Tears again stung her eyes. Only this time she managed to control them.

THEY BURST into the house on a ripple of laughter, Kyle carrying Sharon piggyback—her coltish legs supported by his arms. Only Florence's quelling look halted their fun.

"You're back early," she said. "I thought you were going to be gone for a couple of hours."

Kyle held still while Sharon slid to the floor. "I had to save Daddy from Jenny's mother," the girl said brightly, giggling. "I think she was eyeing him for husband number...four? Five? I forget how many husbands Jenny said she's had."

"Five. She told me five," Florence said disapprovingly.

"Anyway," Sharon continued with a swiping glance at Hallie. "She's very pretty and she's on the hunt again. She was practically sitting on Daddy's lap when I came downstairs from visiting Jenny."

"That's not quite true," Kyle defended himself. "She was showing me photos of her trip to Denmark. She thought I'd be interested."

"You looked interested, all right!" Sharon teased.

Hallie was amused by the obviousness of the girl's tactic. To display the ease with which she could counter that particular ploy, Hallie moved closer to Kyle and slid a casual arm around his waist. "Didn't you once say that Denmark was one of your favorite countries to visit?" she asked, smiling sweetly at him.

Kyle tucked her against his side. His answering smile melted her toes.

"Copenhagen in particular," he murmured.

He liked it that she'd come to claim him. Sharon didn't. The girl's bright smile disappeared.

"Then how come the photo album was closed?" Sharon taunted, still trying to score a point. She was no longer talking to her father, only through him...to Hallie.

"I don't remember it being closed," Kyle said, effectively removing Hallie from the line of fire. If Sharon wanted to continue with her taunts, she was going to have to deal with him.

Sharon's bottom lip began to quiver. She seemed upset that her father had contradicted her, as if in doing so he'd taken Hallie's side. She started for the door.

Kyle released Hallie and caught up with his daughter. "Is our ride still on for this afternoon?" he asked after gently tweaking her nose.

"Do you still want to go?" Sharon challenged him solemnly.

"I'm looking forward to it," Kyle said, and smiled at her.

Happiness was reborn on Sharon's young face, and this time when she turned to leave the room it was with much greater confidence.

Florence made a dismissive sound and resumed her lunch preparations. Kyle crossed back to Hallie.

"Everything all right with you?" he asked, tipping his head slightly toward Florence.

"As right as rain," Hallie replied. She had much more than that to tell him, but now wasn't a good time.

While Hallie finished setting the table, Kyle drifted into another part of the house, Florence having made it apparent he wasn't welcome in the kitchen. A short time later Hallie heard a television set come on and a familiar voice—Kyle's voice—come over the airwaves. She went to investigate.

On screen was a replay of one of Kyle's reports from last summer, the heart-wrenching story of children caught up in the worst of their parents' war. She stood beside Kyle's chair, watching him talk to one and then another, marveling at how good he was with them, getting their stories and yet not forgetting the human side of their misery. In the middle of one interview, he used the remote control to click off the set.

"It wasn't over," she said softly.

"It was for me." His voice was clipped.

She perched on the wide upholstered arm of his chair. "Do you ever wonder what became of them? If they're still alive?"

"Sometimes."

"Has the war broken out again? Is that why the network replayed the piece?"

He stood up, cutting off her words. He went to the window and looked outside, then he paced back across the room. He might have been an animal, frustrated by the imposed boundaries of his cage.

An icy fear clutched at Hallie's heart. All it would take would be one word from him, and the network would gladly assign him to the world's newest hot spot. Within two days he could be in the thick of fighting.

"Kyle?" she breathed. "You're not thinking of—"

He turned on her. "How many times do I have to tell you? No! We're here now. Trying to get our lives in order. What people do over there..." He motioned toward the television set, then he took a deep breath and released it. "There aren't any new hostilities. The network is just using old clips to fill time. But even if there was an outbreak, it doesn't concern me now. Not directly. Not anymore." He pulled her into his arms and murmured regretfully, "I wish I hadn't turned the damned thing on."

Hallie let him hold her, assured yet not assured. She searched for something to say, something that might give him encouragement. "I talked with Florence," he said. "And she said Timothy has agreed. He won't pick a fight if Sharon is nearby."

"Just watch out when she's not," Kyle murmured.

"And," Hallie continued, not commenting on Kyle's highly probable summation, "I'm making some progress myself. Florence and I are on better terms. At least now she doesn't bite my head off if I happen to look her way."

"I don't see how that particularly matters."

Hallie frowned slightly. "Well, I thought it was obvious. She's Sharon's grandmother. All contact between them isn't going to cut off when we leave here. The better we can make the relationship between us, even if it's only between Florence and ourselves— leaving Timothy out of it—the better it will be for everyone, particularly Sharon."

"Florence will never warm to me."

"All right, then," Hallie snapped in frustration. "Me! If she and I can get along, it has to help!"

"As long as you're married to me, she's not going to accept you, either."

Hallie's frown deepened. "Are you saying you don't want me to be friendly with her?"

"I didn't say that."

"That's the way it sounded. Kyle, why didn't you tell me about the month's visitation Sharon is allowed to have with the Langs each summer? And no, Florence didn't tell me. Walker did. But why did it have to be him who told me? Why not you?"

"I thought I had."

She shook her head. "No, you hadn't."

Kyle considered the seriousness of her expression, and he answered just as seriously. "I sincerely thought I had, Hallie. I learned about it shortly before we were married. I guess there was so much going on at the time. With us, with Sharon. We were looking for a house, remember?"

Hallie conceded the point. With all that had been happening in their lives some details could easily have been lost, even a fairly important one. Wasn't it a cliché that in some wedding ceremonies the bridegroom forgot the bride's ring? At least that hadn't happened to them.

Kyle was waiting for her reply. She reached up and cupped his face with both hands. Her wedding band gleamed golden next to her diamond-and-emerald engagement ring. "Yes," she said softly, "I remember." Then she kissed him, telling him with more than words that she accepted his explanation.

The kiss lengthened and deepened, and it took Kyle to gently but firmly push her away. "That's enough, Mrs. McKenna," he said, his green eyes dancing with a devilish light, "unless you want to horrify the Langs by having them find us flagrante delicto in their front room."

Hallie's heart swelled with her love for him. Her body didn't feel big enough to contain it. She giggled. "I don't think Florence would approve."

"No," Kyle laughed. "Florence definitely would not approve!"

TIMOTHY DIDN'T JOIN them for lunch that day. Florence waited on him for half an hour, then she told everyone to help themselves to the warmed-up leftovers from last night's dinner.

"That man's not taking care of himself properly," Florence declared, and sent Kyle a pointed look.

Kyle set his jaw, but he didn't say anything.

Sharon seemed to have cheered up fully, chattering to her grandmother and father, needing little encouragement to skip from one subject to the next.

Hallie offered an occasional comment, but Sharon frequently cut her off. Finally Hallie said nothing at all, which was exactly what Sharon wanted.

By the end of the meal Hallie knew that the girl's attitude had to be challenged if there was to be any chance that they could live together as a family in the future. She no longer expected to gain the girl's affection, but she couldn't allow herself to be treated as an interloper in her own home. That was too close to the reality of her childhood, something she had fought long and hard to put behind her.

Once again Sharon disappeared when it came time to clear up. Florence started to gather the dishes and Hallie helped. At home she and Kyle took turns with the cooking and cleaning. Living on his own for so many years under so many difficult circumstances, Kyle was extremely self-sufficient. He was also a good cook and had introduced her to the various cuisines from the countries where he'd been assigned—Indian, Middle Eastern, African, Southeast Asian, Eastern European. He knew better than to offer any kind of assistance to Florence, though. In her world a man entered a kitchen only to eat.

Hallie and Florence passed the time with a degree of pleasantness that up to this point had been missing from their relationship. They were far from being fast friends, but Florence no longer treated her like a pariah. She even smiled slightly at her once or twice.

When they finished Hallie declared her intention to take a walk.

"Good idea," Florence said approvingly, but she didn't offer to come with her, a fact for which Hallie was grateful since a short time before she'd seen Sharon disappear into the stable. She had yet to see her leave.

The sun was warm on Hallie's face as she let herself out through the house-yard gate. Across the way, she saw Walker bent over the front fender of Timothy's truck. His size made him unmistakable. When he saw her he waved, a wrench in his hand. Hallie waved back but continued toward the stable. She was on a mission.

Once inside the stable it took a moment for her eyes to adjust to the dimness. As she waited her senses were assailed by the pungent smell of hay, animal feed and the animals themselves—a not unpleasant combination.

When her vision sharpened she saw that stalls took up most of the space along one wall, while on the opposite side, past the walkway, a fenced-off area provided shelter for the horses when they came in from the corral. An open door let them enter and exit as they pleased.

Like many of the other outbuildings on the farm, the stable was beginning to show its age. Wood had weathered, hinges showed rust and needed repair. Old leather harnesses and bridles hung from sturdy nails on the far wall. Larger, less identifiable implements sat abandoned on the floor. A saddle had been slung over a wooden sawhorse.

Hallie heard Sharon before she saw her. The girl was in the farthest stall, talking to someone, her words warm and intimate. "You understand. You're the only one I can tell these things to because you *always* understand."

Hallie moved until she could see her. Sharon was bent over, brushing the great brown horse's front leg. She used long, sure, rhythmic strokes.

The horse whickered softly, enjoying the attention. Then sensing Hallie's presence, the animal rolled her eyes and tried to dance away.

"What is it, girl?" Sharon straightened, catching sight of Hallie. "Oh, it's you," she said. There wasn't a trace of welcome in her stance or her tone. "What do you want? How did you find me here?"

"I saw you come in and I thought I'd—"

"Well, don't!" Sharon tried to cut her off.

"—come talk to you," Hallie continued. She motioned toward the brush in Sharon's hand. "Candy seems to be enjoying that."

Sharon didn't move, nor did she answer.

Hallie held the girl's gaze and decided to plunge right in. "You know, Sharon, this antagonism between us can't go on. Whether you like it or not, I am your father's wife. And when we get back to Atlanta we're going to share the same house. You can't continue to pretend I don't exist."

The rhythmic brush strokes started again.

Hallie continued speaking to the girl's back. "I don't intend to try to take your mother's place, or your grandmother's. That would be stupid of me. What I'd hoped—what I *hope*," she corrected, "is that one day we might become friends."

Hallie thought she heard the girl mutter something, but she couldn't make it out. Still, she pressed on. "You're almost fourteen," she said. "In a few years you'll be an adult. You'll be able to make up your own mind about everything. Go where you want, do what you want. You're almost at that point now. But you haven't quite reached it yet. All right, you don't like me. Or you think you don't like me. You don't really know me well enough to make a judgment. But if we're going to live under the same roof—"

"What makes you think we're going to do that?" Sharon asked tightly, turning to face her.

Hallie answered slowly, "In Atlanta...we've bought a house...and we're going to live there."

"Daddy and I are going to live there," Sharon said coldly. "I have no idea where you're going to live."

Hallie blinked, taken aback by the girl's certainty. "Sharon," she said, "I live there, too."

"Not for long."

An uneasiness stirred deep within Hallie, a feeling both alien and familiar. Like something she didn't want to remember, yet couldn't quite forget.

The girl was quick to take advantage. "Daddy told me he only married you to get me. And that once we're back in Atlanta, he's going to make you move out."

"That's not true," Hallie said.

"Ask him," Sharon retorted.

"I *know* it's not true!" Hallie said more heatedly.

Sharon shrugged and turned back to the horse.

Hallie grabbed her arm and jerked her around. She laughed at the look of surprise on the girl's face, but the laugh held no amusement. "You enjoy hurting people, don't you, Sharon? What have I ever done to you to make you hate me so much? Do you have any idea what your father would do if he knew? Has it entered your mind that I might tell him? What do you think he'd say? Do you think he'd still want you to come back with us?"

Sharon's defiance melted. The naked fear in her eyes made Hallie feel ashamed. The girl had wounded her, so she'd struck back. But she couldn't forget who her adversary was, or the relationship they needed to build.

"Don't worry," Hallie said, relenting. "I won't tell Kyle. I want us to be friends, Sharon, and friends don't carry tales."

"We'll never be friends!" Sharon hissed, regaining a measure of aplomb.

"Why don't we wait and see?" Hallie suggested.

"Why don't *you* go take a flying leap?" Sharon retorted, tears of anger and frustration welling in her eyes.

Hallie smiled slowly, this time allowing some humor to show through. "Could have been worse," she murmured, then turned and walked away.

All the way to the door she expected the brush to go sailing past her head or, worse, ricochet off it. But she broke into bright sunlight unscathed.

CHAPTER SEVEN

WALKER CAME to dinner that night, and his easygoing presence was a welcome relief. Even Timothy seemed to appreciate his old friend's company, conquering his hostility to Kyle and Hallie enough to join everyone in the living room for after-dinner coffee.

Sharon sat curled on the rug at her father's feet, her head resting against his knee. She'd avoided Hallie's eye throughout most of the meal, but Hallie had sensed Sharon looking at her several times when the girl thought she wouldn't be noticed. Had Sharon thought about what she'd been told earlier in the afternoon? Hallie wondered. Had it given the girl pause—just as it had her?

Hallie and Kyle held hands as they sat side by side on the couch. She looked at their fingers, threaded together. She couldn't stand it if anything ever happened to break up their marriage. She could barely think the words. Kyle had married her because he loved her. For no other reason. He hadn't needed to marry her in order to regain his parental rights. The Langs had been granted only temporary guardianship, not formal custody. But what if they *had* decided to fight? *Wouldn't it have looked better in a court of law if he had a wife and could offer a stable home?*

Hallie shook her head, suddenly fighting a growing nausea. Her skin felt clammy. No! It was a stupid idea. Unworthy of her, unworthy of Kyle. She couldn't let herself think things like that.

She must have made some kind of sound because all conversation stopped.

"Are you all right?" Kyle asked, leaning toward her.

Hallie drew a trembling breath. It was silly, but she truly did feel ill. There was a roaring in her ears, and her body felt weak, unresponsive.

"I—I don't know," she whispered.

Some of the color left Kyle's face. His freckles, normally hidden beneath his tan, were clearly visible.

Florence came over to feel her forehead, the coolness of her hand offering temporary comfort. "No fever," she said. "Maybe you should take her upstairs, get her to bed."

"No, I—" Hallie tried to protest.

"Florence is right," Kyle said.

Walker was on his feet, filling the room. "Listen to what Florence and Kyle say, Hallie. You don't look as if you're doing too good. Coulda been something you ate didn't sit well with you."

"The fish?" Florence frowned. "Does anyone else feel poorly?"

Heads shook all around.

"She probably ate too fast," Sharon offered. "You always tell me to eat slowly or I'll make myself sick."

For the first time in anyone's memory Florence snapped at the girl. "That's enough, young lady. Hallie needs help, not a smart mouth."

Sharon gaped at her grandmother, blinking.

Kyle stood up and reached for Hallie. She tried to stop him from lifting her, claiming, "I can walk."

"About two steps," Kyle replied tautly. Then he swept her into his arms and started for the door.

"Should we get the doctor?" Hallie heard Walker ask as Kyle stepped into the hall.

"I'm not that bad," Hallie said quickly, talking into Kyle's neck. She needed to be close to him. Her heart ached with the need to *stay* close to him. It was instinctive, like breathing.

"Let's wait a few minutes and see how..." The rest of Florence's answer was lost to her as Kyle carried her into the hall and up the stairs.

Hallie could hear his heartbeat, steady and strong. She caught a trace of his cologne. His arms, supporting her, were at once powerful and comforting.

He placed her on the bed and removed her shoes. Then he unbuttoned her blouse, unzipped her skirt and helped her free of both. Hallie shivered in her slip as he tucked her under the covers.

With her head resting on the pillow, she looked up at him. He sat on the edge of the bed at her side, leaning lightly on the one arm stretched across her.

"Better yet?" he asked.

She tried to smile. "I feel like an idiot. What must everyone think?"

"That you're human and sometimes you don't feel well." He studied her face. "You're not as pale as you were a few minutes ago. Was it your stomach? Did something not agree with you?"

Hallie shook her head but with little conviction. "I truly don't know. One moment everything was fine and the next..." She couldn't possibly tell him what she'd been thinking. Or explain why it'd had such a dramatic effect on her. She couldn't fully explain it to herself!

"Maybe we should call the doctor like Walker said," he suggested.

"No, really, it'd be a waste of his time. I'm almost all right now. I'm probably just tired. It's been a difficult few days."

His lips tightened. "You're trying too hard to make this work. The Langs—"

Hallie reached out to stay his lips with her fingertips. "I didn't sleep very well last night," she said. It was a lie, but he wouldn't know it. He'd gone to sleep before she did.

Someone tapped on the door.

Kyle muttered a curse beneath his breath and went to open it. Florence came hesitantly into the room.

"I wanted to see how Hallie's feeling. Walker isn't about to leave until he knows for sure."

Kyle answered stiffly, "She's as well as can be expected under the circumstances."

"Circumstances?" Florence echoed, her gaze switching instantly to Hallie. "Are you pregnant?"

As Hallie struggled to sit up, Kyle responded angrily, "I meant the difficult circumstances because of you and Timothy!"

"No, I'm not pregnant. I'm just tired, that's all. Nothing else. I—I didn't sleep very well last night. Tell Walker not to worry. A good night's rest is all I need. I'll be back to fighting trim by morning."

"You're sure?" Florence glanced warily at Kyle.

"Perfectly sure," Hallie said firmly. Did the woman honestly think Kyle had caused her near collapse?

"Well, if you should need anything in the night..."

"We'll call you," Hallie said.

Florence nodded, and after giving Hallie another all-encompassing glance, she stepped back into the hall and closed the door.

"Old witch," Kyle muttered.

"At least she came to check on me."

"She's probably afraid we're going to sue her for serving tainted fish."

"Kyle, you're not being fair."

Kyle rubbed his neck. "Okay, I'm not being fair. There was nothing wrong with the fish. But she can still be a witch when she wants to be. Or worse."

Hallie scooted back down in the bed and closed her eyes. A second later Kyle was sitting beside her, his arm once again draped across her waist. "And I can be an ass. Why don't you tell me that? Here you are, in bed because you're upset, and all I do is upset you even more."

There was real regret in his voice and in the way he gently touched her arm. He loved her. How could she ever have doubted it?

Hallie reached out for him and held on tightly, as if her life depended on it. Burying her head against his chest, she whispered, "Kyle, come to bed with me now. Please? Don't go back downstairs. Stay with me . . . stay with me?"

She knew she was asking for much more than that. She needed to feel the security of his continued presence for the days and years to come, the reassurance they would be together always. She couldn't stand the thought that he might turn away. She couldn't face his rejection.

She might have been a child again, desperate for love, *aching* for love, willing to do anything, and afraid that, as before, there would be nothing there.

She lifted her head and looked up at him, her light brown eyes huge. Instinctively, she cupped his head in her hands and started to kiss him—quick, eager, hungry little kisses. Kisses that fell like raindrops in a building storm. His mouth, his chin, his cheeks, his nose, his eyes, his throat, branding him as hers and, at the same instant, nearly devouring him. She tore at his shirt, uncaring if the button threads snapped.

Kyle sat very still, his breathing quickening, growing ragged. Then he moved, his body jerking as he strained to meet the wildness of her passion. Within seconds her remaining clothing had been discarded along with his. His shirt lay half on, half off the bed, her slip puddled on the floor. Bra, panties, briefs, slacks, Kyle pushed them all off the bed with his bare foot, making room as he leaned back and pulled her on top of him.

Sanity prevailed for only a second. "We shouldn't be doing this," he whispered rawly. "You need to rest."

"I don't want to rest," Hallie replied, threading her fingers through his hair and guiding his mouth to her breast.

Kyle's low moan was almost animalistic as he surrendered to their shared lust.

HALLIE'S BODY was covered with a thin film of sweat. Her skin fairly burned with heat. In one or two places, she felt a tiny sting from the roughness of Kyle's day's growth of beard. Her muscles throbbed from excessive use. Her breasts tingled. She felt alive, almost more alive than she'd ever felt before!

She reached out to touch his chest. His body, too, was hot and covered in perspiration. He lay still, breathing hard. He lifted his head to look at her. His green eyes were bright beneath dampened strands of reddish brown hair. A pleased smile curved his lips.

"My God, woman," he breathed, "are you trying to kill me?"

Hallie giggled and pulled herself next to him, resting her head against the crook of his shoulder. "I didn't notice you protesting earlier."

He gave a low whistle. "I was too busy."

"So I noticed," she teased.

He wrapped an arm around her shoulders, too spent to do anything more than let it rest there. Hallie burrowed closer. She had been silly earlier. Two people couldn't share what they'd just shared and not have it based on the rock-solid surety of affection. He loved her as much as she loved him. Sharon didn't know what she was talking about. She was just being a spiteful child, and anyone who listened to her was an idiot.

Kyle kissed the top of her head. "Are you okay?" he asked huskily. "We didn't..."

"I'm fine," Hallie answered. "Even better than before."

He chuckled. "Just call me when you need another prescription filled."

Hallie smiled and within seconds she drifted into a contented sleep.

"WELL, YOU LOOK BETTER this morning. That's one thing for sure," Florence pronounced, her eyes moving assessingly over Hallie as she came into the kitchen. "More color in your cheeks."

"Thank you," Hallie responded. "I do feel a lot better."

Florence motioned for her to sit at the pedestal table. "Everyone else has already had breakfast, but there's no reason I can't rustle up something for you." Her hands, resting palms out on her ample hips, were already covered with flour. This was another bread-making day.

"Some coffee and a biscuit will do fine," Hallie said. "I'm sorry to come down so late."

Florence dismissed her apology. "Pffft. I'm glad Kyle had the good sense to let you sleep in."

Hallie thought of the way they'd spent much of last night and was glad that Florence had no way of knowing. She started to get up to help herself to coffee, but Florence stopped her.

"You sit there," she said, rinsing her hands. She then filled two cups and brought them to the table. The first she placed in front of Hallie, the other she slid into a spot just opposite. "Biscuit, you say?" she asked, still standing.

"Yes, please," Hallie said.

Florence brought several flaky samples on a large plate, flanking them with butter and two different types of homemade jelly. She settled in the chair behind the second cup.

"Time for a break," she murmured.

Hallie wasn't hungry, but she made herself eat most of one biscuit, slathering it liberally with blackberry jelly.

"Have another," Florence urged.

"One's fine."

"You're such a tiny little thing," Florence commented. "One good puff of wind and you'd be off."

"It would have to be a fairly substantial puff." Hallie laughed.

"Not as big as the one needed to lift me. Hurricane force, most likely."

Hallie laughed again, and Florence joined her, then said, "I was worried about you last night. Getting sick so suddenlike." She paused, frowning. "This aunt you grew up with. Has she ever met Kyle?"

"Aunt Catherine? Yes, of course she has. She was at our wedding."

"What kind of wedding did you have?"

"Small. Just family and friends."

"Your family?"

"My aunt," she repeated. "And a few cousins. My parents...well, my parents weren't available. And since Kyle doesn't have any family left except for Sharon..."

"What does your aunt think of him?" Florence asked carefully.

"She likes him. Florence—" Hallie used her given name for the first time "—don't."

Florence folded her hands. "Tell me about this aunt of yours," she requested, backing off a little.

A smile touched Hallie's lips, despite her uneasiness.

"She 's my father's youngest sister, and I love her very much. If it hadn't been for her..."

Florence waited for Hallie to complete her thought. When she didn't the older woman said quietly, "I'm not really being a nosy old woman. I have a reason for asking. But I'll honor your privacy, if that's what you want."

"It's just..." Hallie shook her head, as if to clear it. "Aunt Catherine married once, but her husband died when she was young, and she never married again. She has no children, so she treats me like the child she never had."

"In the place of your parents," Florence concluded.

"I'd rather not—"

Florence stood. "That's enough. You've told me all I need to know."

"We're all perfectly respectable," Hallie assured her earnestly. "What Timothy said that first day—"

"Timothy said a lot of things, some of which he shouldn't have. You're not the kind of woman he accused you of being. I know that, and he does, too—now. Kyle on the other hand—" She stopped, her lips tightening.

Hallie braced for what was coming next. The Langs might have changed their opinion of her, although she had yet to see any sign of that in Timothy, but they both still hated Kyle.

Florence picked up her coffee cup. Discretion seemed to have won out. She motioned to the plate. "Have another biscuit," she said. "To keep up your strength."

Unspoken seemed to be the warning *You might need it.*

Hallie tried to smile. "No, thanks," she said, and she hoped that her reply was just as easy to interpret—that even though she was willing to become friends with Florence, her first loyalty was to Kyle, and she would continue to resist vigorously any defamation of his character.

Hallie wandered outside a few minutes later, leaving Florence to her bread making and her thoughts. The morning was crisp and sunny. Chickens pecked busily in the dirt, the sheep were already moving up and over the nearest hill, and a couple of cows grazed in a pasture a short distance away.

Hallie had never thought about living on a farm herself, but she could see the allure—a special closeness to nature, a rhythmic cadence to each day, a chance to slow down and appreciate the beauty of the land.

She saw Kyle in the corral. He stood beside the big black horse, adjusting the position of a short-sided blanket on its back. Dressed in jeans and boots and a workmanlike shirt, he seemed right at home with the task. Each motion was carried out with skill as he reached for a saddle and slung it on top of the blanket, then adjusted it, as well.

If he hadn't been her husband Hallie would still have found him fascinating to watch—the potent promise of a sexually attractive male. That he *was* her husband increased the thrill. She knew the promise to be reality. She knew what it was like to be kissed by him, to be touched by him, possessed by him.

He reached beneath the horse's belly for a strap to secure the saddle, fastened it, then followed that with a sharp slap to the horse's rump. The horse jumped and in one quick motion Kyle jerked the strap tighter.

"Why did you do that?" Hallie asked, frowning as she climbed up on a fence rail.

Kyle swung around. He hadn't known she was there, but his instant smile showed her she was welcome.

"Henry, here, likes to take a nice deep breath when he's being saddled. That way he thinks he can keep it from fitting too snugly. But if the saddle is loose, it'll slide around and under his belly—something he wouldn't appreciate and neither would his rider. In this case, me. So to save ourselves the trouble, I give him a little tap, he exhales, and I cinch him up before he can take a deep breath again."

"How do you know it's not too tight?" Hallie asked, curious. She had a fondness for animals, even if she wasn't intimately acquainted with any.

"You can tell by the way the saddle fits. Come here, I'll show you."

"That's okay. I believe you."

Kyle walked toward her, leading the horse by its reins. "You look quite appealing this morning, Mrs. McKenna," he murmured as he stopped directly across from her. His green eyes did a quick exploration of her face and form. "Good enough to take a nibble of."

He reached over the top rail and, unmindful of her giggling protests, lifted Hallie off her feet. He chuckled as he pretended to take a bite of her earlobe.

"Just what I suspected—delicious!" he teased, continuing to hold her off her feet.

"*McKenna!*" The name snapped out like the crack of a whip. "You're making a display of yourself in front of the girl." Timothy stood just outside the stable door in the corral, his bearing righteously angry.

Sharon was a step or two to one side of him, holding on to the reins of a dancing Candy.

"I kissed my wife, Timothy," Kyle replied. "What's wrong with that?"

Timothy's eyes narrowed into slits. It was obvious he had forgotten his agreement not to argue with Kyle in front of Sharon. "It's behavior best left to another time and place—that's what's wrong with it!"

"Your attitude comes from the Dark Ages, Timothy," Kyle said, making sure that Hallie found steady purchase on the bottom rail. "Maybe Florence would be happier if you'd give her a kiss in public now and then. Or have you forgotten how?"

Timothy looked ready to explode when Hallie intervened. "Is something wrong with Candy's leg?" she asked, frowning as she pointed to the horse who continued to skitter this way and that while at the same time slightly favoring her right front leg.

"Candy?" Sharon echoed with concern. She tried to get the horse to settle.

Kyle crossed to his daughter's side. Timothy also hurried over, squatting down and reaching for the leg. He ran both hands down its length, concentrating mostly on the knee.

"Feels a little warm," he pronounced. "Let's get her back in her stall and rub her down."

"Let's call the vet," Kyle suggested. "Sharon told me yesterday the horse has had trouble with this before."

Timothy eyed him with disgust. "You've been in the big city too long, boy. You've forgotten all you used to know about animals. Or is it that you wanted to forget?''

''I've forgotten nothing, Timothy,'' Kyle said, straightening to his full height. ''But I've also learned that sometimes it's necessary to ask for help. The old ways aren't always the best ways.''

Timothy stood up to face him. ''They've been good enough for me all these years.''

''Let loose of a dime now and then, Timothy,'' Kyle chided him. ''It's not going to kill you.''

''Granddad,'' Sharon broke in, ''maybe we should call Dr. West.''

''I'll pay his fee,'' Kyle volunteered.

Timothy's lip curled into a sneer. ''Isn't that just like you,'' he observed, his eyes glittering. ''You think you can buy your way in or out of anything. Well, it's not going to happen with me, McKenna. I've never touched a penny of your filthy conscience money, and I don't intend to start now.''

Hallie saw Kyle's back stiffen, and she immediately jumped down from the fence. She had trouble with the locking mechanism of the metal swing gate, but she finally overcame it and got inside the corral. Just as she started across the dirt, she saw Timothy take the reins from Sharon's hands and head for the stable door. When Kyle reached out to stop him, Hallie was afraid that both men had forgotten their promises and that this could turn into something very nasty.

''Kyle,'' she said breathlessly as she came up beside him. ''Kyle, don't.''

He shook her hand off as he might a fly. She'd never seen him so angry.

"Are you telling me," he asked Timothy with a dangerous slowness, "that you haven't touched any of the money I've sent for Sharon's upkeep all these years?"

"Not a cent!"

"You've made her suffer, do without, all because you're such a stubborn, vindictive—"

"She hasn't done without!" Timothy denied. "I've paid for everything, McKenna. By the sweat of *my* brow, not yours!"

Hallie looked from one man to the other, then at Sharon, who seemed frozen in place.

"Does she look like she's suffered?" Timothy challenged, motioning toward the girl. "There are no tears in her jeans, no frayed edges on her shirt."

"And you accuse *me* of trying to buy her love?" Kyle countered.

"I'm only doing what Cynthia would have wanted," Timothy retorted.

"Cynthia!" Kyle repeated, giving the name a bitter edge. "Cynthia would have spent the money on herself."

Timothy jerked forward. "Take that back!" he demanded, ready to do Kyle physical injury. Then suddenly he winced, jamming a balled up hand to his stomach.

Kyle stayed as he was, fists flexing at his sides, but he made no move to take advantage of the older man.

"You take it back, McKenna," Timothy ordered in a gruff hiss. It was obvious he was in pain.

"Sharon, take your grandfather's arm," Hallie said, stepping forward.

The girl stared at her blankly.

"Do it!" Hallie commanded, and the girl shook free of her stunned state and reached for her grandfather's sleeve.

"There's nothing wrong with me!" Timothy protested, trying to brush them both away. But his strength wasn't what it once had been and they had no trouble catching hold.

"I'll look after Candy," Kyle murmured.

Timothy glared furiously at him, but he let the reins slip from his fingers.

Kyle opened the gate for them and they slowly made their way toward the house.

"Damned troublemaker," Timothy grumbled after the first few steps. "I should have shot the bas—" He glanced at his granddaughter and shut up.

Florence must have seen them through the kitchen window. She rushed out the screen door, letting it bang shut behind her, and met them halfway across the yard. She took in her husband's pale face, forehead beaded with sweat and protective hand held just above his belt buckle.

Hallie saw the fear in her eyes.

"Thank you...thank you for helping him," Florence said as the two women exchanged places. "Did you take your medicine this morning like you were supposed to, Timothy?" she asked as they started off for the house. Then she noticed Sharon keeping up. "It's all right, dear. I'll take over from here. He's going to be just fine. You don't have to worry about a thing. He'll be just fine."

She seemed to be talking more to reassure herself than to comfort Sharon.

"Are you sure I can't help?" Hallie called after them. She and the girl stood a few feet apart, both left behind.

"No, we're fine . . . we're fine."

It was a mantra that Florence would probably keep repeating, so Hallie fell silent. She watched as the older couple passed through the gate and walked along the flagstone path and into the house.

She felt compelled to say something reassuring to the girl. "I'm sure he'll be—"

"—fine. I know," Sharon said hollowly.

Hallie turned to look at her, and for the first time read concern in the girl's eyes. Up to now Sharon had seemed interested only in herself—in what was happening to her or was going to happen to her. Her grandparents' needs and wishes hadn't mattered.

"Has this happened before?" Hallie asked.

"A couple of times. He's trying to get an ulcer, Grandma says. He takes his medicine, lies down for a while, then he's better."

Hallie didn't know what to say next. This was the first real conversation the two of them had ever shared.

Sharon moved uncomfortably, as if she, too, was aware of that fact. "I—I think I'm going to see how

Candy is,'' she announced, and after a moment did exactly that.

Hallie stood alone in the yard. Florence didn't seem to want her in the house, and Kyle and Sharon probably needed some time to themselves in the stable. She looked around and decided to take a walk.

CHAPTER EIGHT

HALLIE FOLLOWED the quiet rural road that fronted the farmhouse. Not relishing the idea of becoming lost, she kept to a path that would be easy to retrace.

Her thoughts were restless. They were barely four days into the week that she and Kyle were to spend here, and it already felt like a lifetime. This certainly wasn't the sort of trip you could write home to friends about with a quickly scribbled "Having a great time, wish you were here." She wouldn't wish this experience on anyone!

She thought of her aunt Catherine. How would she react to Florence and Timothy? As inherently sweet as her aunt was, she would probably feel sorry for them. But she wouldn't invite them to her home. Conflict was something her aunt avoided. That she'd stubbornly held her ground with her brother and sister-in-law and eventually persuaded them to let Hallie come live with her was a sign of how deeply she cared.

It had taken months for the little girl Hallie had been then to respond to her aunt's loving ways. Not that she hadn't wanted to respond; it was just that she couldn't. She was too afraid her aunt might reject her. But her aunt's love had remained constant, and ultimately she'd gained Hallie's trust.

Hallie longed to see her, to hear her reassuring voice, to look into her gentle brown eyes. But her aunt was on a driving tour of the Northeast, and she had no idea how to get in touch with her. Not that she would want to interrupt her aunt's vacation. If anyone had earned the right to send home a batch of "Having a great time" postcards and to laugh at the corniness of the expression, it was her aunt.

The first sign of a vehicle on the road was a thin plume of dust in the distance. Because of the speed of its approach, Hallie moved onto the shoulder to give it plenty of room to pass. But instead of shooting by, the pickup slowed and stopped.

Walker Bucannan jumped down from the cab. "Hey, pretty lady, I was wondering about you! I was just coming by to see how you are."

Hallie's dimples deepened. "Much better, as you can see."

"Uh-huh. Still look a little green around the gills to me."

"I'm not a fish," Hallie protested.

"You're telling me. If you were a fish, I'd be the first one on the side of the bank with a fishing pole. 'Course I'd probably have to fight off Kyle. And being that he's a younger man, he'd probably win."

Hallie grinned and theatrically placed a hand on her chest. "There'll always be a special place in my heart for you, Walker."

He snorted. "I've heard that before! Usually before the lady tells me to take a hike."

"I'd never do that."

"Uh-huh."

Hallie giggled.

"You just out for a little exercise?" Walker asked.

"I wanted to explore a bit."

Walker busied himself with lighting a cigar. "How are things at the Lang house today?" he asked casually. Too casually.

Hallie knew that if she pretended everything was all right Walker would spot the lie in a second. "Not very well," she admitted. "I'm trying, but nothing seems to be working out. Timothy upset himself just a little while ago, and his stomach started giving him trouble. Florence still thinks Kyle is the devil incarnate, and Sharon . . . well, Sharon thinks the same of me."

A puff of smoke obscured the craggy lines of Walker's face, but she thought she saw a dry smile. "Did you think it was going to be easy?" he asked.

Hallie shrugged. "No. Walker, I don't think it's ever going to work out. Timothy and Florence aren't going to budge. Neither is Kyle."

"I noticed that Florence had thawed a bit toward you last night, which is something."

"That's what I keep telling myself."

"Well, believe it. It's a lot."

"But Timothy—"

"—can act like a danged fool sometimes. So can Kyle. I've seen it all before, when Cynthia was alive. She played those two like they were violins and she was the concertmaster."

"Did she and Kyle—" Hallie stopped. "No, never mind. I shouldn't pry."

"Why not?" Walker's gray eyes narrowed.

"Because it's part of Kyle's life before we were married. He doesn't like to talk about it, so neither should I. Particularly not behind his back."

"But if I talk it's okay, isn't it? What do you want to know?"

Hallie felt guilty, but she couldn't help herself. "Did they fall in love right away?"

Walker leaned back against the truck and propped a boot heel against the tire. "Some people might call it love. I call it something else, but they were both fairly young. She was nineteen and Kyle was twenty-six. They met when Kyle arrived to cover a bad twister that came through the area and killed some folks. You heard about it, right?" At her nod, he continued, "He worked for a TV station in San Antonio. Came with a full crew, cameras and sound. Talked to people all over. Caused quite a stir. Almost more than the storm. Then he kept coming back—evenings, weekends, whenever he could get time off—to see Cynthia. Mind you, she was something to see. Ask Florence—she'll show you a picture. She put most of them away after the girl died. I guess because it was too hard to look at them and they had Sharon, who looked a lot like her mother did when she was that same age. Anyway, Florence and Timothy hit the roof when Kyle kept coming around. They had plans for Cynthia that didn't include him."

"What kind of plans?" Hallie felt like a thief, stealing knowledge.

"Well, they wanted her to marry my boy."

Hallie stared at him. "Were they engaged?"

"No. Not even close. This was more in Florence and Timothy's minds than it was in anyone else's."

"Did you want it?"

"Nope. She was my goddaughter, but I didn't particularly want her as a wife for Jimmy. I could see there was going to be trouble."

"So you weren't upset when Kyle and Cynthia married. Was your son?"

"Nope. Jimmy was just starting graduate school to be an engineer. He'd probably fooled around with the girl a time or two, but she fooled around a lot. Not just with him."

"Did Florence know that?" Hallie asked, her eyes widening as she thought about how straitlaced Florence was.

"There's a lot of things Florence and Timothy never knew about that girl of theirs."

"And you never told them?"

"Not my place." He puffed on his cigar. "It was hard for the two of them to give up their dream. I think Timothy wanted to join up the two farms, as well as the two families. It was like he could see that things were going to be hard in the future for farmers and ranchers—harder than usual—and he was trying to get things set up properly for all of us. He wouldn't admit that now of course. Probably wouldn't <u>have</u> then. He also wanted to keep Cynthia close to home. If she married Kyle, Lord knows where she'd end up."

"Did they try to stop them?"

GINGER CHAMBERS   135

"Tried as hard as they could. Tried so hard Kyle and Cynthia ended up running off. 'Course Sharon was already on the way, and that was something else for Timothy and Florence to be embarrassed about and to blame Kyle for."

"And you don't? Blame Kyle?"

"Things happen because they're meant to happen. That's it."

"What about after they married? How did the Langs react then?"

"Cynthia didn't let them see the baby for at least six months after Sharon was born. She hadn't called or written them for an entire year. Guess who they blamed?"

"But if they disliked Kyle so much, isn't it only natural he'd resent them?"

Walker carefully extinguished the half-smoked cigar and placed it in a narrow metal case he carried in his shirt pocket. "I don't know how much responsibility Kyle bears in all this. What happened in the marriage is his secret to tell. I'm not privy to it. All I know is there's been a lot of hell created and he's been at the center of it. But he's not alone."

Hallie was quiet, thinking about all she'd learned. "Why did you tell me this?" she asked.

Walker straightened. "Because if you're going to be in the thick of the battle, you need a weapon or two on your side." He smiled slowly. "Would you like a ride back to the farm?"

Once again Hallie saw the compassion in his eyes. It wasn't something he would easily admit, but he truly cared for the Langs. They were among his oldest friends. Yet he also cared for her and for Kyle and for Sharon. He was doing his best to see that in the end everything worked out.

Hallie crooked her finger, a request for Walker to bend down. When he did, she quickly kissed his whisker-roughened cheek. "You're a good friend, Walker," she said softly. "To all of us."

To her amazement color bloomed in his cheeks as he quickly pulled away. He seemed not to know what to do with his hands or feet.

She smiled at him fondly. "Thanks for the offer, but I think I'll keep walking for a little longer. You've given me a lot to consider."

Walker nodded and strode back to the cab of his truck. After restarting the engine, he pulled slowly away so as not to stir up a lot of dust.

Hallie waved, thinking what a wonderful considerate man he was, and wondering how on earth any woman in her right mind could have left him.

SHARON SAT on a hay bale at one side of the stall and watched her father examine Candy's leg. It was strange how he seemed to fit in no matter the circumstance. He was like a chameleon, capable of adapting to any situation—on the farm, in a faraway city, in places that had no names. Kyle McKenna, her father. His face and voice was known to millions of people around the world. Sometimes she resented the unknown millions. The fact that she had to share him with them. He was her father. Hers!

Sharon moved, uneasily aware that he had straightened and was now looking at her.

"What do you think we should do?" he asked. "Call the vet, or do as your grandfather said and rub her down?"

Sharon considered the options. "Call the vet," she said. "Granddad said we might have to if it kept getting sore."

"When did he say that?" Kyle asked.

"The last time it happened."

Kyle laughed shortly and shook his head. "Stubborn old—" He laughed again.

He came over to the hay bale and sat down beside her, leaning back against the worn wall planking just as she did. Sharon moved over to give him room. He reached for her hand and placed it on his knee, patting it lightly as he said, "He'd just as soon wrestle a mountain lion as take a suggestion from me."

"Daddy?" she ventured. "Why doesn't he like you? Is it because you and Mommy ran off to get married?"

Kyle looked at her from the corner of his eye. "How do you know about that?"

"I found one of Mommy's letters. It was the one she wrote them when you two were getting ready to run away. She said you were going to do it and that nothing they did or said could make her change her mind. And for them not to come after you, because she'd run back to you again and again until they finally left you alone."

Kyle said nothing.

Sharon murmured, "It was very romantic." She pulled her hand away from his, unsure that she should have mentioned the letter. Maybe it was something he didn't want to talk about. It was definitely something her grandparents didn't discuss with her. She might have hatched from an egg as far as they were concerned, with no mother or father at all.

She had memories of living with her parents when her mother was alive. She remembered two houses, one she later learned was in San Antonio, the other in Houston. One was large, the other larger, with trees and flowers and a little boy next door she played with when she got home from day care.

Her mother was beautiful with dark hair like her own, and she always smelled good. Her father liked to carry her on his shoulders, making her giggle as he took her upstairs to bed.

But she also remembered something else. Something that seemed like a faraway dream—anger, tension, raised voices as she hid under the sheets. She was only four or five, but she knew enough to be frightened.

"Your grandfather doesn't like me on general principles," Kyle answered. "He didn't like me the instant he first set eyes on me."

"But why?" Sharon persisted, frowning.

"Have you ever asked him?"

"No, I asked Gran."

"And what did she say?"

"She said not to bother her with questions like that. Daddy, she doesn't like you very much, either."

Kyle laughed dryly. "I'm the least popular person in the area."

Sharon leaned forward. "But that's not true! People who know me, who know who you are, they all think you're the best reporter on TV. They've told me so. It's just Gran and Granddad who..." She didn't finish the sentence.

"...hate me." Kyle finished it for her.

Her chin dipped. "Yes," she agreed, barely above a whisper.

Her father placed a comforting arm around her shoulders. It felt so good to be protected, even if the moment was fleeting. Her heart thudded strongly, her throat tightened with emotion.

"Honey," her father said quietly, "a person can't always be liked by everyone in life. Sometimes a person does things that other people don't agree with. But just because people don't agree, doesn't mean things shouldn't be done. Do you understand?"

Sharon nodded, but what he said wasn't entirely clear. Was he talking about himself and her grandparents and her mother? Or was he talking about something else? Something she didn't know about and was unable to understand?

"I hope so," he said. "Right now, I can't explain it any better. Maybe one day, when you're older—"

Sharon closed her eyes. *One day, when you're older!* She was almost fourteen! Wasn't that old enough?

"—we'll have a long talk and I'll try to explain."

Even though Sharon wanted to protest his depiction of her as a child, she listened to his huskily spoken words. *One day...I'll try to explain.* That promised a future for them. Together.

She wrapped her arms around her father's waist and held on tightly, like the child she didn't want to be mistaken for.

HALLIE FOUND Kyle in the stable. He was brushing Jill, and from the satisfied toss of Henry's head, the black horse had been brushed, as well. With ears working to catch every sound, Henry stood at the front of his stall, his head hanging over the top board, interested in everything going on. He greeted Hallie with a friendly whicker.

"Where did you disappear to?" Kyle asked, coming to stand at the front of Jill's stall.

"I took a walk. Where's Sharon?"

"In the house calling the vet."

"I didn't see her."

"She's probably using the phone in the living room so she won't disturb her granddad. How is he, by the way?"

"Florence said he's resting comfortably."

"Man's too ornery to rest comfortably."

Kyle went back to brushing Jill, smoothing the bristles over the horse's rump. Hallie patted Henry and then Jill when she came forward and poked her head out. Hallie cooed to her softly, appreciating the velvety touch of the horse's muzzle as she nudged her hand, looking for a treat.

"Next time bring her a carrot," Kyle said.

"I will. One for Henry, too. How's Candy?"

"Not any worse."

"Does this mean that Sharon won't be able to ride her again before we leave? It would be such a shame if she couldn't."

"We'll have to see what the vet says."

Hallie continued to stroke Jill, but she wasn't paying as close attention to what she was doing as she'd been before. "Kyle," she said eventually, "does the offer to teach me to ride still stand?"

The motion of the brush stopped. Kyle looked up, his pale eyes curious. "What's brought this on?"

Hallie shrugged. "Well, it's like you said. There's not a lot to do and...and I thought it might help with Sharon if I'm able to do something she loves."

"Hallie, you're trying too hard. I told you last night—"

"It's not that," she denied. "I really would like to learn. Horses are...nice."

"You probably think cows are nice, too."

"If I knew one, I probably would." Hallie lifted her chin.

Kyle grinned. "Sure, yeah, the offer's still open. When would you like to start? Now?"

"Why not?" Hallie said. She saw Sharon come into the stable and thought that now was just as good a time as any.

Kyle saw her, too. "Sharon, Hallie wants to learn to ride. Which horse would be better? Jill or Henry?"

"Either one," Sharon answered noncommittally.

"Jill, please," Hallie requested.

"Jill it is," Kyle agreed.

Jill must have realized that something was up because she lifted her head and started to stamp around.

Kyle slipped a bridle over the horse's head and secured it in place. Then he led her outside to the corral, where he soon reached for a blanket and saddle.

Hallie started to get cold feet. What was she doing? she asked herself as she and Sharon followed him into the corral. She wasn't dressed for riding. Her wide-legged black crepe-de-chine slacks were more suited to an afternoon spent browsing through an art museum than clinging to the back of a powerful steed. Her blouse—simple, snowy white; her shoes—black flats, not cowboy boots.

She watched nervously as Kyle completed the job of saddling the horse. She could feel Sharon's eyes on her, judging her, so she tried to keep her trepidation to herself, but she doubted she was successful.

When Kyle finished he turned to her. "Still want to do it?" he asked quietly.

Hallie gulped and nodded.

Kyle held her gaze and said, "Come over here and pet her again. She's still the same horse she was a few minutes ago."

Hallie crossed to the horse's side. Jill greeted her with an inquisitive head nod. Hallie jumped back, then forced herself to reach out. Up till now there'd always been a fence or the wooden slats of a stall separating them, a barrier that offered more psychological protection than real safety. At present there was just her and the horse and Kyle, nothing in between.

Jill nuzzled her hand, again looking for a treat. Hallie laughed a little anxiously. "Maybe I should go get a carrot."

"She's fine," Kyle said. "She's just a mooch."

Hallie bit her bottom lip to keep it from trembling. She patted the smooth cheek. "You don't think she'll mind if I ride her?"

"She's used to it," Kyle said.

Sharon had taken a seat on the top rail of the fence near the gate, her heels hooked on the railing below. Hallie glanced at her—at her skeptical expression—and felt her own determination grow. "What do I have to do?" she asked tightly.

"Do you want a boost, or do you want to do it yourself?"

"Do it myself."

"Then put your left foot in the stirrup, stand up, swing your right leg up and over and find the stirrup on the other side. Do you want me to show you?"

Hallie nodded.

"Okay," he said. "Stand back a space."

After she complied, he swung easily into the saddle, doing exactly as he'd said. Jill skittered slightly, then became still.

Hallie gazed up at him. He seemed so high up, so in command. He made it look simple. Once he swung down, he even said, "See, it's easy. Nothing to it."

Hallie wasn't deceived. She knew nothing was as simple as people accustomed to doing an activity claimed it to be.

Nevertheless she said, "I put my foot in here—like this?"

The position was awkward.

"That's right," Kyle approved. "Now, grab hold of the saddle horn and pull yourself up."

Hallie could feel perspiration break out over her body, from fear, from expectation. She took a deep breath and tried to do as he said, but she ended up hopping about on her right foot as Jill skittered sideways.

Kyle curbed the horse with a tug on the reins and a quick reproving word. Then he took Hallie's arm to steady her as she brought her left leg back down to the ground.

"I don't understand," she said, heat growing in her cheeks. "I can't seem to..."

Hallie heard Sharon's giggles from across the way and felt her cheeks grow even hotter.

"All it takes is a little practice," Kyle said firmly, throwing his daughter a quelling look. "Give it another try."

Once again Hallie lifted her left leg and slid her foot into the stirrup.

"I have the reins. Don't worry," Kyle assured her as she started to bounce on her right foot. "Use your hands," he instructed. "Pull yourself up."

Hallie bounced and pulled and got nowhere. She felt like a fool. How had she ever thought to gain Sharon's respect when she looked like a participant in a comedy act? But suddenly she felt a hand applied to the seat of her pants and a second later, her right leg swung over the horse's back and she plopped down in the saddle. She then veered crazily from one side to the other, until finally, miraculously, she gained some control.

Jill moved forward several paces, eliciting another cry from Hallie. The ground looked so far down!

"Whoa, girl," Kyle crooned, trying to soothe the horse. "Settle down. Everything's fine."

Jill stamped her hooves a few more times, then stood still, her great chest heaving.

Hallie clung to the saddle horn. It felt so strange to be perched on the back of such a large animal—an animal, who though sweet and friendly, was immensely strong. And who, if she wanted, could take it into her head to run off and Hallie wouldn't be able to do anything to stop her, only hang on for dear life. There was no doubt about who was in command here—and it wasn't Hallie!

"You okay?" Kyle asked, his eyes dancing with amusement.

Hallie nodded jerkily. "I'm fine. What's next?"

"We have to make sure the stirrups are the right length. They're a little long, from the look of them. Slip your foot out for a minute."

"You mean...take it out of the stirrup?"

Kyle grinned at her. "You won't fall off, I promise."

Hallie did as he directed, her fingers clutching the saddle horn desperately. She prayed that Jill wouldn't move.

Kyle worked on the leather strap that supported the stirrup, and after a moment told her to slip her foot in again. Then he moved to the other side and did the same thing.

"Now stand up," he said.

"Stand up?" Hallie repeated, but this time she did as he requested without making him explain.

He nodded, satisfied, and signaled that she could sit down. Then he put a hand on her knee. "We're going to walk you around a little bit. Let you get used to the feel. You don't have to worry about guiding her or anything. I still have the reins. Are you ready?"

Hallie gave a short nod.

At first it took all her concentration not to fall off. Jill's gait seemed exaggerated, each foot stomping the ground like a battering ram, sending shock waves up Hallie's spine. Then slowly Hallie became accustomed to the motion, and what had felt like stiff-legged jabs became surefooted plops.

Kyle walked slowly around the corral, glancing frequently at Hallie to see how she was holding up. Finally she sent him a glowing smile.

"This isn't so bad!" she enthused, and even found confidence enough to pat the side of Jill's neck close to her mane. That was as far as she wanted to reach.

Jill's ears moved independently of each other, one tuned to Kyle in front and one tuned to Hallie on her back. Hallie laughed.

The first couple of times they went past Sharon, Hallie had been too preoccupied to look at her. This time Hallie couldn't help but grin at the girl. But Sharon didn't smile back and Hallie's grin faded.

Kyle went around the corral another time, then drew to a halt near where they'd started. "Now for the next step," he said. "You get to do this by yourself."

Hallie immediately panicked. "Oh, no, Kyle. I'm not ready... am I?"

"Relax," he said, patting Jill's shoulder as he moved toward Hallie. "You're ready. As ready as you'll ever be."

"But, Kyle—" Hallie started to protest again.

"Maybe you shouldn't make her do it, Daddy," Sharon chimed in. "She might spook the horse and cause all kinds of problems."

Kyle reached around Jill's head, splitting the reins properly. Then he held them out to Hallie. "It's a piece of cake," he said softly. "Take the reins in one hand—your right hand since you're right-handed and will feel more comfortable that way—and let your other hand rest on your thigh."

"But I'll fall off when she walks!"

"No, you won't. Hold on with your knees. You won't fall."

Hallie looked at him, then glanced at Sharon, who seemed pleased at the prospect that Hallie might chicken out. She looked back into Kyle's confident gaze.

"All right," she said tightly, and accepted the reins. He showed her exactly how to hold them.

"Now let go of the horn," he said.

"What do I do if she runs away?"

"She won't."

Mercifully when Hallie removed her hand from the horn and placed it, trembling, on her thigh, Jill remained perfectly still.

"Pull left when you want to go left and pull right when you want to go right. When you want to stop, pull back. But not too hard. You don't want to startle her." He began to walk away.

"Where are you going?" Hallie squeaked. At this moment she didn't care what Sharon thought. She only wanted to survive.

"I'm just giving you some room to maneuver."

Hallie could feel sweat break out over her body again. This was it. This was really the full experience. She waited for Jill to start forward.

When nothing happened, she looked blankly at Kyle.

"Just give her a little tap with your heels," he suggested.

Hallie followed his instruction timidly. Nothing happened.

"A little harder," Kyle said.

"I don't want to make her angry," Hallie pleaded.

Kyle laughed, genuinely amused. "Hallie, you're wonderful! But if you don't tell her what to do, she's not going to do it. You're the boss."

Hallie tapped a little harder, and this time Jill started off to the accompaniment of Hallie's fearful moan. She wobbled drunkenly in the saddle, forgetting everything she'd been told.

"Keep firm hold of the reins," Kyle called from a short distance to one side. "Your free hand should be on your knee. No! Don't reach for the horn. Let her know which way you want her to turn."

They were fast approaching the fence and Hallie had to make a decision to go either right or left. She pulled right and amazingly the horse turned in that direction.

Hallie's heart thudded, her breathing was jerky, and she didn't know if she wanted to laugh or cry. But she'd done it! She'd gotten the horse to do what she wanted!

They continued, Kyle jogging alongside, tracing more of a square in the corral than a circle, but each time the fence loomed, Hallie pulled on the reins and Jill responded.

As had happened earlier, Hallie soon adapted to the process. She even tried stopping and restarting Jill, and it worked! Then for variety, she had her turn left. And that worked, too!

At some point Kyle stopped keeping pace, and when next she noticed him he was leaning back against the fence, grinning proudly.

"This is fun!" she cried.

He grinned. "Of course it is."

She went around the corral again, this time actually forming a circle. Then she went around it again.

"That might be enough to begin with," Kyle suggested after she'd completed yet another circuit. "You've really done very well. Hasn't she, Sharon?"

Sharon hopped off the top rail. "Not bad," she admitted begrudgingly.

"Not bad at all," Kyle emphasized.

Strangely Hallie didn't feel like getting off. For someone who'd been terrified only a short time before, she was decidedly beginning to enjoy herself.

She reached out and patted Jill's neck, farther down this time and while Jill was still moving. She'd gained that much confidence. "You're a wonderful horse," she cooed. "Thank you for letting me ride you. Later, I promise, I'll bring you that carrot!"

Her face was glowing when Kyle came to collect the reins.

"You get down the same way you got up, only in reverse," he said.

Hallie lifted her right leg. It felt heavy, but she managed to bring it over the saddle. Then she kicked her left foot clear of the stirrup, as she had seen Kyle do, and jumped.

It was only when both feet hit the ground that she realized her muscles had turned to jelly. It was all she could do to stay upright.

She automatically reached for Kyle for support. He eyed her with concern.

"I was afraid that might have been a bit too much," he said. "You're going to stiffen up even more later."

"But... I'm in good condition."

"These are different muscles than you usually use."

Sharon, who'd been watching them from a short distance away, stomped toward them and exploded,

"For heaven's sake! Here! Let me take care of Jill so you can help *her* to the house."

"I don't need to be helped," Hallie claimed.

As Sharon took the reins from her father's hand, her eyes traveled over Hallie disparagingly. "You look like you're going to fall down."

"Well, I'm not!" Hallie let go of Kyle's arm to prove her point. She swayed slightly, but didn't collapse.

"Sharon, behave yourself," Kyle warned.

The girl looked at her father, her pretty face a mix of emotions. Guilt, because she knew she was being unfair. Anger at Hallie, for being Hallie. Anger at him, because he was the one who'd brought this intruder into the scene. There was also a plea for understanding. A plea that her father show he loved her best by taking her side.

Recognizing the girl's vulnerability, Hallie searched for a way to defuse the tension. "Do they still make those awful liniments? The kind you put on horses, but sometimes use on humans, too? They're supposed to smell terrible." She wrinkled her nose.

Kyle tore his gaze from his daughter's. "Where did you hear about that?" he asked, amused.

"Some book I read."

"Would you like us to ask the vet when he comes?" Kyle teased. "When's he due, Sharon?"

"He said he'd be out in a couple of hours," the girl answered peevishly. She wasn't ready to concede anything to Hallie, not even her attempt to be a good sport.

"A long soak in a tub of hot water would probably do you more good," Kyle said seriously. "And the sooner the better. Can you walk?"

"Of course," Hallie answered with all the dignity she could muster.

"The question later will be, 'Can she sit down?'" Sharon murmured, seemingly just beginning to relish the thought of getting to watch Hallie suffer.

CHAPTER NINE

HALLIE CAME DOWNSTAIRS slowly and settled into her place at the dinner table with extreme care. The long hot soak in the tub had done wonders, but it hadn't been a magic cure-all. Muscles she hadn't even known she possessed protested at their abuse.

"Are you sure you want to do this?" Florence questioned, frowning. "I could easily bring a tray upstairs."

Hallie sent her a grateful smile. "I'm fine, thank you."

Timothy, who looked to have fully recovered from his own disorder, sat at the head of the table, his icy blue eyes taking her measure before moving away.

"Are you feeling better, Timothy?" Hallie asked. She was determined not to let him keep such a firm upper hand. He had intimidated her at first, but she had to start standing up to him.

"Yes," he answered tersely.

Sharon watched her with undisguised glee. "Would you like to go for another ride after dinner?"

"I'll pass."

"First and last lesson," Sharon mocked.

Hallie accepted the bowl being passed around the table and spooned a serving of mashed potatoes onto her plate. "No, not at all," she said, offering the bowl to Timothy. "I quite liked it. In fact, I'd like to go again tomorrow."

"Tomorrow might be too soon," Kyle said.

Hallie accepted another bowl and added a spoonful of green beans to her plate. "I mend quickly."

Her hand collided with Timothy's as she passed the bowl on. His moved away immediately.

"It would be a silly thing to do," Florence said. "No use making matters worse."

"Let her do what she wants," Timothy decreed. But he wasn't supporting Hallie in her decision. His reasoning sprang from spite—as in, let the witch get what she deserves.

"Yes," Sharon agreed, quick to pick up on her grandfather's meaning. "If she wants to, let her."

"Why don't you decide when the time comes?" Kyle suggested.

"That would be much better," Florence said.

Timothy looked at his wife with incredulity. "Did I hear that right? You're agreeing with *him* now?"

Florence's lips tightened. "I'm not agreeing with him, Timothy. I'm agreeing with what he said. Hallie should wait a couple of days before she tries to ride a horse again."

"You two gals are getting mighty thick," he said reprovingly.

Florence said nothing, but her jaw jutted stubbornly.

The table was silent as they started to eat. Hallie noticed later that Timothy had finished only his po-

tatoes. She wasn't hungry, either, but she forced herself to clean her plate. After almost passing out the
night before and then being in pain tonight, she didn't
want them to think she was in any way fragile.

That was why, at the end of the meal, she insisted
upon cleaning the table as usual.

"Sharon will help me tonight," Florence said,
stopping the girl halfway through the doorway into the
hall. The men had already left the room, so it was only
the three of them there.

Sharon looked at Florence archly. "I didn't think I
counted anymore, Gran. You and your new friend are
getting along so well I'm not needed. Granddad's
right. You two are getting thick."

"I'm asking you to help me, Sharon."

"Why should I if she's willing? Let her take my
place." She snapped her fingers as if an idea had just
occurred. "I know! She can take my place after this
week, too! Daddy and I will go to Atlanta and she can
stay here with you. Even exchange. Then everybody
will be happy. You won't miss me at all!"

Deeply wounded, Florence asked, "Why would you
say such a thing?"

"Because it's true!"

"Sharon..." Florence began, but the girl didn't wait
for more. She disappeared into the hallway and then
they heard her feet pounding upstairs. Seconds later
the door to her room slammed shut.

Hallie watched as gathering pain etched itself on
Florence's face. Was she beginning to see the past
blossom once again in the present? All the trouble with

Cynthia before she left the farm, and now the trouble brewing with Sharon? But Sharon's anger sprang from a different source. Sharon didn't want to share anything, particularly with her, Hallie. Not her father, not her grandparents.

Hallie rose slowly from the table. It wasn't easy, but she managed to take a stack of plates into the kitchen.

"You shouldn't be doing this," Florence complained.

"It's better to keep moving."

Hallie started back into the dining room only to meet Kyle in the hall.

"I don't suppose it'd make any difference if I asked you go upstairs and get into bed," he said.

Hallie grinned, dimpling. "It would depend on your motivation."

"Do you honestly think you're ready for me to be motivated?" he murmured.

Florence appeared in the kitchen doorway, preventing Hallie's answer. Kyle glanced at her, then shifted his gaze back to his wife. "Later," he growled with mock ferocity, and turned to walk away.

All the love Hallie felt for him was in her eyes as she watched him disappear from view. Turning, she saw that Florence had followed his departure with barely contained disapproval. Still, this time, the older woman said nothing.

Hallie collected the glasses and brought them to the kitchen. But as she started off once again to continue clearing the table, Florence shooed her away from further effort.

"That's enough. Go to the living room and watch TV if you insist on staying up. I'll finish here."

Hallie finally relented. It was one thing to prove a point and another to act like an idiot. As she'd claimed earlier, she did mend quickly, but her body, like everyone else's, required a certain amount of time to recover.

She chose a magazine from the chest and settled on the couch. She was just finishing an article when Florence joined her.

"That's done for another day," Florence said as she took a seat in her favorite chair. She rubbed her hands together, spreading a soothing lotion.

Hallie lowered the magazine and smiled. "Do you ever get tired of life on a farm?"

"Not so I notice."

"But it's the same thing day after day."

"Isn't that the way it is with what you do?"

Hallie shrugged. "I meet different people. Interesting people."

"But you do the same thing day after day."

"In a way I suppose so. People need their seat assignments, need their tickets changed, lose their luggage." She thought of Kyle and how they'd met.

"That's how it is with me. I feed the chickens, gather the eggs, keep the house clean, cook the meals."

"But it's so solitary."

"I don't mind. I'm used to it."

"And you've never wanted anything else?"

Florence hesitated, then she said starkly, "I want to keep my granddaughter with me."

A knot formed in Hallie's stomach. For one second she'd let down her guard. She'd asked a question that almost forced Florence into giving a brutally honest reply.

"But she's the one who wrote to Kyle asking to come live with him," Hallie said quietly, not wanting to inflict additional pain, but knowing that she, too, had to speak the truth.

Florence waved that away. "Sharon is at an age where she's confused. One day she's up, the next she's down."

"She hasn't changed her mind," Hallie insisted.

"She just doesn't know." Florence dropped her hands to her lap and fell silent.

Hallie was silent, as well. The Langs' hatred of Kyle was so blind, so all-encompassing, there was nothing she could do to change it. And that was the only key to the situation.

When she'd first come here she'd thought the Langs were terrible people who were actively harming Sharon. It hadn't taken her long to revise that theory—to learn that Florence and Timothy truly loved Sharon almost more than was healthy for any of them. Their hateful actions were rooted in fear—fear of losing the young girl's love, as well as her physical presence.

"Florence—" Hallie began, but the older woman spoke at the same time.

"We haven't told her what we know about Kyle. We didn't think it would be good for her."

Hallie considered Kyle's fears, his belief that his in-laws might at any time try to poison Sharon against him. "That's...good," Hallie said hesitantly.

"Now I wonder if we did the right thing. If only she knew even just a little, it might make a difference to how she looks at him."

Hallie sat forward, forgetting for the moment her bruised flesh. "No! That wouldn't be a good idea, Florence."

"Why not? Hurt her now so that she isn't hurt more in the future. How is that wrong?"

Hallie shook her head. "No, Florence."

An odd smile tilted Florence's lips before disappearing. "Probably would do you some good, too."

"Florence...I don't want to hear any more lies."

"What if it's not a lie? What if it's the truth?"

"Your truth!" Hallie retorted, becoming angry. They just wouldn't stop. They had to keep pushing and pushing. That was one of the main reasons Kyle had made the decision to take Sharon away. Not content to have her live with them, they had to interfere with his visits—shortening them, canceling days without notice. Anything to keep Kyle and Sharon apart, to cut him out of her life.

"What if I was to tell you that it's Kyle who's doing the lying?" Florence taunted. "And I can prove it."

Hallie shook her head again, only this time the knot in her stomach reappeared. She wanted to run from what might follow. She felt herself losing control.

"Earlier you said something about Kyle's not having any family except Sharon to invite to your wedding. Is that what you believe?"

Hallie couldn't answer.

"Well, it's not true," Florence said. "I debated telling you about this, but now I see I have to—it's an obligation. Kyle not only has a stepmother, but a half brother and half sister. They still live out on that ranch where he grew up west of San Antonio. I've met them. They came for a visit a few years after he and Cynthia got married. There was trouble between them, too, bad blood. Kyle was trying to cheat them out of some money. They wanted Timothy and me to do something about it."

Hallie's throat tightened. It wasn't true! Kyle had told her there was no one!

"I can also show you some of Cynthia's letters," Florence continued. "You can read them for yourself. You can see how he drank, how he womanized—"

"No!" Hallie jumped to her feet. She didn't care about her aching flesh.

"—how he hit her. I never did tell Timothy about that. I didn't want him to end up in jail."

Tears filled Hallie's eyes.

Florence got up to put an arm around Hallie's shoulders, but Hallie evaded her. Sighing, the older woman crossed to the small desk in the corner of the room and opened a narrow drawer. She withdrew a packet of letters, extracting the top two.

"Here," she said, holding them out to Hallie. "These came near the end. Cynthia died shortly after writing them. When you read what she has to say you might ask yourself the same questions we did, and you might come to the same conclusion." She took a moment to continue. "I don't want to hurt you. I know you think you love him. But he can't be allowed to get away with it again. When I asked about your aunt before, I did it for a reason. I wanted to see how close you two are, to see if she objected to your marriage, to see how she felt about Kyle. But if she likes him... You have to have *someone* looking out for you, Hallie! Particularly if you won't do it for yourself!"

Without noticing where she was going, Hallie started to back away. She bumped into a chair, a table. "I don't want them," she said huskily. "I believe Kyle. I believe..." Her throat closed on the rest.

Florence gazed at her sadly. "I'd have to answer to God if I didn't try harder to make you understand."

Hallie gave a small cry and hurried from the room.

The stairs were difficult for her to manage because of the flood of hot tears that blurred her vision, but she climbed them. She hurried down the hall into her bedroom. Hers and Kyle's.

She opened the door, then used it for support once she was inside. She didn't believe a thing Florence said! Not for a second! Tears continued to flow. She hated this place! She hated Florence! She hated

Sharon! She and Kyle had been happy before they'd come here!

She forced the tears to stop, forced herself to wipe her cheeks and take several deep breaths. She had to regain control.

She went into the bathroom and splashed water on her face, then she combed her hair and went back downstairs. She found Florence in the living room, still sitting in her chair. The quilt piece slowly lowered as Hallie entered the room.

"Hallie?" The woman seemed as if genuinely concerned by the way she looked.

"I thought we were becoming friends," Hallie said, her voice shaking with emotion.

"We are," Florence agreed.

"Friends don't treat other friends that way. They don't try to hurt them. That's not what a real friend does."

"I agree, but—"

"There are no buts! Your conscience can be clear now, Florence. You've warned me. More than once. So don't do it again."

"Hallie, it's only because I'm worried."

"I can take care of myself! It took a number of years, but now I finally think I'm worth taking care of! I married Kyle because I love him. And he loves me. *He* loves *me!*"

Florence watched her sadly. "If that's what you think," she said.

"It's what I *know!*" Hallie declared. "Now...are we going to stay friends? Are you through putting your nose in where it doesn't belong?"

"There's one more thing." Florence hesitated, apparently reluctant. "Hallie, I have to ask—when did you meet Kyle? Was it somewhere near the end of July this last summer?"

"What difference does that make?" Hallie demanded stiffly.

"Because that was when Kyle's lawyer first contacted us and told us Kyle wanted Sharon back. If that was close to when he met you, it means—"

"It means nothing," Hallie said coldly. "All right. You've made your decision. We go back to being enemies. Which is a shame, really, because it's you who's going to be the big loser. You're forcing Sharon to choose between you or us—and it's very clear what her decision will be."

Hallie turned away.

"I want us to be friends!" Florence cried, abandoning the chair.

Hallie turned back. "All right," she said quietly. "We'll be friends—on condition." Then she spun on her heel and walked out the door.

HALLIE LAY curled in bed later that night, curled away from Kyle. She had used sore muscles as justification for her need not to be touched. But it was more than that.

Long after Kyle had fallen asleep, she lay there awake. She didn't want to believe a word Florence

said, but something in the back of her mind kept stirring. She'd met Kyle in late July. In late July his at-
torney had contacted the Langs. Did that mean
anything? Did it have the sinister turn Florence inti-
mated?

No! Hallie's mind cried as her fingers twisted in the
pillowcase beneath her cheek. It didn't mean a thing!
It was just ... coincidence. But what about his telling
her he didn't have family when he did? Or forgetting
to mention the visitation rights? Or saying he should
have come for Sharon years ago? At the time he'd said
it the thought had flashed through her mind: Did that
mean he would have brought along a different wife?
But she had immediately rejected it as being disloyal.
Now she wondered ... was it?

Hallie bit her knuckle to keep from crying out. She
didn't want to think things like that! She didn't want
to believe that Kyle could in any way deceive her. It
was impossible. He loved her. *He loved her!*

But why should he? a voice from long ago
prompted. Why should he—a man like Kyle Mc-
Kenna, who'd obviously been pursued by numerous
beautiful women—look twice at someone like her?
Someone who even her own parents had found difficult to love?

She wasn't pretty, not really. Her nose was too
small, her eyes too big. Pale skin, pale hair, flat chest.

She'd never shined at anything the way other children did. Her parents had tried. They'd dragged her
to events at their club, dressed her up, sent her out—
always putting a brave face on it, of course, because

they knew in their heart of hearts that she'd never win. And when she didn't, it was as if she had failed on purpose, just to be obstinate. She'd done nothing but cause problems for them from the moment she was born.

She'd had some kind of difficulty shortly after delivery and almost died. As a child, she'd sometimes wondered if she had disappointed them by surviving. A dead baby was easier to speculate about—to create a monument to—than a living, breathing failure. How could parents explain that to their friends? If she was a failure, they were a failure—because they'd given birth to her. She was always lacking in their eyes. She didn't walk soon enough, talk soon enough, make good enough grades. She wasn't athletic. They had wanted to use her like a trophy they could take out and show off, only it didn't work out that way. Her life to the age of ten had been a series of failures.

Hallie drew an unsteady breath. Even today, when with Aunt Catherine's help she understood that it was her parents who had the problem, not her, the memories were hard to deal with. She'd been a basket case, a girl with a devastating lack of self-worth, when she moved to Atlanta from Richmond. Only years of patient, loving kindness had changed that. College had helped; so did getting a job at the airline and doing well in it. Then, years later, meeting Kyle.

Hallie heard him breathing steadily behind her. She wanted to reach out to him. She ached to touch him, any part of him—his arm, his shoulder, his neck. She wanted him to open his eyes and look at her, to tell her

he loved her and only her. That Cynthia didn't matter
to him anymore, that Sharon was his daughter and he
loved her, but not in the way he loved Hallie, his wife.
She wanted him to hold her close, to never let her go.
But she couldn't touch him. Not now. Not while she...

Hallie shied away from the word *doubt.* It was too
scary. *Questioned,* that was better. She was questioning herself, questioning him.

Late July. They'd met in late July. And the next two
months had passed at astonishing speed. Kyle had
taken over her life. He'd consumed her.

Had he sensed that because she'd been wounded
badly in her youth he would have an advantage and
could manipulate her?

"No!" Hallie cried again, only this time out loud.

In his sleep Kyle reached for her. He slipped an arm
around her waist and pulled her against him.

For a second Hallie resisted, then she allowed herself to relax. Feeling his strong body pressed to hers
was like coming home. Home and Kyle. For her, they
were synonymous.

SHARON STOOD at the corral, her arms folded on the
top rail as she watched the horses munch on the carrots she'd been sent to give them.

A short time before, her father had discovered Hallie at the refrigerator holding a bunch of carrots, and
instead of letting Hallie feed them to the horses as
she'd planned, he'd told Sharon to do it.

Sharon kicked the dirt with the toe of her boot. *She*
hadn't been the one who promised the horses carrots

yesterday. *She* wasn't the one who was acting such a ninny, gaining all the attention just because she was sore. Anyway, Hallie didn't look all that sore this morning. She moved slowly, but easily. She certainly didn't merit special treatment!

A noise came from behind her. It was her grandfather trying to start the truck. Sharon turned away. She was *not* going to go to church this morning. Everyone knew she was leaving for Atlanta, and she didn't feel like being the object of curiosity. So she would stay home, exchange no goodbyes. Anyway, most of the people she wanted to say goodbye to she already had. The remaining ones—her very best friends—she would see again before she left.

Tuesday was the day they were planning to leave, and this was Sunday. By Tuesday night she would be in Atlanta with her father and *her*.

She swung away from the fence and spotted her grandfather bearing down on her. She waited for him to close the gap.

"I saw you over here," he said, taking off his hat to fan his face. The lighter band of skin at the top of his forehead was the mark of an old-time farmer, one who didn't believe in smearing creams on his skin to protect it from the sun, but who religiously wore his hat. It had been a part of him for as long as Sharon could remember.

"Daddy sent me out here with some carrots. Hallie wanted to thank Jill for letting her ride her and she didn't want the other horses to feel slighted." Ironic contempt colored her words.

Her grandfather snorted, as she'd expected. There was no way Hallie was going to get around him. She might have wormed her way into her grandmother's good graces, but she'd better not try it with her grandfather. He was made of sterner stuff.

"City people," her grandfather grumbled.

"Yeah," Sharon agreed.

"You're not dressed for church," he observed, taking stock of her jeans and cotton sweater. "You're not coming?"

She shook her head.

"Your grandmother isn't going to like it."

"I don't care."

Timothy shifted position. "You might go a bit easier on her, little girl. She's taking this pretty hard."

"We've been through all this before, Granddad."

"I still don't know why you're leaving. Haven't your grandmother and I done everything we can for you?"

"It's not that!" Sharon returned with unconcealed impatience. Why was it so hard for him to understand?

"Then what is it? Why don't you try telling me?"

"I have, Granddad! You just won't hear! I want to live with Daddy now!"

"You'll be safer here."

"Maybe I don't want to be safe!"

"That father of yours hasn't been much of a father up to now. What makes you think he'll change?"

Sharon had had enough. Her fuse seemed to be much shorter these days, her temper a burst of flashing energy. "Look! You don't like him. I know that. But it's what *I* want to do! I want to live with him!"

"And his new wife?"

Sharon turned back to the horses. "She may not be around for long."

Her grandfather frowned. "What makes you say that?"

"Intuition, okay? Nothing else," she snapped.

Her grandfather continued to look at her, his eyes ice blue slits in his darkly tanned face. Wrinkles creased his cheeks, his neck. He was sixty-seven, Sharon knew, but he might have been older or younger. Years of hard work in the sun and wind had made him ageless like the land.

He stuffed his hat back onto his head. He was wearing a suit this morning, his only suit, which he saved for Sunday services. And his hat was his "good" hat, a cream-colored Stetson in pristine condition. "Well, little girl," he said quietly, "you just remember—you can always change your mind."

"But I don't want to—" She stopped herself from saying more. She'd just be wasting her breath.

Her grandfather nodded shortly and started to walk away, but he stopped when he saw her grandmother huffing and puffing toward them from the truck. It was obvious she'd spotted Sharon and the way she was dressed, and she was coming over to berate her.

"I'll take care of this," her grandfather said, and went to intercept his wife.

A heated conversation took place with much waving of arms by her grandmother. Sharon could hear very little, but she knew her grandfather had won when he took hold of his wife's hand and drew her toward the truck. Florence sent several angry glances back over her shoulder, but Sharon brushed them off with easy nonchalance.

A few seconds later the pickup pulled away, and Sharon rocked back on her heels, watching it.

She did love them. But she also loved her father. And in a contest between the two, her father would always win. She couldn't let herself be concerned about anything else.

CHAPTER TEN

IT WAS A RELIEF to Hallie to have the morning free. The only fly in the ointment was that Sharon had decided not to go to church with the Langs. The girl had made herself scarce, though, leaving Kyle and Hallie with the house to themselves.

"It's so quiet here," Hallie said, sitting at the kitchen table, a cup of coffee at hand.

"You're the one who's quiet," Kyle said, sitting across from her. "Just exactly how sore are you?"

"I'm not," Hallie claimed quickly. "A little stiff, yes. But that's all. I could go riding again this evening."

"Not if I have anything to say about it."

"Kyle..."

He grinned. "I know. I don't have anything to say about it. You're an independent woman and can make up your own mind. Take it as a strong suggestion."

Hallie sipped her coffee and let her eyes settle once again on the scenery outside the screen door. "It almost feels like spring," she murmured.

"Not for long. Another norther is due tonight. It's supposed to be freezing by morning."

"That's hard to believe."

Her reply was so listless Kyle frowned. "Are you sure you're all right?" he demanded.

Hallie tried to shake free of the moroseness that had been hovering like a dark cloud all morning. She'd lain awake so long last night, her mind battling against itself, that her body felt limp, her mind exhausted. She offered what she hoped was a bracing smile. "I'm fine."

Kyle's gaze was skeptical.

To keep him from questioning her further, Hallie mused, "Do you think Sharon remembers anything about the accident?"

"Accident?" Kyle echoed.

"The one that killed her mother."

As always when the accident was mentioned, Kyle's expression changed. It sent clear signals that he didn't want to discuss it. "She wasn't old enough to remember," he said shortly.

"She was six."

"But she wasn't in the car. She was staying with Timothy and Florence."

"Still, it had an impact on her. One day her mother was there, the next she wasn't. And she never came back."

"She and her mother weren't close."

Hallie looked at him, surprised. "What do you mean?"

He shrugged. "Just what I said."

"They weren't close?" Hallie repeated. Under other circumstances she wouldn't have continued to pry, but today it seemed important.

Kyle pushed his coffee cup away. "Cynthia wouldn't have won any prizes as a mother. That's it. Okay?"

"What happened, Kyle? Tell me about the accident. I know Cynthia was killed and you almost were, too, but that's all I know. And I think it's important for—"

Chair legs scraped against the floor. "It was all a long time ago, Hallie," Kyle said. "It's dead and buried now. Just like Cynthia."

"But is she?" Hallie asked softly. At his puzzled look she added, "Dead and buried? Sometimes she seems very much alive to me." She wanted him to talk. To answer all her questions. To put her mind at rest. Instead, he reacted with anger.

"Dammit, Hallie, just leave it alone!"

"Why won't you talk to me about it?" she persisted.

"Leave it alone, Hallie. I'm warning you..."

"Or you'll do... what?"

Kyle sat back, stunned by the implication.

Hallie was equally shocked. She hadn't meant to say that. She sounded as if she didn't trust him. She wanted desperately to correct the impression.

"Kyle—"

He cut her off. "Leave it, Hallie. That's enough. Before one of us says something we'll regret."

Was it already too late? "Kyle! I didn't mean..."

He stood up and walked to the door.

"Kyle!" she cried, jumping from the table to run after him, to throw herself against him. She held on to him desperately, willing him not to push her away.

Without hesitation his arms came out to hold her, to pull her even closer. "It's this place," he said huskily, dropping his head next to hers. "These people. That's why we have to get Sharon out of here."

"I didn't mean— I didn't—"

"I know you didn't," he murmured.

"I *trust* you, Kyle," she whispered ardently.

His arms tightened.

Sharon walked up to the screen door and they were forced to separate to let her inside. She looked from one to the other, her green eyes narrowing as they rested on Hallie.

Kyle tried to hide the fact that there'd been a misunderstanding, only he tried a little too hard. Hallie heard the edge in his voice, as did Sharon.

"So," he said stoutly, "did the horses enjoy their carrots?"

"They said to tell Hallie thanks," Sharon said mockingly.

Kyle made no rebuke. He seemed preoccupied with the need to get away. He said something about seeing the horses for himself, then left.

"Trouble in paradise?" the girl asked, her satisfied smile speaking for itself. "I did try to warn you, you know. He only needs you until he has me safely in Atlanta." She shook her head in pretended pity. "Poor Hallie."

Hallie wanted to slap the impudent smile right off the girl's face. But everything combined—from her worry last night to her altercation with Kyle just now—made her vulnerable. And Sharon wasn't one to let an opportunity pass.

The girl's smile broadened as she looked Hallie up and down. "I'm surprised he picked you. He's sent me pictures of some of his girlfriends. Believe me, you're nothing like them. But then, Gran and Granddad might not have approved of the others, and you're so...bland they couldn't possibly object. Oh, and you can tell Daddy what I've said if you want. It won't make any difference. I'm still going to Atlanta with him."

The hit was aimed to inflict the most damage. Hallie felt it slice through her like a knife.

The girl didn't wait to see the results. She had so much confidence she'd wounded her adversary that she strolled from the room without a backward glance.

Hallie groped for a chair and sat down. Maybe it *was* this place. Maybe it *was* these people. Instinct screamed for her to grab Kyle and leave right away. But she knew Kyle wouldn't go without Sharon. And Sharon wouldn't be free for two more days.

Two days. In these circumstances it seemed an eternity. And after that, what? If Sharon was to be believed, Kyle would ask for a divorce the moment their plane landed in Georgia. And if he didn't do it then, he certainly would soon.

He was using her, Sharon claimed. He was using her, the Langs pronounced.

Hallie covered her ears, but it didn't help. The cacophony came from strife within her, not from an outside source.

WHEN THE LANGS RETURNED from church Timothy went to change his clothes, while Florence bustled about the kitchen still dressed in her Sunday best. She made fresh coffee and buttered several thick slices of bread, which she then popped into the oven to toast.

"Is Sharon about?" she asked.

Hallie, who'd entered the room a moment before, shrugged. "I have no idea where she is."

Florence paused to look at her. "Has something happened?"

"Nothing that would make you unhappy."

Florence tsked. "It doesn't make me happy to see you upset."

"That's not the way it looked yesterday."

"I had to say what I did, Hallie. It was my obligation."

"So you told me."

Florence turned away, shaking her head.

Timothy came back into the room, transformed from gentleman farmer to working farmer. As he sat at the table his gaze ran over Hallie.

Hallie noticed that he didn't even murmur a thank-you when Florence served him a steaming cup of freshly brewed coffee and a plate bearing his after-church snack of crispy buttered toast. The food seemed to be something he expected.

Hallie's expression must have reflected her disdain because when his wife brought her own toast and coffee to the table he jerked a thumb at Hallie and asked, "What's wrong with her?"

Before Florence could say anything, Hallie snapped, "I can answer for myself."

"Never said you couldn't," Timothy grumbled. He bit into his toast and chewed with satisfaction.

Florence watched Hallie warily.

Hallie sat down and folded her arms. "Do you really want to know what's wrong with me?" she challenged Timothy.

"Not particularly," he said.

"Too bad. You asked, so I'm going to tell you. I think you're an unmitigated boor. Your wife comes home and before she even thinks to see to her own needs, she prepares something for you to eat and drink—and you can't even say thank-you, or 'This certainly does taste good,' or even better, 'Here, Florence, let me serve you for a change.' You take everything she does for granted."

Timothy's eyes widened and then widened some more. The piece of toast in his hand was forgotten.

If Hallie had been in a different frame of mind she might have found his reaction amusing. As it was she waited for him to explode. True to form, it took only seconds.

"You're saying I'm ungrateful?" he demanded.

"I do it because I want to, Hallie," Florence said.

"*I'm* ungrateful?" Timothy repeated, his voice rising.

Hallie wasn't about to back down. "How long has it been since you've complimented Florence about anything? Can you even remember?"

Timothy threw the toast on his plate and scraped back his chair.

"Don't bother to strain your brain," Hallie continued before he could get up. "I'm sure Florence can remember." She looked at the older woman, signaling encouragement.

Florence's face was an array of contradictory feelings. She didn't want to make the situation worse, she didn't want to make Timothy angrier, but the truth was difficult to evade.

"It *has* been a long time," she admitted quietly.

Timothy stared at her before transferring his gaze back to Hallie. "Seems to me you live in a pretty big glass house yourself, girlie." At her frown he continued, "If there's anyone ungrateful around here it's you and that husband of yours."

"Kyle and I don't live here every day. You do. We're only here for the week, and we're not exactly guests."

"Sharon lives here. Have you forgotten that?"

"Timothy!" Florence instantly reproached him. "I won't have you saying something like that! Sharon hasn't been a burden."

"That's not what I'm getting at!" Timothy denied. "I'm saying they're not very grateful!"

"They don't have to be grateful! I didn't agree to take Sharon on for any reason except I love her!"

"Of course not. I'm not saying that, either!"

"Then what *are* you saying?" Florence demanded.

Timothy's frustration peaked. It was easy to see that he was unaccustomed to looking inside himself. "Oh, to hell with it!'' He got up and stomped angrily out the screen door.

''I shouldn't have done that,'' Florence said softly as she watched him go.

''He's wrong not to thank you once in a while,'' Hallie said.

''But he does, in his own way. Just not with words.'' She paused. ''I don't want to make him sick again.''

Florence's words pricked Hallie's conscience. Did it matter that Hallie was right if, in the end, she lost the larger contest? But her goal of bringing peace to the situation was growing fuzzy. As usual, her efforts just might not be good enough.

HALLIE COULDN'T SHAKE her gloom. It was as if more than the norther was moving in on them, ready to bring about a drastic change. Tuesday was looming and everyone seemed to feel its approach.

A number of Sharon's friends dropped by Sunday afternoon to visit her, including Jenny and her mother. Florence received them all politely, but Hallie could see that the woman was having a hard time bearing up under the strain. Sharon of course seemed oblivious to her grandmother's difficulty—telling everyone, when they asked, how excited she was about moving to Atlanta.

Timothy did little work that day, in accordance with Florence's strict principles. He sat in a corner of the living room, aware of the many arrivals and departures, but rarely taking part in the conversations. The television was on with the sound turned down and his attention seemed mostly on it. But he, too, grew more on edge as afternoon evolved into evening.

All the visitors wanted to talk to Kyle. He'd met some of them before; others he met for the first time. They held him in a mixture of curiosity and awe, allowing his celebrity to obscure the man. Hallie never moved far from his side. She could sense that he wanted this day to end. Just as she did.

Jenny's mother flirted with him. So did several of the other women, but in a more circumspect way. Kyle related some of his tamer experiences in the field. One of the fathers, who'd been pressed into driving his daughter over to the Langs, prodded him for a more detailed account of his last assignment. The man had picked a side in the small country's political disagreement and wanted Kyle to tell him his assumptions were correct, which Kyle refused to do.

Finally the last visitors went home, leaving the Langs and their unwanted houseguests to limp through a late-evening meal.

"Sunday dinner is usually my specialty," Florence apologized, "but this!" She dismissed the quickly put together meal they'd just eaten as being wholly inferior.

"Sharon has a lot of friends. It takes a long time to say goodbye," Timothy said. Everything about him seemed to warn of bad temper. He was like a disgruntled porcupine, quills at the ready.

"She's not going to lose them," Kyle said firmly.

"Tell them that," Timothy retorted.

"I did!"

"Stop it!" Hallie snapped almost before the last word had left Kyle's mouth. She'd thought the admonition numerous times in the past few days but had never said it. The growing tension was starting to tell on her, too. "Arguing doesn't solve anything!"

Everyone looked at her, but she held her ground. First she'd taken on Timothy, now she was willing to take on both Timothy and Kyle.

Kyle stood up, drawing Hallie with him. "Come on," he said gruffly. "We've all had enough for one day."

"But it's so early!" Sharon protested. She'd said little throughout the meal. Actually she'd said very little since her last friend had left.

"We're still going upstairs."

"But I wanted you to come for an after-dinner ride with me. I can't ride Candy since the vet said not to today, but I can ride Jill."

"It's getting dark, Sharon."

"So what?"

"So we're not going riding," Kyle answered shortly.

"Since when are you afraid of the dark?"

"I'm not. I'm also not afraid to tell you no. We can go for a ride first thing tomorrow morning if you like. But not now."

"It's because of her, isn't it?" Sharon turned to glare at Hallie. "She's the reason you won't do it!" Huge tears hung, suspended, on the girl's dark lashes. "Why don't you tell her what you told me, Daddy? That you only married her to get me! Why don't you tell her that?"

Kyle stiffened.

Sharon rushed on. "You don't love her! You *can't* love her. Not after the way you and Mommy fought so hard to get married." When Florence made a soft sound of distress she turned to her and explained, "I know! I have the letter she wrote!".

"That's enough, Sharon," Kyle said harshly.

She jumped back from the table. "Why won't anyone talk to me about my mother? Whenever I ask a question, everyone shuts up! You, too, Daddy! You won't talk about her, either. Why not? If you loved her so very, very much—"

"This isn't the right time," Kyle said tightly.

"Will it *ever* be the right time?" she demanded, the hovering tears starting to roll down her cheeks.

Hallie felt like crying, too. There was so much tension pulling in so many different directions. She knew she didn't shine enough; she didn't sparkle! And once again she hadn't measured up. Sharon didn't like her, and it was Sharon who was important. Unless, as the wicked girl had just publicly proclaimed, Kyle wasn't planning to keep her, Hallie, around. Then it wouldn't matter whether Sharon liked her or not.

Somehow, with her world spinning, Hallie moved toward the door. When Kyle caught up with her, she mumbled something about how he should stay and talk with Sharon and tried to pull away. But he wouldn't let her go. He took one look at Sharon and said resolutely, "We're going upstairs." Then he placed a hand on Hallie's back and accompanied her from the room.

Hallie climbed the stairs and walked down the hallway and into the bedroom without conscious thought. Once inside the room she crossed to stand at the window, whether from a need to see that the world outside remained steady and true, or as an avenue of possible escape, she didn't know. A part of her—the part she'd fled to when she was a child and hurt by something her parents did or didn't do—welcomed her back. The remaining self searched for any possible reason not to believe the worst.

Kyle stood beside her. "Hallie, what Sharon said just now..."

Her spine automatically stiffened. Kyle must have felt it because he turned her to face him. Running a hand over the back of her short hair, he let his fingers rest on her neck, then he tipped up her chin, trying to make her look at him.

"Hallie..." he said again.

She lifted her gaze and searched the familiar features. Worry and concern were reflected on his face, but there was also something else. Something he tried to cover with a smile.

"Today was hell, wasn't it?" he said bracingly. "All those people. I'd almost forgotten what Sunday can be like in the country."

"Tell me what's going on, Kyle," Hallie said flatly, disregarding his effort at small talk.

"And today was doubly worse because Sharon is leaving."

"Kyle!"

His smile disappeared.

"This isn't some kind of game, Kyle. Real people are involved here. Real feelings."

"What Sharon said—" he began earnestly.

"It's not just that!" Hallie interrupted him, pleading for him to understand. "It's everything! You, me, Sharon, Timothy, Florence. Cynthia!"

"Cynthia is dead!" he burst out.

"So you keep saying! But didn't you hear Sharon just now? She has questions, too, questions that no one will answer. Tell me, Kyle. Please tell me!"

"I warned you when we came here that they would say things." He laughed harshly. "So what exactly is it you want me to tell you? Do you want me to confirm that I'm a murderer?"

"No!" she cried. "I don't believe that! It's...it's other things."

He looked at her and shook his head. "They've really done a number on you, haven't they? A little word here, a little word there. Spread their poison—and it worked!"

"It's not that!"

"What else is it, then?" he demanded.

She hesitated, trying to think of the right way to express herself. "It's you," she finally whispered.

Kyle laughed again, only more softly, but still with no humor. "And you say this isn't a joke."

"I said it's not a game," she corrected him.

A long silence passed between them. Long enough for Hallie to regret ever having brought up the matter. It would have been so much easier to ignore it. To ignore all the questions and wait and see what happened. But how could she? While the vulnerable child she'd once been was still a part of her, Hallie was also the woman she'd fought so hard to become. Maybe Kyle *had* married her because of that vulnerability— because she'd be easy to manipulate. Or maybe that was merely what the Langs were trying to make her believe. She'd thought of Florence as a budding friend, but was she? Who was on *her* side? Was anyone?

Kyle, dealing with his own hurt, missed the painful conflict reflected in her eyes. "I'm the same person I've always been, Hallie," he said quietly. "I haven't changed."

Left unspoken was the question *Have you?*

Hallie held his gaze for only a moment before looking away. She couldn't answer him.

IF SHE EXPECTED HIM to leave the bedroom, she was wrong. It would take a truckload of dynamite to blast him out, and even that might not work. Kyle didn't know what he felt most at the moment—anger or fear. In one short week—actually, less than one week— everything he'd worked so hard for was in danger of disintegrating.

He should be used to it, though. Hell, he should expect it, considering the way he'd spent his life. For years he'd been paid to witness other people's miseries, to report on their stunned pain, to get pictures and put words to those pictures, to express the inexpressible, to explain the shattered ravages of what once had been ordinary lives. One day, a city or a town, the next, a bombed-out no-man's-land. He also knew from his personal life how easily happiness can change to despair.

Kyle moved the book he had propped on his stomach, pretending to adjust its position. From over the rim of his reading glasses he could see Hallie's back. He couldn't tell if she was asleep or awake.

They hadn't exchanged a word for hours. They'd gotten ready for bed, settled in their usual spots and maintained their positions ever since.

He watched the soft, even movements of her rib cage as she breathed, and a flash of desire burned through him. If he were a savage, he'd take what he wanted. He wouldn't consider the consequences. He wouldn't care what she thought, what she felt. But he wasn't a savage—at least, he didn't like to think he was. So he controlled the urge by refocusing his gaze on the book and did his best to concentrate on the story.

Before long, though, his mind once again wandered. Was there still the possibility that this was going to work out as he'd planned? Or would it end in ashes at his feet? All they had to get through was two more days. They were scheduled to leave on a four-o'clock flight to Atlanta on Tuesday. Himself, Hallie and Sharon.

Sharon. As Hallie had said, the girl was getting old enough to demand answers. His stomach tightened reflexively. It was something he didn't look forward to having to deal with.

He glanced at Hallie. She was still lying on her side, facing away from him. But he could tell now, from the soft ease of her breathing, that she was asleep.

He closed the book, placed it and his glasses on the end table and turned out the lamp. Then he moved carefully until he was lying next to her.

Unable to stop himself, he leaned over her and kissed the exposed curve of her shoulder. But he was unprepared for her reaction. In her sleep, she captured his arm and held it to her waist, securing him against her.

"Don't leave me, Kyle," she whispered faintly.

"Hallie?" he said, hope rising.

But her reply was garbled, indistinct.

Kyle released a pent-up breath. How many times had he gone to sleep in the past hoping that things would be better in the morning? Countless times. So once more wouldn't hurt.

"Just hang in there for a few more days, baby. Just a few more days," he said. And he knew he was talking as much to himself as he was to her.

CHAPTER ELEVEN

KYLE HAD ALREADY LEFT the bedroom, as well as the bed when Hallie awakened the next morning. She had no idea what time it was, and as memories of last night came flooding back, she didn't care. She didn't know who to believe anymore, and she was tired of trying to figure it out. If she could, she'd stay right there with the covers pulled over her head until it was time for them to leave for the airport the next day. If Sharon wanted to come, good. If she didn't, then good, too. If Timothy and Florence were upset, they had only themselves to blame. It was their hatred that had driven Kyle to act. And Kyle? Hallie didn't want to think very long or very hard about Kyle. It hurt too much.

She stayed exactly where she was for another half hour, then decided it was worse torture wondering what was happening downstairs than it would be to actually find out. She dressed, put on her usual light application of makeup and let herself into the hall. Only to find Sharon walking toward her.

The girl's face was pinched, as if she, too, hadn't slept well. And lack of sleep had done little to improve her disposition.

"I was just coming to look for you," she announced.

"Oh?" Hallie was determined not to react unduly. She was tired of expending energy where it did no good.

"Gran seemed to think you might have died in your sleep or something."

"Sorry to disappoint you."

Sharon gave her a funny look.

Hallie pushed past her and started down the stairs. Sharon followed close on her heels.

Florence was in the kitchen, once again making bread. She looked up from her work when Hallie entered and watched closely as she helped herself to a cup of coffee. "I wasn't sure if you were ill again or not," she said. Had her previous reserve made a slight reappearance?

"I'm rarely ill," Hallie claimed. "It's only been since we've come here."

Florence frowned. She glanced at Sharon, who'd settled into a chair at the table before turning back to Hallie. "Maybe something here doesn't agree with you," Florence suggested slowly.

"I've been thinking that myself," Hallie replied.

Timothy stomped in from outside for his usual midmorning break. He looked at Hallie, made a dismissive sound and sat down at his place at the table. Florence hurriedly washed the flour from her hands, then brought him a cup of coffee.

He took a sip.

"Thanks," he acknowledged belatedly, after another glance at Hallie.

Her lips twisted in a wry smile. He'd remembered.

Caught off guard, Florence blinked, then she returned to her bread dough and began to knead it, apparently forgetting that she'd already completed that step.

Hallie caught Sharon watching her. Where before she might have looked away, today she raised her cup in a mock salute. The girl's eyes widened but her gaze didn't falter.

"Are you still too sore to ride today?" Sharon asked.

"I'm not sore at all."

"Then how would you like to ride with me?"

"When?"

"Now?"

"Fine."

The girl's eyes glittered. "Don't you have to ask Daddy?"

"No."

"I'll go saddle the horses."

Timothy took another sip of coffee as his granddaughter ran off to the stable. Hallie drank her coffee slowly, determined not to let herself be rushed.

"So, what are you going to do once you're on your own?" he asked—on one level evincing interest, on another leading with a quick jab. "I certainly hope you made Kyle sign one of those premarital agreements. Something to keep you in the style you're accustomed to. Nice clothes, nice jewelry, nice place to live. Make Kyle cough up a little of that money he's been busy raking in."

Hallie put down her cup, her eyes flashing. "Let's be honest, Timothy. If I ended up out on the street begging for food, you'd think it was exactly what I deserve. But that's not going to happen. You forget, I have a job. I'm financially independent."

His eyes narrowed. "So you admit he's going to turn you out."

"I admit nothing!" Hallie snapped.

She stood up and brought her cup to the sink. Florence, who'd continued to knead the bread dough throughout their conversation—in all probability ruining it—caught her eye and said quietly, "We're not angry with you anymore, Hallie."

Hallie's smile was sardonic. "You could've fooled me."

"We don't blame you!"

Hallie met her gaze coolly, then she said, "You know, Florence? At the moment...I just don't care what you think."

Whereupon she pushed her way through the screen door and into the still, springlike morning. She'd spent most of this last week watching other people exit the house in high dudgeon. It felt wonderful to do it herself.

THE NORTHER predicted to blow through the night before had stalled, and the weather forecaster now said it would arrive sometime later that evening.

As Sharon readied the horses for their ride, she noticed that both Jill and Candy were a little more skittish than usual. They sensed the coming change and were reacting to it. Henry was his typical placid self, more interested in conning her out of food than he was the weather. For a second Sharon pondered saddling Henry for Hallie, instead of Jill. But she decided against it. Let Hallie have a little trouble.

When Hallie presented herself at the corral Sharon motioned to the woman's dove gray dress slacks. "Don't you have any jeans?" she demanded.

"This is it, I'm afraid."

"You could ruin them," Sharon warned.

"I'll take that chance."

Sharon snorted. "All right then, fine!" Silly woman! Without another word she handed over Jill's reins, then bounced into position on Candy's back. From her superior height, she looked down on her despised stepmother and watched with secret delight as the woman strained to pull herself into the saddle.

It took several tries before Hallie managed it. And once in place, she didn't look nearly as self-possessed and confident as she had previously. Her cheeks were bright pink and her forehead was damp from exertion.

"Are you ready now?" Sharon asked, doing nothing to hide her impatience.

The woman nodded, which was probably all she could do. Sharon could almost smell her fear. For a friend new to riding, Sharon might have suggested that they take a refresher circle or two around the corral.

But because it was Hallie, Sharon urged Candy to the gate and leaned down to swing it open.

"After you," she invited, holding Candy back.

One light tap from Hallie's heels and Jill jumped forward, nervous energy causing the horse to respond quickly. The next second, horse and rider were jogging through the opening, Hallie bouncing hard in the saddle, elbows out and flapping up and down even as she groped with her free hand for the saddle horn.

Sharon urged Candy through the gate at a more leisurely pace and leaned down to close it. Then she caught up to Hallie with the ease of an experienced rider.

"Follow me," she said cheerily, and urged Candy into a fast trot.

"Sh-Sharon!" Hallie called after her.

Sharon didn't respond.

When she looked back a few minutes later, Hallie was still having difficulty. Her elbows were flapping, her body bouncing. Sharon stopped to let her catch up.

"Did you say something?" she asked with pretended innocence as Hallie and Jill drew near.

Hallie looked in even worse condition than she had before. Her face was now almost entirely white, her hair was tousled, and her blouse was half in and half out of her slacks. Sharon couldn't contain a self-satisfied smirk.

"Could we go...a little slower...please?" Hallie puffed. "I'm not— I can't— I'm going to fall off!"

"You said you wanted to go for a ride."

"A ride, not suicide! I think I should go back to the stable. This isn't going to work out." She started to execute an awkward turn.

"What's the matter?" Sharon taunted. "Don't you trust me?"

Hallie stopped. "Can you give me one good reason why I should?"

A little of the natural color had returned to Hallie's face. She was pretty, damn her, Sharon thought irritably. Not beautiful, like the photos she'd seen of her mother, but pretty all the same. Was that why her father was so attracted to the woman?

"All right! We'll go slower!" Sharon conceded crossly.

Hallie hesitated for only a second. Then she tipped her head and settled her weight more comfortably in the saddle.

Sharon urged Candy forward and within moments heard the other horse fall into place behind her.

AS THE RIDE WENT ON—stretching well past the half hour Hallie had expected and taking them much farther into the isolated countryside—she wondered why in the world she'd agreed to come. Had it been momentary madness? Was it because of the alienation she suddenly felt toward everyone here? A rebellion against her own untenable position?

Sharon had stayed ahead of her throughout the ride, content, after their initial contretemps, to plod along at a steady pace. Not once had the girl looked behind her. Hallie wondered what would have happened if she'd toppled off—would the girl even know? She wouldn't care, that was for sure.

Hallie decided to break the silence. "Sharon!"

The girl glanced back over her shoulder.

"Where are we going?"

"Are you getting tired?"

If the question had been posed by someone other than Sharon, Hallie might have thought her answer mattered. From Sharon it was a challenge.

"A bit, yes," Hallie answered honestly. Some of the bruised and strained muscles from two days before were starting to make themselves known again, along with a few new ones.

"It's not much farther," the girl said.

"What's not much farther?" Hallie asked. This was the first time she'd known of a destination.

"I thought I'd show you one of the cave openings I've found."

Why? was the first thought that popped into Hallie's head. She remembered some talk about a cave from earlier in the week, and her principal memory was that exploring one could be dangerous. Kyle had mentioned some amateurs coming "to a drastic end." That didn't exactly make her want to forge on, but she wasn't about to object, either, since that was what Sharon was waiting for her to do.

"Sounds like fun," she lied, to which Sharon made no reply.

The surrounding countryside became a little hillier and a lot more rugged, with jagged outcroppings of rock.

"It's up there," Sharon said, stopping at last at a grove of scraggly trees. She pointed halfway up the side of the nearest hill.

Hallie squinted her eyes. "I don't see anything."

"The black slash that looks like a mouth. Close to the second clump of brush."

Hallie searched for the opening, then exclaimed, "Yes. I see it!"

"We'll have to leave the horses here," Sharon said. She threw a leg over Candy's neck and slid to the ground.

Hallie knew her descent would be much less graceful. Her leg felt like lead as she lifted it over the saddle and her knees like marshmallows when she tried to stand, but she managed to do both without wholly disgracing herself.

Sharon made no comment. Instead, she quickly secured the horses and said, "Come on."

The incline grew steeper as the hill built. Hallie groaned as she looked at it.

"Come on!" Sharon urged again from her already much higher vantage point.

Hallie gauged the distance between them, took a deep breath and plunged ahead. Brush caught against her legs and tore at her slacks. As Sharon had warned, they were going to be ruined—were ruined already— but slacks didn't matter right now. This was a contest between Sharon and herself, and she wasn't about to cry foul because she wasn't properly dressed.

The last bit of climbing wasn't easy. It was difficult to find firm footholds on the rocky ground. Hallie slipped at least twice, banging her knee and an elbow. Still, she kept going.

Sharon waited for her at the cave opening. Hallie completed the last few yards and, panting, turned to take in the view. She couldn't see the Langs' farm, but she could see the cattle pond they'd passed and the old windmill nearby. Other than a few grazing cattle, they'd seen no other living thing. If Sharon planned to abandon her, to get her out of the way for a while, this was the perfect place. It would take her hours to walk back, *if* she chose the right direction. And if she didn't...

Hallie turned to face the girl. "What's next?" she asked.

A slow anticipatory smile touched the mouth that was a feminine version of Kyle's. "We go inside."

Hallie examined the opening. It was only about three and a half feet high and six feet across. Close up, it looked even more like an open mouth.

"You've been inside before?" Hallie asked.

"Lots of times."

"What about a light?"

Sharon pulled a miniature flashlight from her shirt pocket.

"You've thought of everything," Hallie murmured.

Sharon smiled. "Would you like to go first?" she asked.

The whole idea of entering the cave appalled Hallie. She didn't like dark enclosed places where God knew what might be lurking. But she wasn't going to tell Sharon that. Whatever the girl wanted to do, Hallie was game for—except anything truly dangerous. She wasn't a total fool.

"Sure," she said. "Give me the flashlight."

Sharon handed it to her. Hallie turned it on, checking the beam. She flashed it a little way into the entrance. "Is the floor level inside?"

Sharon nodded.

Hallie held her gaze. "Is it?" she repeated softly.

"Yes," Sharon replied.

Hallie held her gaze for a moment longer, then after taking a couple of deep breaths, she directed the beam of light ahead of her and bent low to slip inside the gaping maw.

Her first sensation was of coolness. It was as if the cave had a refrigeration unit. The next thing she noticed was a damp, earthy smell, mixed with something else she couldn't identify.

She heard Sharon move outside. "Sharon?" she called, her voice echoing hollowly through the chamber. "Sharon?"

For a second Hallie thought her fears had been realized. The girl had run back down the hill to collect both horses and ride away. But a jeans-clad leg appeared in the narrow entrance, soon followed by the rest of the girl as she dipped her way inside.

"Did you call?" the girl asked, grinning wickedly.

Sharon knew darned well that Hallie had called, but Hallie was so relieved to see her she didn't fuss.

"I wasn't sure if you were coming," Hallie admitted.

"Oh, I wouldn't miss this for the world."

"Miss what?"

"I love to explore caves."

"I thought you told your grandmother you didn't go inside very far."

"Gran worries too much."

"With good reason, it seems."

"Are you going to tell her?"

"Me? No."

"Why not?"

"Because it's not my business."

In the tiny glow of the miniature flashlight Hallie saw the girl shrug.

"There's something I want to show you," Sharon said.

Hallie frowned. She'd gone about as far into the cave as she wanted to go. Farther back the inky blackness seemed even more threatening. "What?" she asked.

"What I brought you here to see." Sharon snatched the flashlight from Hallie's hand.

If Hallie had known what the girl had planned, she would've held on tighter. She felt extremely vulnerable without the light.

"The cave gets bigger as you go farther back," Sharon said. "But watch out for your head here." She flashed the light to reveal a protruding rock.

Hallie was of two minds about what to do. One part of her said that since she'd gone this far she might as well go farther. The other part of her, the part that hated enclosed dark places, shrieked for her to get outside.

"Come on," Sharon jeered. "Nothing's going to eat you."

"How far?" Hallie asked, moving toward her, careful to watch out for the jutting rock.

"Just a few feet."

Hallie nervously watched the cave's entrance grow smaller. A few steps later she said, "This is far enough, Sharon. I don't want to go any deeper. Not without proper equipment."

Sharon made sounds of a chicken clucking.

"No more!" Hallie declared, stopping.

Sharon laughed. "Oh, all right! It's here, anyway." She hunkered down on the cave floor and shined the light on something. "Look!"

Hallie couldn't identify what it was from where she stood, but when she, too, hunkered down she saw a collection of animal bones.

"Oh . . ." Hallie breathed.

Sharon watched her closely, as if waiting for her to show some sign of revulsion. But Hallie wasn't at all perturbed by the find.

"It's a skeleton," Sharon said needlessly.

"Yes, I know."

"It's a *skeleton!*" Sharon repeated dramatically. "Of a dead animal!"

Hallie smiled slightly. "Am I supposed to faint or scream?" She examined the collection more closely. Part of a skull, a fairly complete jawbone, teeth, several vertebra, a long thin leg bone, numerous other aller bones. "It's probably a wolf or a coyote," allie speculated. "A female or a young male."

"How do you know that?"

"Because of its size. It could be a dog, too."

"How do you know *that?*"

"Because—"

"No! I mean, how do you...?" She waved her hand encompass more than just the animal bones.

Hallie smiled thinly. "My mother and father were ry involved in civic affairs. Their favorite project as raising money for our local museums—art, natu- science. Whenever they were in meetings, I was sent f on tours. I went on a lot of tours. Saw a lot of an- al skeletons."

"Do you think you could put it back together?"

"Is this all you've found?"

"Yes."

"Then probably not. Too much is missing."

Sharon stood up and after a moment Hallie did, as ll.

"What do you think happened to it?" Sharon ked.

"For it to die here?" Hallie shrugged. "I have no ea."

Sharon went a little deeper into the cave. "What out this?" she asked after a moment, and directed e light toward something else.

Hallie stepped closer to the pool of light and stared the whitish conglomeration collected along the top a long rock. She frowned when she realized that the underlying sharp odor she'd noticed earlier had grown steadily stronger. "What is it?" she asked.

"Guano," Sharon replied with relish. "Bat dung."

"Bat dung?" Hallie repeated. And this time Sharon received the reaction she'd been waiting for when she flashed the light quickly upward, exposing the ceiling of the cave. Literally hundreds of bats hung suspended above their heads. As the light disturbed them some started to move, adjusting their dark wings stretching and twitching.

Hallie made a horrified sound and started to run toward the opening. She forgot about everything but the need to get out of the cave. Dark, enclosed.. teeming with bats! She knew she was playing right into Sharon's hands, but that didn't seem to matter. Neither did the fact that she'd read articles, seen documentaries, purporting that bats were truly benign little creatures. But it was one thing to sit in your living room and watch the sweet little furry things respond to their human keepers and another thing entirely to have them lurking above your head!

In her haste Hallie forgot about the protruding rock. She sensed it just before she hit it. The blow wasn't enough to cause serious damage, but hard enough to stun her. She fell to the ground.

She had no idea how long she lay there, staring dazedly into the darkness. It could have been seconds before Sharon was kneeling beside her, or it could have been half an hour.

"Are you all right? Hallie! Say something!"

Sharon's rising panic broke through Hallie's fog. Hallie looked at her, blinked and said, "What happened?"

"You hit your head. I didn't mean it. I just wanted to scare you, that's all. Just scare you."

Hallie looked around, confused by the darkness. "Where are we? The cave—are we still in the cave?" She tried to get up. "Bats! They were moving. We have to get ou—"

"They're fast asleep again," Sharon interrupted, trying to restrain her. "They only woke up because I disturbed them."

"I still want out!"

"Okay, okay. Do you think you can stand?"

"Of course I can," Hallie snapped.

When Sharon's hands fell away, Hallie struggled to her feet. There was a bump on the right side of her head, just above her hairline. She felt woozy, but she could walk, especially if it meant getting out of here.

Bending to step through the narrow entrance caused her head to throb. She was probably going to have a horrible headache.

Hallie leaned back against the steep hillside, closed her eyes and took large gulps of air. Sharon hovered next to her.

"Are you sure you're all right?" the girl asked anxiously.

"Never better in my entire life."

"I didn't mean for that to happen, Hallie. I never thought you'd run."

"Sorry. It's my typical reaction when I'm truly frightened by something."

"The bats wouldn't hurt you."

Hallie looked at her. "So I've been given reason to understand."

"Then why did you run?"

"Primal instinct."

Sharon looked down the hill to the grove of trees where the horses waited. "Are you going to be able to ride home?"

"It's the only way I'm going to get there."

Sharon frowned. "Stop answering like that."

"Like what?"

"Like that! You're just doing it to get back at me. You blame me for everything! *Everything!*"

"Sharon, I'm answering like I am because I need a few minutes to pull myself together. Everything is still a little—"

Sharon wrung her hands. "Daddy's going to be so mad at me. Gran, too. Especially when they find out where I took you."

"Why should they find out?"

"Because you'll tell them!"

"Why should I do that?"

"For revenge. Because I've been so nasty to you."

Hallie sighed and touched the bump on her head. When she checked her fingers there was some blood, but only a couple of drops. "Sharon, you're a young girl caught in a very bad situation. I don't blame you for being upset."

"I'm not *that* young!"

"I know." Hallie sighed again. "Look, do you think we could climb down to those trees and sit for a while?"

Sharon stamped a foot in general protest against life, then said, "Sure, yeah," and started down the hillside ahead of Hallie. Only this time she took very good care to monitor Hallie's progress.

Hallie watched the girl with almost as much interest as she did the treacherous ground. It was hard enough being thirteen these days. But add to that a bevy of adults who were fighting over you and life became almost impossible.

For the first time since coming here and being subjected to Sharon's atrocious behavior, Hallie felt a stirring of sympathy for the girl.

CHAPTER TWELVE

THE HORSES WHICKERED a soft greeting when, at last, Sharon and Hallie approached. Sharon went over to give each a pat, Candy first and then Jill, while Hallie found a place to sit at the base of a spindly tree.

"Watch out for rattlesnakes," Sharon warned belatedly. "They like to come out on warm days and sun themselves."

Hallie searched warily around her. "Bats... snakes..." she grumbled.

Sharon grinned. "Scorpions, too."

"Oh, great!"

"Texas can be an unfriendly place sometimes."

"So I've noticed," Hallie murmured, but she wasn't thinking only of the wildlife.

She knew that Sharon took her meaning. The girl bent to examine Candy's leg.

"What did the vet say?" Hallie asked.

"Not much. Just to watch it."

"Did we hurt it this morning?"

"I don't think so."

Hallie watched the girl continue to minister to the horse. There was a real bond between those two. She thought back to what she'd overheard the day she'd followed Sharon into the stable. Sharon looked upon

andy as a special friend; she didn't want to hurt the
orse, she wanted only what was best for her. Did
haron's sensitivity extend only to Candy?

Hallie once again checked the bruise on her head.
he bleeding had stopped, but the bump was still
here. Next she examined her elbow and knee. The top
ayer of skin was scraped on each, but not deeply. Her
lacks were a complete write-off, though. She tried to
rush some of the streaks of dirt away. She wished she
ad a mirror.

A small hand mirror appeared before her.

"I use it to send signals," Sharon murmured.

"Who to?" Hallie asked, surprised by this show of
ourtesy.

"No one in particular. Sometimes a friend."

Hallie took the tiny mirror and peered into it.
"Good God," she breathed. "It's worse than I
hought."

"Yeah, you look pretty bad."

Hallie smiled ironically. "Thanks."

Sharon fished a bottle of water out of a plastic net
ack hanging from her saddle horn. "Here, use some
f this."

"I didn't know we had any."

"Gran never lets me go far without water."

Hallie wetted a tissue that she found in her pocket
nd cleaned her face, even managing to wipe most of
he dried blood away from her bruise.

"That's a little better," she said as she finished.

"Does it hurt?" Sharon asked.

"A bit."

Sharon perched on a flat rock a short distance away and began to draw aimlessly on the ground with a stick.

"I won't tell anyone, Sharon," Hallie assured her.

"I would."

Hallie shrugged.

"Do you really love Daddy?" the girl burst out after a moment. It was almost an accusation.

Hallie's reply was immediate. "I love him, yes."

"I love him, too!"

"I know that."

"And my mother!"

"I know that, too."

"And my grandparents!"

Hallie looked at her.

"I do!" Sharon reinforced her previous claim.

Hallie shrugged again.

Sharon threw away the stick in one angry motion. "You don't believe me!"

"I don't really care."

Sharon's frown deepened. "You're different today."

Hallie brushed at her slacks again. "I'm tired of trying when it doesn't do any good. I'm tired of people who—" She stopped.

"Who what?" Sharon prompted.

Hallie stood up, not without some difficulty. "I think we've been gone long enough, don't you?"

"You didn't answer my question."

Hallie smiled. "No, I didn't."

The girl jumped to her feet. "Because you don't think it's any of my business?" she demanded.

"Because I just don't want to talk about it anymore. Come on. Let's go back."

Hallie walked to Jill, pulled herself into the saddle by some miracle of determination and turned her in the direction of the farmhouse. She didn't wait to watch Sharon mount.

KYLE SAW THEM in the distance before they saw him, and if truth be told, he had to admit to a flash of relief. He hadn't spoken to Hallie since last night. She'd been sleeping so deeply this morning he hadn't wanted to disturb her. Then she'd disappeared with Sharon before he'd returned from picking up a few things in town.

He'd been concerned by their prolonged absence but hadn't mentioned it until he'd noticed Florence's growing agitation.

"Sharon didn't say anything about staying out long. And frankly, Hallie didn't seem in a good enough mood to want to, either," Florence told him when he'd pressed her. "I'm worried that something may have happened."

So he'd saddled Henry and started off in the direction Florence had said they'd gone. He didn't have to go far.

He urged Henry forward and cantered closer to his wife and daughter. "Hello," he called.

Neither looked at him with welcome. Sharon seemed worried about something, although she was doing a fairly good job of covering it. And Hallie glanced at him and then quickly away.

"You've been gone a long time," he said.

Sharon seemed to pull tighter into herself, as if bracing for something.

"I had a small tumble," Hallie murmured.

Kyle was aware of the glance Sharon sent her. He frowned. "Were you hurt?"

"Only my dignity."

He maneuvered Henry closer. Hallie did look ruffled and her gray slacks were torn and dirty. "What happened?" he asked.

She shrugged. "I just... fell."

"Did Jill throw you?"

"No."

He looked at his daughter. "Where were you when all this happened? You know Hallie's a new rider."

"Just drop it, Kyle, okay?" Hallie said. "It wasn't Sharon's fault."

Kyle had a strong sense that there was a lot more to the story, but he didn't press it, not if that was what Hallie wanted.

He reached out to ruffle her hair, but she evaded his touch. His hand dropped away.

He let Henry walk abreast with the others as they started off again. "It won't be long now," he said after a moment. "Late tomorrow night and we'll be in Atlanta."

If he'd expected enthusiasm, he didn't get it. Not from either one of them. "Let's don't all applaud at once," he said wryly, trying to strike a humorous chord.

"That sounds great, Daddy," Sharon responded huskily.

Hallie said nothing.

Kyle felt a spurt of irritation. They were so close to the end! Once again he tried to touch Hallie, reaching for her arm. As before, she evaded him.

His lips tightened. Irritation turned to anger. "What the hell's the matter with you?" he demanded, keeping his voice low.

"She fell, Daddy!" Sharon cried. "She hurt her arm."

Kyle looked at Hallie and then at his daughter. For Sharon to come to Hallie's defence, something strange was really going on.

"Let's see," Kyle said. He pulled on Jill's reins at the same time as he stopped Henry.

Tears were glittering in Hallie's eyes when she looked at him, and it was all he could do not to draw her out of the saddle and onto his lap. To cradle her head against his chest and try to erase any hurt she might feel. But he couldn't ignore the other message in her eyes—the one that kept him at arm's length, the one that said the rift between them hadn't healed. She wanted something from him, something he wasn't prepared to give.

He examined the superficial scrape on her elbow. "It shouldn't leave a scar," he joked in another attempt to lighten the situation.

"Not all scars show," Hallie returned thickly. Then she tapped Jill's sides with her heels and started off at a much faster clip than Kyle had ever seen her ride before.

Kyle and Sharon watched her leave. Father and daughter, side by side, thinking their own private thoughts.

"What did she mean, Daddy?" Sharon asked after a moment. "Do you think she's hurt worse than she said?"

Kyle didn't know how to answer. His daughter might think herself very grown-up, but the more complex thought processes of an adult weren't yet a part of her.

"I don't think it's that," he said firmly, trying to reassure the girl who seemed very badly in need of reassurance.

Sharon heaved an unconscious sigh. Then with unspoken agreement, they both prodded their horses after Hallie.

As THE AFTERNOON WORE ON, Sharon watched Hallie's every move, waiting for something to be said about the cave, but it never was. Not that she wanted her to say anything; she didn't want to get into trouble. But the idea that Hallie had kept her word was unsettling.

So, too, was Sharon's notion that there was something wrong between Hallie and her father. The easy rapport the two had once shared was gone, its place taken by a rising tension. There were no more loving touches or looks, only an uncertain hesitancy. A god-send like this should have made Sharon ecstatic. It was what she'd wanted all along. But somehow seeing it had the opposite effect.

As they finished the last evening meal they would all be forced to share, Sharon continued her watch. Conversation had been sporadic—tiny spurts, mostly to do with the necessities of eating. Pass this... pass that. There was enough strained politeness around the table to make a person gag!

Her father didn't seem happy, his features set, his lips thinned. Hallie was clearly trying not to look miserable, but she was so quiet it was hard not to notice her unhappiness. Her grandmother had returned to her previous gravity. Her grandfather, well, her grandfather hadn't changed. He'd been angry from the beginning and had stayed that way.

At the end of the meal, as Sharon started to leave, her grandmother put a hand on her shoulder, keeping her in her seat.

"Sharon will help me," she said pointedly to Hallie. "I want to have a word with her."

Sharon squirmed. How—and when—had her grandmother learned the truth? But after everyone dispersed, all seeming to go in different directions, her grandmother sat in the chair nearest Sharon's and took her hand. Her grandmother's hand was strong from a life spent working on the farm. Sharon's was soft, uncallused, untried.

"You know that I've let you have your way about this," her grandmother began sternly. "And you know it's not what I want for you. I want you to stay right here with us. But it's not something that can't be put right. You can change your mind at any time—either now or later."

"My mother didn't change her mind," Sharon said levelly.

Her grandmother looked at her. "What would you say if I told you she had?"

Sharon pulled her hand away. "You're just saying that!"

"No, Sharon, I'm not."

"No! I have her letter! She says she's going to marry Daddy whether you want her to or not! She loved him so much she was willing to give up everything!"

Her grandmother answered calmly, as if she'd prepared herself for this. "I'm not saying she wasn't besotted with your father. Yes, she was determined to marry him. More than determined. And you're a lot like her, Sharon. You think you know what you want and you go after it. But sometimes...maybe you should think a little more before you act. Emotion gets in the way. It blinds people. Your mother found that out."

"I'm not blind!" Sharon denied.

"To your father's faults you are."

"He doesn't have any faults!"

"Everyone has faults!" Florence snapped. "Everyone on this earth, Sharon. That's what I'm trying to make you see."

"Then you and Granddad do, too!" Sharon countered. "And maybe your main fault is that you judge people too much!"

"If you're speaking of your father, we have our reasons."

"What reasons?" Sharon demanded. "You never tell me anything!"

"Sharon—"

"No!" She pulled her arm away when her grandmother tried to catch hold of her. "Every time I ask, you change the subject or you pretend not to hear. Why do you hate Daddy so much? Why don't you want me to live with him?"

True to form her grandmother evaded the question. "Because we love you and we'll miss you."

"See?" Sharon cried, stumbling to her feet. "I ask, and you tell me nothing!"

"Sharon, please..."

Her grandmother's face was aging before Sharon's eyes. The wrinkles seemed deeper, the stoop to her shoulders more pronounced.

"I won't change my mind. I won't!" Sharon shrieked. "You're being just as mean to me as you were to my mother!"

"We're not! We weren't!" her grandmother said. "Sharon, you don't know your father! You don't know what he's capable of!"

"I'm not going to listen to this!"

"Sharon!"

"No!" Sharon yelled as she ran to the door.

She ran all the way up to her room. She'd never before had so serious an argument with her grandmother. They rarely exchanged a cross word.

She threw herself on the bed, sobs racking her body. Did her grandmother suddenly not love her? Everything seemed to be spiraling out of control. All she wanted to do was live with her father, to be close to him as other children were close to their fathers. To not feel so *different*. What was wrong with that?

It wasn't selfish, as she had overheard the mother of one of her friends say. That woman didn't know what it was like to live with people who were so much older...who didn't understand what a girl felt or needed...who were so set in their ways. She loved her grandparents. She loved them terribly, but...

If a heart could break, hers was breaking. She knew it. She could feel it. Things couldn't get any worse!

A light tap sounded on the door.

"Go away," she said, her voice muffled by the pillow.

"Sharon?" Hallie prompted softly.

Sharon's first instinct was to groan.

"Please...may I come in?" Hallie asked.

"Did Gran send you?" Sharon demanded.

"No. I'm here on my own."

Sharon paused to think how strange this was all turning out to be. At the beginning of the week, she'd never have thought she'd be pushing herself away from the bed, tear tracks still wet on her cheeks, to let her father's new wife into her room. But that was exactly what she did.

She cracked open the door and looked at Hallie, then she swung it wide and stepped back.

Hallie took only a second to glance at the jumble of keepsakes Sharon prized. At that moment Sharon saw the room herself through the eyes of a sophisticated stranger, and she was uncomfortably aware of how childish it must seem. Her stuffed animals and dolls piled on top her old toy chest, the Victorian dollhouse her father had sent her from England, framed photographs of herself at different ages wearing a variety of dance costumes, a huge poster from her trip with a church group to the Six Flags Over Texas amusement park near Dallas, a plastic flower lei from a friend's birthday party hanging from a tack on the wall near the collection of postcards her father had sent her from all over the world.

"May I sit down?" Hallie asked, motioning to the foot of the bed.

"Sure." Sharon shrugged. Feeling suddenly foolish, she wiped at her cheeks.

"Is this a quilt your grandmother made for you?" Hallie asked, tracing the bright star pattern radiating outward from the center. When Sharon nodded, she said, "It's beautiful."

"Yes." Sharon looked away. She stared at the second-floor bedroom of the dollhouse, at the intricate wallpaper, the delicate scrolled fireplace.

She turned back in time to see Hallie settling carefully on the quilt with a slight grimace. This time Sharon didn't take pleasure in her discomfort.

"I heard you run by, then I heard you crying," Hallie said quietly.

"Did Daddy hear?"

"He isn't upstairs."

Sharon relaxed somewhat.

"Sharon, I just thought—" Hallie began, then stopped to rephrase. "You're a very lucky person, did you know that? Your grandparents love and care for you. Your father loves and cares for you. Not everyone has that."

Sharon didn't say anything.

"You've always been loved," Hallie continued. "The people who love you do things for you because they care. I know sometimes it may not seem—"

"Gran said I don't really know my daddy."

Hallie watched her carefully. "What else did she say?" she asked slowly.

"That I can always change my mind. Granddad said that, too."

"It's true," Hallie confirmed.

Sharon stared at her. "You're . . . saying that?"

"I have to. It's your decision to make, Sharon. No one else's."

Sharon continued to stare at her as conflicting thoughts raced through her mind. "You don't want me to come?" she whispered.

"That's not what I said."

"Yes, you did."

"No, Sharon."

"Why don't you want me to come?" she demanded. A worse panic than she'd ever experienced

seized hold of her. "Has Daddy said something to
you? Is it because I asked questions about my mother?
I won't do it again! I promise! I won't ever do it
again!"

Hallie stood up. "It's not that."

Sharon shook her head. "Everyone gets upset when
I ask about Mommy. Why? Do you know?"

"Sharon—"

"You do!"

Tears again welled up in Sharon's eyes. She'd felt
bad before, but now she felt worse. A burning anger
began to grow. She wanted to strike out. To hurt
someone as she was hurt. Anyone. Hallie!

She ran over to open a wooden box where she kept
her most secret possessions. She searched through the
contents until she found what she wanted.

"Here!" she said, thrusting the old photo forward.
"I heard Gran tell Granddad that you didn't know
anything about Daddy's family. Well, here they are! *I*
know about them! They're his stepmother, his half
brother and his half sister! Donna, William and Sara."
She pointed to each one in turn. Then she turned the
photo over. "See, their names are on the back. They
live on the ranch where Daddy grew up."

Hallie had paled considerably. Sharon felt a burst
of pleasure, followed almost immediately a sense of
shame. She frowned, confused by her own confusion.

She slowly drew the picture away, looking at it herself. The woman was a petite brunette with a sharp
face and intelligent eyes. The young boy, about eleven,

had the same sharp features as his mother, but there was also a slight resemblance to Sharon's father in the way he was built, in the way he stood. And the girl, two or three years younger than the boy, had the same russet-colored hair as her father.

Sharon looked back at Hallie and saw that she was still pale. She, too, had seen the familial similarities. Not knowing what to do next, Sharon turned to put the photo away. When she swung back, the door to the hall was just snapping shut.

HALLIE WALKED BACK to her room in a daze. She had gone to comfort Sharon. The sobs she'd heard coming from the girl's room had been too much like her own when she was a child for her to stand by and do nothing. Now she wished she hadn't gone. It was one thing to try to deny the information that Florence had given her by claiming it as prejudiced. It was another thing to be presented with actual evidence.

Why hadn't Kyle told her the truth? Why was he trying to keep his family's existence a secret?

She let herself into her room and sat down on the bed next to the nightstand. Almost as if in a dream, she withdrew the folder Kyle had brought with them from Atlanta. She knew it contained copies of the paperwork the lawyers had exchanged about the transfer of Sharon's custody. He'd brought it with them in case it was needed. Well, now it was needed. By her.

She turned to the very first letter and looked at the date: July 19 of the previous year. The letter was a replica of the one sent to the Langs, telling them—as

Florence had said—that Kyle was reclaiming custody of Sharon. July 19—exactly five days after Hallie and Kyle had met.

Hallie slipped the papers back into the folder, which she then replaced in the nightstand. So this, too, was true. She closed her eyes.

Silent pictures played in her mind: Kyle, the first time she'd ever seen him, when he'd looked up from the magazine he'd been reading in the airline's VIP lounge, those green eyes that had instantly stolen her heart; the days and nights that followed, when he'd come back to the airport to see her, to arrange a meeting outside of her place of work; the first moment she'd realized that her sentiments were returned, that he was serious about their relationship; their first kiss and the rest that had followed; the moment he'd asked her to marry him; the way he'd looked at her as they left the church after the ceremony; their honeymoon...

Had it all been a sham?

Her body was already aching from the long horseback ride, not to mention her fall. Her head throbbed. It had been all she could do to sit through dinner and act as if nothing was wrong. Kyle had watched her—she'd thought because he felt badly about their argument last night. She'd even considered apologizing! She was being oversensitive, she'd told herself, she'd been listening to the wrong people.

Nothing they say or do can ever change the way I feel about you—her exact words. They screamed above the babble in her mind. He'd told her not to believe the Langs. But how did one not believe when presented with facts? When the person you so desperately wanted to trust, lied to you or told you half-truths?

Hallie groaned and got to her feet. She couldn't just sit there. She had to get out of the house, out of the situation. She had to have time to think!

She lurched toward the door and hurried downstairs and out the front door. She didn't want to take the chance of running into anyone, especially Kyle.

She walked until she couldn't walk any farther. This time she didn't care if she got lost. She didn't care if clouds from the delayed norther were building above the horizon. She didn't care that the evening sun was rapidly becoming obscured, creating a premature sunset. She didn't care about anything!

It was only when exhaustion stopped her that she realized how foolhardy she'd been. She looked around, panting, and in the fast-falling dusk, searched for somewhere to shelter. The wind had picked up, blowing leaves and bracken, swirling them against and around her body. The air smelled fresh and cold, and soon large drops of rain began to fall.

A building of some kind was in the distance, and she started to run toward it, forcing her tired muscles to respond.

CHAPTER THIRTEEN

THE BUILDING turned out to be a house, moderate in size and faced with rock. At first Hallie tried to shelter in the attached open carport, but the cold wet wind drove her to the front door. A weak light filtered through the window curtain of the nearest room, giving her hope that someone was inside.

Her teeth started to chatter. She stood on the porch, half-soaked, her hair hanging in damp trails to her neck, her blouse plastered against her shoulders and back, her slacks sticking to her legs.

The door opened and Hallie looked hopefully at her deliverer. Her gaze had to travel a long way up—the man literally filled the doorway. Walker! She gave a joyful cry of relief.

Walker stared back at her dumbfounded. "Hallie?"

"Oh, Walker! Yes, it's me!"

He frowned and checked behind her. "You're alone?" he asked, then he took in her bedraggled state. "You're wet!" he cried, and quickly drew her inside.

"I got caught in the storm," she explained, shivering even more now that she'd found welcome shelter. "I saw the clouds, but I didn't think."

"Come on. I just lit a fire. It's not going very goo
yet, but it'll help warm you."

He led her across the room. Hallie had the impres
sion of well-kept bachelor quarters, much lived-in an
comfortable.

"I'll get a blanket," he said gruffly.

Still shivering, Hallie tried to smile at him before h
turned away, but her attempt failed. She huddle
closer to the hearth. Of all the places for her to hav
ended up. In her pain and confusion she'd struck ou
into the unknown. Had instinct taken a hand in guid
ing her here? She'd known that Walker lived nearby
but not where.

Walker came back into the room. On his arm was
large wool blanket and red-and-black plaid flanne
robe.

"It'll swallow you, but not as much as a pair of m
jeans and a shirt. You'd disappear in them." H
handed her the robe, then held up the blanket
spreading it wide between his extended hands. "
won't look," he promised. "Anyway, I'm too old.
talk a better game than I play." He raised the blanke
above his head, giving her full privacy.

Hallie quickly divested herself of her wet oute
clothing, kicking off her shoes in the process. The rob
was huge—the hem draped the floor, the sleeves set
tled a good eight or ten inches beyond her fingertips
But she could roll the sleeves back and wrap the la
pels around her at the waist, securing them with th
matching belt. The effect might look comical, but sh
felt swaddled with care and goodwill. When she wa

done, he wrapped the blanket around her shoulders and took her wet clothing to hang in the bathroom.

"Here," he said, tossing her a towel upon his return. "For your hair."

Hallie caught it and tried to smile again. "Thanks," she said. The word came out thickly, whispered through a tightening throat. He was being so kind.

He looked at her a moment, but didn't ask probing questions. "How about something warm to drink?" he urged, instead. "Some coffee or tea?"

Hallie nodded, leaving the choice to him.

He disappeared into the back of the house again and she transferred her gaze to the fire. The warmth of the dry clothing, as well as the fire, was finally banishing her chill.

He came back into the room. "It'll just be a minute," he said. "Better dry that hair."

Hallie did as he directed, her head disappearing under the towel. Afterward she combed her short locks with her fingers to tidy them.

"Thanks," she murmured.

Again, he looked at Hallie, but he still seemed content to wait for her to confide in him. He wasn't going to press her.

He pulled two comfortably worn chairs closer to the fireplace and indicated for her to sit. Hallie curled into the nearest chair, tucking the excess length of robe around her toes.

"This is wonderful, Walker. Thank you."

"Not a problem," he said mildly, and took the other chair.

Hallie stared at the flickering flames. So much had happened today. She touched the bump on her head. "Did you hurt yourself?" Walker asked, noticing.

"Not really," she said.

He was silent a moment, then asked, "Do you think we should let the others know you're here?"

"No!" she said quickly, then amended, "Not just yet. I'd like to sit quietly for a while."

The whistle of the kettle called Walker to the kitchen. A few minutes later he returned, carrying two large mugs. "Sugar or cream?" he asked, handing her a cup.

"Black's fine," she replied.

She sipped the hot coffee, feeling the warmth reach her stomach and radiate outward. She glanced at Walker, who was staring intently at the fire. She wanted to confide in him, but she didn't know where to start.

"Walker—" his steady gray gaze shifted to her "—I... Things..." She hesitated. How did she explain such a terrible suspicion about someone she loved?

"Things aren't working out?" he guessed when she didn't go on.

She nodded, swallowing.

He sighed. "Well, sometimes they just aren't supposed to, I guess."

"I tried."

"I'm sure you did."

"It's really... quite a mess."

"Anything I can help with?"

Hallie shrugged.

"Anything I can help *you* with?" he amended.

She looked across at him, her fingers wrapped tightly around the mug. "I don't know what to do, Walker," she confessed, her voice wobbling. "When we first came here everything seemed so straightforward. Kyle had every right to custody of Sharon, especially considering the way the Langs were behaving. Then as time went by, it wasn't so straightforward anymore. Florence and Timothy weren't the monsters I'd thought them to be. Everything they did, even if it was wrong, was because they loved Sharon." She paused as Walker nodded agreement. "Then . . . then I found out that Kyle . . ." Her throat closed. She backed away from what she'd been about to say. "Sharon hates me. I thought for a time today things might have a chance of working out, but . . . they won't. We're back to where we started and tomorrow is when we go to Atlanta. I don't know what's going to happen then. Or if there's even going to *be* a then! Kyle and I—"

The telephone rang. Walker put his cup aside and went to answer it. Hallie heard only his part of the conversation, but she knew immediately who the caller was.

"Yeah, she's here," Walker said. "Came in looking like a drowned rat. I gave her some dry clothes and some coffee and she's starting to look better." He listened. "Yeah, I'll tell her. See you then." After he hung up, he settled back in his chair. "Kyle," he explained unnecessarily. "He says he'll be by to pick you up in a few minutes. Wasn't anything I could do about it. He sounded pretty determined.''

Hallie's stomach tightened.

"Should I have told him not to come?" Walker asked after a moment of reading her miserable expression.

"No," she whispered. She couldn't have Walker fighting her battles for her. She had to face Kyle sometime. It might as well be tonight.

"Do you remember what I told you once before?" Walker asked, interrupting her thoughts. "About the way things aren't always as dark as they first seem?"

"I remember, but they still look pretty dark."

"Well, just don't forget what happens right before the dawn. It gets pretty dark then, too. Then up pops the sun and everything's all right!"

Hallie laughed because he wanted her to. Tears glistened in her eyes. "I'm going to miss you, Walker," she said softly.

"I've never been to Georgia," Walker mused. "Somewhere in the next year or so I just might buy myself a ticket there. Would it be all right if I paid you a visit?"

Hallie reached out to squeeze his hand. "You're welcome in my life anytime, Walker."

A car pulled into the driveway and cut its engine. Seconds later, there was a rap on the door. Walker got up to answer it.

Kyle swept into the room, his gaze centering immediately on Hallie. He took in the oversize robe, the blanket and her damp hair.

Walker came to stand beside him. "See, the little gal's fine. She just got caught out in the rain."

Kyle's lips tightened.

For the first time since meeting him, Hallie didn't want to run into Kyle's arms. Maybe he saw that in her eyes, because his expression grew even grimmer.

"Thanks, Walker," he said. "Hallie?"

Hallie uncurled from the chair. She knew she must look a sight. She struggled to keep her hands free of the long sleeves.

Walker set about gathering her wet garments, which he placed in a plastic bag. "Shoes are in here, too," he said. "Don't worry about the robe. I'll stop by and collect it sometime in the next few days."

Kyle didn't give Hallie any choice. He stepped forward and picked her up in his arms before she had time to protest.

"May we take the blanket?" Kyle asked. "It's cold out there."

"Sure," Walker agreed, wrapping it around Hallie's body and tucking it under her chin. He winked at her. "Remember that old sun and how powerful it is."

Hallie nodded under Kyle's puzzled gaze.

Walker held the door open for them. The rain had let up, and only an occasional drop fell. But the wind, which had increased, was cuttingly cold in the moonless night. Hallie shivered beneath the blanket. Noticing that Kyle wasn't wearing a coat, she almost said something solicitous, but then she clamped her mouth shut.

Kyle placed her in the passenger seat before circling the car to slide behind the wheel. He started the engine without comment. Similarly, he backed out of the long drive and accelerated down the road. But they didn't go very far. At the first opportunity he pulled the car to the side of the road and turned to face her.

"Would you like to tell me what that was all about?" he asked flatly.

She could see the tightness of his expression. Her first instinct was to shrink further down in the blanket.

"Are you still angry about last night? Is that what it is?" he demanded. When she remained mute, he continued, "I had no idea where you were. I came back to the house and everyone was there but you. You weren't in the barn or the stable or any of the outbuildings. I looked."

"I'm sorry," Hallie whispered.

He heaved a frustrated sigh. "I don't want you to be sorry. I want you to tell me what's wrong. All day you've been..." He didn't finish. Instead, he reached for her, pulling her against him.

Hallie closed her eyes, her cheek buried against his chest. She could hear the strong beat of his heart, feel the cool dampness of the rain that had soaked into his shirt. She didn't want things to be this way! She didn't want any kind of problem between them.

He took her by the shoulders and pushed her back. "Hallie... talk to me."

She wiped the trace of a tear from her cheek. She had trouble meeting his eyes. "This isn't working out very well, is it?" she whispered shakily.

"What isn't?"

"This. Everything!"

"It's almost over."

She shook her head. "No."

"Tomorrow afternoon we leave here, we get on the plane, and three hours later we're in Atlanta. That seems pretty over to me."

Hallie continued to shake her head. "No," she said again.

He shifted his hands to the steering wheel. She could see the steely set to his jaw.

"Kyle," she began, "why did you tell me you didn't have any family left when you do?"

"Sharon."

"No, not Sharon. When I asked if you had anyone left at the ranch where you grew up, your answer was no. But I've seen a picture, Kyle. Of Donna and William and Sara. Why did you lie to me?

"I didn't lie!"

"And what about when we first met. Why didn't you tell me then you'd decided to demand custody of Sharon?"

"When we first met?" he repeated incredulously. "Do you honestly believe that would have been a good dating move? *Oh, and by the way, I have a daughter I may have to get involved in a real battle to regain custody of, but you won't mind that, will you?* I don't think it would have worked."

"Why didn't you tell me later?"

"I *did* tell you!"

"Only about getting Sharon, not about when you'd decided to do it."

Kyle ran a hand through his hair. "I don't see where that makes a difference."

"It was only five days after we met, Kyle. Five days! I've seen the copy of the letter your lawyer sent to the Langs."

"You checked the file?"

"I had to."

He said nothing. Hallie stared at the road ahead. The rain had increased again, and now, illuminated by the car's headlights, fast-falling drops splattered against the ground.

She didn't want to look at him. She came close to losing her nerve every time she did. But finally, as the silence lengthened, curiosity forced her to see what he was doing.

He, too, stared straight ahead, his body tense, his fingers clenched on the steering wheel. Sensing her glance, he turned to look at her.

Hallie had expected a further display of anger. Huge, towering. After all, she was calling into question his word. What she hadn't expected was real evidence of pain. The deep hurt that showed in his pale green eyes. It was quickly covered, but the memory was indelible.

"Kyle?" she whispered uncertainly.

He gave his head a shake. "You had to check," he repeated dully.

"Kyle, I—"

He raised a hand, stopping her. "Let's just leave it at that for now, Hallie."

Hallie couldn't. Too much remained unanswered. "The visitation rights...you didn't tell me about that. And Cynthia. Sharon's right! No one will talk about Cynthia, especially you! I've asked, and you still won't explain. I'm left to wonder—"

She stopped abruptly when he rammed the car into gear and it shot forward, the windshield wipers working like angry bees.

Kyle roared down the road, unmindful of the slippery conditions. Hallie felt a spurt of fear. He was angry again, with cause. She shouldn't have said what she had. She hadn't meant to. It'd just slipped out.

"Slow down," she pleaded. "Don't kill us bo—" A thought suddenly occurred to her. She stared at him. "Is this how you and Cynthia crashed? Were you arguing and she made you angry, and you..."

Kyle immediately slowed the car. He turned into the Langs' driveway and parked in the usual spot before he answered. "You can come up with all kinds of theories, Hallie. I'm sure the Langs have any number and will be happy to share them with you—if they haven't already."

How did he manage to make her feel in the wrong? As if it was her fault that she didn't trust him enough? "I didn't—"

"At the moment I just don't care, Hallie. I should never have brought you here in the first place. It was a bad idea."

He got out of the car and strode around it, seemingly oblivious to the falling rain and the cold. He opened her door, scooped her up, along with the bag of wet things, and carried her into the house.

"Would you like me to take you upstairs?" he asked formally, manservant to mistress.

The stress, the long ride, the adventure in the cave, her fall, the lingering throb of a headache, her encounter with Sharon, her brush with the storm, her brush with Kyle. It was more than one person should have to endure in a day!

"I'm perfectly fine now," she returned, with just as much stiff formality. Which was difficult considering that she looked like a hapless refugee. When he put her down she somehow managed to contain the long sleeves and gather the extra length of robe, then start up the stairs, with the light from the second-floor hall guiding her way. She was very much aware that he watched her.

At the landing she turned to look back, but he had already faded into the shadows.

HALLIE LAY AWAKE for hours, waiting to see if Kyle would come upstairs. The wind continued to howl, driving the scattered raindrops against the windowpanes. She could feel the cold creeping into the old house and snuggled deeper under the covers.

Where was he? she wondered. Had he gone out? She hadn't heard the car, but it was parked on the other side of the house, so she probably wouldn't. She had seen and heard no one since her return. She might have been completely alone.

Questions continued to circle in her mind. Had she done the right thing in confronting him? Was she right about the accident and the way it had happened? But if that was so, why wouldn't he talk about it? People would understand, because it *was* an accident. The Langs... No, she decided, the Langs would never understand.

She couldn't get the image of his pained look out of her mind. It hadn't been faked. He'd been truly hurt that she could side with the Langs. But she didn't want to side with anyone! Not *for* them. Not *against* him. All she wanted was the truth. She couldn't stand lies, not when they made her doubt his love.

She examined her own feelings. Throughout so much of her life all she'd ever wanted was for the people she loved to love her in return. It was such a simple thing. All she wanted was to be loved.

And, God help her, she still loved Kyle! It was deep in her being, a part of her. She would always love him, no matter what. It was her trust that had been shaken. And it was trust that made a marriage work. Without trust, a marriage fell apart.

She turned her face into the pillow and tried to run away from that thought, from all thought.

The next morning broke very cold with the sky crystal clear. Ice had formed on the puddles left over from last night's rain and dressed tree branches and shrubs with a thick film of frost.

Hallie awoke hoping that yesterday might have somehow been a dream, but Kyle's continued absence told her otherwise. Dressing quickly, she went downstairs. A fire crackled in the fireplace and she walked straight toward it.

After warming her hands, she turned and saw him stretched out on the sofa, the decorative quilt draped over him. If this was where he'd spent the night, he couldn't have been comfortable. But she doubted that anyone in this house had passed an easy night.

Her gaze lingered on him, and she couldn't help the sensual response that shot through her. He was her mate, and her body didn't care that he might have deceived her.

With a jolt she realized that his green eyes were open and fixed steadily on her. A deep flush rose in her cheeks. He knew exactly what she was thinking, what she was feeling.

She took a symbolic step back, an attempt to serve notice to both of them that life had yet to return to normal—if it ever would.

"I—I didn't mean to wake you," she murmured.

"You didn't," he said.

She moved uneasily.

Kyle pushed off the quilt and sat up. He flexed his shoulders and stretched his spine. The couch was a good foot shorter than he was.

Rapid footsteps sounded in the hall and a second later Florence bustled into the room, a flowered robe wrapped around her plump body. "Oh!" she cried, surprised at finding them there. "Is it that late? I don't usually oversleep, but today..." She self-consciously patted her hair, trying to right the silver curls. "I'm glad you started the fire."

Kyle came over to poke the flames and added another log.

Florence looked at Hallie, her gaze a mixture of curiosity, wariness and concern. "I see you made it back in one piece last night."

Boots clomped down the hall and Timothy entered the room. "Should have been up hours ago," he grumbled. Then he saw Hallie and Kyle, and his frown deepened. He started to say something else, but Florence stopped him.

"We need more logs for the fire, Timothy. Would you bring some in when you get a chance?"

"I'll get them," Kyle volunteered.

Timothy shot him a resentful glare. "No, you won't."

Florence stepped closer to her husband. "Timothy..."

He sent his wife a smoldering look before stomping out of the room.

Florence stared after him, and Hallie saw defeat in the set of her shoulders. She was much more of a realist than her husband. She knew when the battle had been lost.

"I'll get breakfast," the older woman said quietly.

Kyle stayed by the fire, one foot, clad only in a sock, resting on the stone hearth, his hand braced on the mantel. He seemed absorbed by something in the flames. He didn't notice when Hallie slipped from the room.

She found Florence in almost the same trancelike state in the kitchen. The older woman stood at the counter, her hands resting on either side of a mixing bowl, staring at the canister of flour. She jumped when she realized she was no longer alone.

"Oh! I was just..." Her words petered away. She shook her head, trying to call herself to order.

"Is there anything I can do to help?" Hallie asked, and she didn't mean only with the preparation of breakfast. Her anger from the previous day had evaporated. It didn't matter anymore whether Florence had tried to use her. A desperate struggle had been waged. And now, at the end, Hallie felt compassion for the woman.

"Why should you care?" Florence said. "You've won."

"Florence—"

"You have! It's all over now. You and Kyle..." Her voice broke.

She reached into the canister and threw measures of flour into the bowl, uncaring if the white powder scattered beyond its rim.

Florence found her voice again, but she didn't lift her gaze from her work. It was as if she couldn't bear to look at Hallie while conceding defeat. "You and Kyle are taking Sharon away today. Timothy and I can't do anything to stop you. We've done our best, but that's the way it is. You choose not to see what's in front of your very eyes. I—I hope that things go well for you. But if the time ever comes when they don't—" she glanced up, her blue gray eyes filled with suffering "—please don't wait as long as our Cynthia did. Don't let it go that far. Go to your aunt. Come to us. One call to us is all it'll take. And for the Lord's sake, please take care of our Sharon. Don't let him..." Her voice broke again.

Hallie shook her head. "Florence, Kyle would never hurt Sharon." She truly believed that.

The older woman brushed away a tear. It was the first time Hallie had seen her so emotional. "I don't know what I think anymore. I don't know what he's capable of. All I know is that every day she's away..."

Hallie wanted to assure her that she would be there, that she wouldn't let anything bad happen to Sharon. She wanted to still the monsters that were poised to haunt Florence's every waking moment in the weeks ahead. But she couldn't do it. Not when her marriage was so fragile. Not when she had no idea what tomorrow might bring.

Hallie offered what comfort she could. "I'll call you," she said.

That small kernel was enough to give Florence hope. "Every week?" she asked quickly.

"Every day that I can," Hallie swore.

Florence gave her a grateful smile.

CHAPTER FOURTEEN

SHARON FOUND HERSELF in another funny mood when she woke up. She should have been on top of the world. This was the day she'd been waiting for—she was going to go live with her father! No longer would she feel so removed from him. She would see him every day. But as she looked around her room, noting the empty spaces, she felt a sense of loss.

She'd lived in this room for seven years, more than half her life. She knew which floorboard squeaked, which window stuck when you tried to open it; she knew how you had to hold your hand, just so, when you wanted to open or close the door without it making a sound. She knew the history of the ink spot on the wallpaper beside her desk, knew about the secret drawing of Candy in her closet.

Her chest of drawers looked ransacked, her shelves denuded. Most of the stuffed animals were gone. She felt emotion tighten her throat. Last night, for the first time, she'd considered what it really meant to be moving away—from her grandparents, from her friends, from the farm. And she'd cried.

She knew it wasn't forever—she'd be coming back for visits—but it would never be the same. She wouldn't be the same. Neither would they.

She rolled over and stared at the wall. She wished the day would hurry up and get over with. To that end, she stayed in bed for as long as she could. Finally, just as she was about to get up, someone knocked lightly on her door. A second later her grandmother stepped inside, carrying a tray.

"I thought you'd like to have breakfast up here this morning," Florence said cheerfully. "So you could stay all snug in your covers."

Sharon struggled to sit up. "What time is it? Is it late?" she asked hopefully.

"Later than usual," her grandmother replied as she settled the tray on her lap. "We've all had a late start this morning."

Sharon looked at the contents of the tray. All her favorites were there: apple and pecan hotcakes, maple syrup, her grandmother's special sausage, a huge glass of fresh-squeezed orange juice. Even a flower that her grandmother must have picked yesterday, before the norther blew in, with just this purpose in mind.

Emotion again tightened her throat. "Thanks, Gran," she said.

Her grandmother couldn't help but notice the bareness of the walls, of the shelves, or the packed boxes pushed against one wall. "You've finished packing?" she asked.

Sharon heard the quiver in the voice, the emotion that colored the words. She dipped her chin. "Yes."

"I was going to ask if you needed any help."

Sharon shook her head. "No, everything's done."
She glanced uneasily at the suitcases open on the floor.
"Just a few last things."

Her grandmother stared at them for a long moment. Turning, she started to rub her right arm from elbow to wrist, an action that Sharon knew signaled intense agitation.

"I'll, ah, wash the clothes you've worn over the last few days and pack them in one of the boxes to be sent on, unless you want me to send them separately. I, ah..." She seemed to lose what she'd been about to say. "Your granddad and I will get everything off to you as soon as we can. Tomorrow, the next day at the latest. We, ah... We..." Again she seemed to lose track.

Sharon cut into the hotcakes, the muscles of her face tightening. She'd never felt so awkward with her grandmother before. "There's no hurry," she murmured.

"Oh, but we want to get them to you so you won't feel lonely. Things from home always—" Florence stopped.

Things from home. Her grandmother must have realized what she'd said. Sharon moved, growing more uncomfortable. The farm wasn't going to be her home any longer. It was the past, and Sharon was moving on to her future.

"It's okay, Gran," she said edgily.

Her grandmother turned as if to leave, but she didn't move away. Sharon watched her for a second, then she transferred the tray to the other side of the bed and slipped out from beneath the cover.

"Gran?" she said, padding closer.

Her grandmother sniffed, rubbed at her plump cheeks and turned to face her, a bright smile pinned in place. "I'm glad you're so organized," she said proudly. "Not every girl your age would be."

Sharon knew her grandmother was only saying that to ease the situation. Once, she would have taken it at face value. She would have preened under the compliment. But over the past few weeks she'd started to realize that people sometimes did things for reasons other than the ones they claimed. That both black and white had shades of gray. Was that what growing up was about? If so, she wasn't sure she wanted to all that much anymore. Being a child was far easier.

She threw herself into her grandmother's arms, obviously surprising Florence. She held on fiercely, then pulled back so that she could look at the older woman. "I love you, Gran. I love you and Granddad and the farm. And when I'm in Atlanta, I won't forget you. I'll write, I'll call. You'll see. You'll get tired of hearing from me!" She tried hard to steady her smile.

Her grandmother worked just as hard. She patted Sharon's back and smoothed her long dark hair. "We'll never get tired of hearing from you," she said huskily. Then she glanced at the tray and admonished, "Better eat that before it gets cold."

Sharon laughed and hugged her grandmother again before scurrying back to the bed.

After her grandmother left, though, Sharon found it difficult to eat. The hotcakes were cooked to perfection, the sausage expertly seasoned, the orange juice fresh and sweet. But she just wasn't hungry.

HALLIE CHECKED her watch for what must have been the thousandth time. Under normal conditions a morning and afternoon could fly by without her being aware of the passage of time. But today each second was excruciatingly slow, minutes took forever, and one hour changing into the next seemed an impossible goal.

Tension vibrated in the air of the house. Kyle was drawn into himself, speaking only when he had to. Sheer force of will kept Florence going. Timothy was almost beside himself with anger. Even Sharon seemed preoccupied, distracted.

Lunch was somehow gotten through, then the telephone calls started. Sharon's friends wanted to say goodbye again. They called on their lunch break and in between classes. If it hadn't been a school day, they probably would have visited. Hallie, remembering the aftermath of their Sunday visits, couldn't help but be thankful.

As the afternoon wore on, Sharon wandered out to the stable. She wanted to say goodbye to Candy, she said.

The adults waited in the living room. Timothy in his recliner, Florence in her chair attempting to work on her quilt, Hallie on the sofa and Kyle moving restlessly about the room.

The outside temperature had hovered around the freezing point all day, and the fire had been kept going. Kyle squatted down to prod the logs with the poker, an act he performed repeatedly.

Seeing him, Timothy snapped, "You're going to run us through a season of logs in one day if you don't stop that. I've already brought in more than I usually do in a month."

Kyle continued to poke at the logs. "I've told you I'd be glad to bring them in."

"It's not bringing them in that I'm complaining about. It's the waste."

"I'll have another cord of wood delivered next week."

Timothy snorted. "I chop my own."

Kyle immediately straightened. "Is that what it is you want?" he demanded. "For me to personally replace what I've burned? I can do it, Timothy. We still have time to spare before we leave."

"Don't be ridiculous, both of you," Florence said tightly.

Timothy rounded on his wife. "Well, I for one am tired of pussyfooting around! I've tried it your way and it hasn't done a damn bit of good. Yes, I said *damn!* And I feel like saying a lot worse! What good does it do Sharon for us to just sit back and let this thing happen? We should be fighting it to our last ounce of strength!" He jabbed the air with a finger. "We shouldn't have listened to what that lawyer said. We should have gone to court, told it to a judge, let him decide. We're old, but we're not that old!" He transferred his angry gaze back to Kyle. "Did you have something to do with that, McKenna? I'm beginning to smell a rat. Did you pay our lawyer to tell us we couldn't win?"

Kyle shook his head. "Timothy, I feel sorry for you."

Timothy's nostrils flared. "Well, don't! I think what we need to do is end this right here. I'm doing what I should've done weeks ago. You're not taking Sharon away from us! *She's not leaving this house!*"

"Timothy!" Florence abandoned her sewing. She didn't notice it slide to the floor.

Kyle continued to shake his head. "You're a deluded old man."

"Deluded, am I?" Timothy shifted to the edge of his seat. All the hatred he felt for his onetime son-in-law was evident on his face. It twisted his features, making them ugly.

"I've never talked to your lawyer in my life," Kyle said, "much less paid him anything. If he advised you not to take your case to court, it must be because he thought it was weak."

"Unlike your case, which is strong?" Timothy demanded. "A man who abandoned his only child because she was inconvenient. A man who preferred his job over everything else. A man who cheated on his wife. A man who *murdered* his wife!"

Kyle's jaws clamped shut. Hallie held her breath.

"We weren't too old to take on a six-year-old child, were we, McKenna?" Timothy continued, out of control. "We weren't too old to care for her for the next seven years while you flitted around the world making a name for yourself. We just got too old when you decided that you wanted her back again. When you got worried that we might tell her the truth!''

Kyle's hands opened and closed into fists at his sides. His body was tensed for action. ''You wouldn't know the truth if it jumped up and bit you in the butt, Timothy.''

''Are you trying to tell us that you didn't kill Cynthia?

''Would it do any good if I did?''

''Hell no!'' Timothy stumbled as he got to his feet, but he didn't fall. It took him only a second to right himself, even as he fought off Florence's helping hands. ''I read her letters.'' He marched over to the narrow drawer in the desk to dig them out. Then he came back across the room, removed the band that held them together and threw them in Kyle's face. ''They were quite an education.''

Hallie's heart beat rapidly, like a butterfly frantic to be set free. She couldn't say anything; she had no part to play. But she had instinctive knowledge that this argument could affect the rest of her life.

Kyle did nothing to retrieve any of the letters. His gaze stayed fixed on Timothy. ''Your daughter was a spoiled little bitch, Timothy. And you're the person most responsible. Our marriage didn't stand a chance.''

''You're blaming me because *you* cheated?''

''No!'' Kyle's voice rang with feeling. ''I'm blaming you for raising Cynthia to expect everyone and everything to always give in to her. She didn't have an unselfish bone in her body. It had to be her way or no way at all."

"You married her. You took her away!"

"Something I came to regret."

"So you started to run around."

Kyle laughed shortly. It wasn't a pretty sound. "I *never* ran around. She did. If it had a pulse, she slept with it. My friends, my co-workers, her co-workers, the paperboy—she didn't miss many."

Timothy let out an outraged bellow. "So you killed her!" he accused.

"No!"

All eyes turned to the doorway. Sharon stood just inside the room, her face a mask of pain and horror. She looked from her grandfather to her father and back again. Her body jerked spasmodically as she tried to breathe. Her eyes were huge, bright, filled with tears.

The adults looked stricken. No one had meant for her to hear. Florence automatically reached for her but seemed unable to get out of her seat. Timothy froze, one arm held in the air like an avenging hammer. Kyle closed his eyes. His worst nightmare had come true.

Hallie, alone, could act. She went over to touch Sharon's arm, but the girl didn't notice. Her attention couldn't be diverted from the angry, hurtful words.

"Daddy?" she said hollowly. A range of questions were unconsciously packed into the inquiry. She wanted him to tell her that nothing she'd overheard was true. "Granddad?" she said. She wanted the identical assurance from him.

Timothy started to breathe heavily. Perspiration popped out on his forehead and above his upper lip. He grew extremely pale. Then he staggered, his hand grasping for purchase on the chair. It slipped off, and he toppled to the floor.

Florence hurried to her husband and dropped to her knees next to him. She screeched at Kyle, "Are you satisfied? Are you finally satisfied? First Cynthia, now Timothy. Oh, God! Please help him. Please help him," she repeated like a chant. "Don't let it be a stroke!"

Hallie grabbed Sharon's arm. "The doctor's number. What's the doctor's number?" she repeated even though the girl seemed incapable of responding.

Almost in a stupor, Sharon pointed to a notebook on the desk. "In there," she whispered. The gaze she turned on Hallie made her shiver. It seemed dead, as if she'd suddenly cut herself off from all feeling.

Hallie wouldn't let go of her arm. "His name." She pulled the girl over to the desk. "Would it be under *D* for doctor?"

Sharon nodded.

Kyle bent down on one knee next to Timothy. He felt his pulse. "Maybe you'd better dial 911. Get an ambulance out here right away."

"We're not in the city," Florence snapped. "It would be best if we drove him."

"I'll get the car," Kyle said, straightening. He paused to look at Hallie and his daughter. "You still should call the doctor, so he'll know to meet us at the hospital's emergency entrance."

Hallie did as he directed while Florence continued to crouch worriedly by her husband's side. Sharon had stopped talking; she wasn't of any more use.

Moments later Kyle strode back into the room. He lifted the unconscious Timothy easily and strode out the door, covering ground quickly. The others followed, Florence having gathered the decorative quilt off the arm of the couch.

Kyle arranged Timothy on the back seat of the rental car. Florence spread the quilt over him and then settled in the passenger seat. Kyle started to slide behind the steering wheel, but Hallie stopped him.

"Do you think he'll be all right?" she asked on behalf of Sharon, who still seemed incapable of speech.

"Who knows?" Kyle said harshly, then glancing at his daughter, he promised, "I'll get him to the hospital as fast as I can."

Hallie wouldn't let go. "Kyle," she said urgently.

He paused again to look at her.

It was necessary that he leave right away. It was necessary that Timothy receive proper care. She knew that, but she had to say something first. All that came out of her mouth, though, was an ineffectual "Kyle...be careful!"

A shutter descended over his pale green eyes. "I always am," he replied tersely, and closed the door.

Hallie and Sharon drew back as the car shot forward. They watched as it turned onto the road, then continued to watch until it disappeared from view.

In a few short minutes so much had happened. There was no question of them leaving for Atlanta this afternoon. When she got a chance she would call the airline and explain. Her thoughts veered. Kyle had said that it was Cynthia who'd cheated, an extension of what Walker had already told her—that Cynthia had been promiscuous before she married. Before... after. It wasn't difficult to accept that, not given the rest of what she knew about Cynthia.

Hallie stood with an arm around Sharon's shoulders and felt a shiver pass through the girl's body. It was cold out, and they'd been too rushed even to think of gathering coats.

"Come on," she said, "let's go inside."

She guided Sharon into the kitchen, only to find the girl's coat discarded on the counter. She must have tossed it there earlier, then come to join them in the living room.

"I'll make us coffee," Hallie said.

"Tea. Gran always makes tea when..."

She didn't finish, but Hallie had a good idea of what she had been going to say—*when things get a little rough emotionally*. She filled the kettle, then prepared the cups, adding an extra spoonful of sugar to Sharon's.

When the kettle whistled, Hallie added the tea bags, poured the water and carried them into the hall. Sharon followed her like a lost puppy. She hesitated only slightly when she saw that Hallie was prompting her to return to the living room.

"Here," Hallie said once the girl was sitting on the rug in front of the fire. "Drink some tea. It'll help. I had some last night myself for the same purpose. Coffee, that is. But it's all the same. It's warm."

She was babbling, but Sharon didn't seem to mind. The girl took the cup, hunched her shoulders and shuddered slightly as she stared at the flames.

Hallie wished she had a blanket to wrap around the girl, but she didn't want to leave Sharon for the length of time it would take to find one. She thought of the girl's coat, hurried into the kitchen and was back before Sharon had even realized she was gone. She placed it over Sharon's shoulders and the girl huddled into it.

Shock had made Sharon sensitive to the cold. It would take a long time for her to warm up, just as it would take time for her to heal emotionally—if she ever did.

What a horrible thing to hear at such a tender age. Just what Kyle had dreaded, only worse, since the added condemnation of her mother had come from his lips. Now Sharon not only knew that her grandparents blamed her father for her mother's death, but that her father considered her mother little better than a tramp.

Hallie settled on the rug beside Sharon and sipped her tea. She noticed that Sharon automatically did the same. After a while Hallie murmured. "I'm sure they'll call us as soon as they know anything."

Sharon said nothing.

"I wonder if we should call Walker."

"Granddad wouldn't like a fuss."

"But Walker is his best friend."

Sharon shrugged, her eyes glued to the flames. "Call him if you like," she said dully.

"We'll wait until we hear something," Hallie decided.

She finished her tea and put her cup aside. Sharon held on to hers, even though Hallie could see that it was empty.

"Want some more?" she asked.

Sharon shook her head.

Hallie sighed and hugged her knees. She didn't know whether she should mention the accusations that had been flung about earlier or not.

"For some reason," Sharon said eventually, her voice oddly dreamy, "I was never sure I would go to Atlanta with you."

"You weren't?" Hallie said, surprised.

Sharon gave her head a small shake. "No. I always thought something would come up. That Daddy would be called away or something." She laughed unsteadily. "I never expected *this*."

"Your granddad—"

"All of it!" Sharon said impatiently, then was immediately repentant. "I'm sorry."

Hallie frowned. Sharon? Apologizing? To her? It must be the shock.

Sharon smiled weakly. "I am sorry," she repeated. "I didn't like the idea that Daddy had a new wife. It wasn't personal. You could have been anyone."

"Why are you telling me this now?"

Sharon's gaze returned to the fire. "Because none of it matters anymore."

"Sharon—"

The girl shook her head with much more force. "I don't want to talk about it!" She started to get up. "I'm going to my room."

Hallie stopped her. "I don't think you should be alone right now."

"Why not? I've been alone all my life."

"Sharon! You have your father, your grandparents..."

"Have I?"

The telephone rang, causing them both to jump. Hallie hurried to answer it. "Yes?" she said, without thinking that the call could come from someone besides Kyle or Florence.

"The doctor is with him now," Kyle said tightly. "We still don't know anything. Probably won't for a while, but Florence wanted to reassure Sharon."

"I'll tell her what you said," Hallie promised.

There was a short silence, then Kyle said, "I'd better go."

Hallie didn't want to let him break off. She searched for something to say. She knew he must be worried sick. He sounded so hollow, so distant. "I—I was thinking about calling the airport."

"Good idea," he agreed.

"I'll tell them we'll have to reschedule."

He didn't say anything. Hallie had the impression that he nodded.

Finally he sighed. "Look, I have to get back to Florence. She's pretty broken up."

"Yes," Hallie said.

A click signaled the end of their conversation.

Hallie rubbed her forehead near her bruise after returning the receiver to its cradle. Until this minute she hadn't been aware of any holdover from yesterday's throbbing ache. But it must have been hovering in the background all along.

She drew a deep breath and turned to Sharon—only the girl wasn't there. Not surprisingly, she'd taken advantage of the moment and withdrawn.

Hallie made her call, then went in search of Sharon. As she'd said earlier, she didn't think it a good idea for the girl to be alone. So much had been left hanging.

Sharon wasn't in the house, so Hallie went to the stable. She had a feeling that if Sharon was anywhere, she was with Candy. She was proved right.

Again the girl stood brushing the horse, in all likelihood because it soothed her as much as it did her charge.

Sharon shot her a look from over Candy's neck. "Is Granddad all right?" she asked.

"They don't know yet," Hallie said. "He's with the doctor."

Sharon bent to brush the horse's front leg, then she came around to start on the opposite side, her back to Hallie.

"Your dad said he'd call later."

Sharon still said nothing.

Hallie watched the practiced strokes and huddled deeper into her coat. It was cold out here, even with all the doors closed.

"I'm not going to do anything silly," Sharon said after a moment. "You don't have to stay with me."

"I didn't think you were."

"Then why are you here?"

"Because I think I should be."

"Because of what I overheard?"

"Because what you heard may not be the way things really are. Were."

"You know that for a fact?" Sharon challenged. She had stopped brushing the horse to look at Hallie.

Hallie shook her head. "This time, Sharon, no. I know very little more than you do."

"Do you think Daddy killed my mother?" She came directly to the point.

"No."

Sharon resumed brushing. "You don't sound very sure."

"I think we should wait to hear what he has to say."

"Is that why my grandparents hate him so much?"

"It would be better if you waited to ask them."

"I think it is. It all makes sense now. I thought they just hated him because he took Mommy away. But if he killed her—"

"Sharon!"

"Well, maybe she deserved it!"

Hallie closed her eyes. "Wait to talk to them," she repeated.

Sharon shrugged.

Hallie sat down on a bale of hay and stretched her legs out in front of her, crossing them at the ankle. She picked up a long piece of straw and twirled it between her fingers. She wanted to go back to the house so that someone would be there to answer the phone when Kyle called again, but she didn't think Sharon would come.

"Do you remember before when I told you that you're a very lucky person to have so many people who love you?" Hallie asked moments later. "Well, you are. I only ever had one person feel that way about me when I was growing up. An aunt."

"What about your parents?"

A dry smile flickered over Hallie's lips. "They were parents in name only. I went to live with my aunt when I was ten."

"Like me, only a little younger."

"Not exactly like you. As I said, my parents were only too happy to pawn me off on my aunt once they decided on a way to explain it to their friends. I believe they said they nobly sacrificed their daughter to my father's sister's care because she was an emotional wreck and in desperate need of someone to mother. They saved her sanity, to hear them tell it."

"Was she an emotional wreck?"

"She's the sweetest, most giving person I've ever met."

"Did you know her before you went to live with her?"

"I'd gone to visit her. My parents made numerous long trips and had to find places to put me. Aunt Catherine took me whenever she could."

Sharon straightened. "That doesn't sound like very much fun."

"It wasn't, except when I was with Aunt Catherine."

"So you wanted to go live with her, like I do with..." She stopped, unsure of the future.

"Yes, I did."

"Is that why you agreed to come here with Daddy to get me?"

"I was in a good position to understand the problem involved, yes."

"What problem?" Sharon asked quickly. "Oh, you mean..."

"That you should have the right to decide who you want to live with," Hallie supplied.

Sharon looked at her. "Do you still feel that way now?" she asked.

"More than ever," Hallie replied.

"Even if I..."

The way she shied away from completing her thought led Hallie to believe that she was considering opting out of the move. Hallie thought of Kyle and how crushed he'd be. But she knew it was Sharon who had to make the decision. And if the girl decided not to come, where did that leave her and Kyle? Especially if he'd married her only to regain custody of his daughter.

Hallie straightened her shoulders. She couldn't visit her problems on the girl. Sharon had more than enough of her own. "Before you make a decision, you have to get all the facts," she advised quietly. "And then, whatever your decision is, I'll support you."

Sharon stared at her, the brush in her hand forgotten.

Hallie returned her look with resolute firmness, knowing that Sharon had no idea how difficult it had been for her to say that.

CHAPTER FIFTEEN

THE TELEPHONE CALL didn't come until an hour later, after Hallie had convinced Sharon to return to the house. The two of them had waited, both now able to show their concern, on the rug in front of the fire. It seemed to be the place that offered Sharon the most comfort, outside of the stable.

Hallie replaced the receiver and broke the good news. "It wasn't a stroke or his stomach or a heart problem. At least, not as far as the tests he's taken up to this point show. Tomorrow they want to do more just to be sure. The doctor thinks it was stress. Your grandfather's body stopped him before he could do too much damage to himself."

Sharon started to cry and Hallie didn't try to hush her. They had all been living under a high degree of stress. It would do Sharon good to have a short release.

After a moment she said, "Your dad and your grandmother will be back here soon. Florence wanted to stay overnight, but the doctor told her she'd end up in the hospital herself if she didn't get more rest."

That news was enough to stop Sharon's tears. "They're both coming back?"

"So it seems."

Sharon nervously twisted several strands of her hair. "I'm afraid," she said simply.

Hallie knew Sharon wasn't afraid of the people, only of what they might say. "It's better to get it over with," she counseled.

"I know," Sharon whispered.

Not a half hour passed before they heard the car turn into the drive. Sharon immediately tensed. Hallie did, too, but she tried not to let it show.

Her heart was pounding as Kyle came into the room, following Florence. His face continued to be tight, noncommittal. His gaze sought her out, but he didn't come over to her.

Florence enveloped Sharon in a flurry of hugs and tears. "He's all right, Sharon. He's all right!"

"That's great, Gran," Sharon returned, her expression troubled.

Florence pulled back. Her hands fluttered to her hair. "I must look a sight. I—I'm going to go upstairs and freshen up a bit." Then before anyone could say anything—not that anyone would—she hurried off to the privacy of her bedroom.

Hallie stood with her fingers laced in front of her. "Would you like some coffee or something?"

Kyle shook his head. After his first quick look at her, his gaze had been exclusively on his daughter. "No, I had enough coffee at the hospital."

Sharon couldn't seem to look at him. She'd scram-
bled to her feet upon hearing the car and hadn't resettled.

Hallie noticed the girl's telltale twisting of her hair.
She thought to leave the room, to leave them alone
together where they could talk over the whole situation without an audience. Kyle had never wanted to
discuss Cynthia with her. "Maybe I should just—"

"Don't go," Sharon said. "Please?"

Hallie looked at Kyle. She saw the suffering in his
eyes. "You and your father have things to talk about,
Sharon. Things that I—"

"You should know the answers, too! I'm tired of
having things kept from me. All secrets do is hurt
people! Please stay!"

Kyle moved stiffly across the room. He dropped his
coat onto the arm of the couch. "Do whatever you
want," he said.

A muscle twitched in Hallie's cheek. "I'll stay," she
said softly.

Kyle shrugged and for a long time said nothing.

Florence slipped back into the room, actually looking a little better. She had combed her hair into neat
curls, and her face was ruddy, as if freshly scrubbed in
cold water. She saw the gravity with which the others
were waiting and immediately understood.

If Kyle noticed her, he gave no sign. A moment later
he started to speak. "I didn't want it to be like this. I
never planned... I don't want you to think badly of
your mother, Sharon. In her defense, she did the best

she could in a poor situation. You said once that you thought the two of us running away to get married was romantic. Well, maybe it was for the first month or so. After that, I think she came to regret it. She wasn't ready to get married. She was only nineteen. A very young nineteen in some ways. And I was busy with my work. Maybe I neglected her, I don't know. Then you came along. One of the best things that happened in my life.'' He smiled tautly, his green eyes fastened on his daughter.

Sharon remained perfectly still, her own green eyes steady. It was as if she was doing what Hallie had suggested, gathering all the facts, hearing everyone out. In one week, the girl had done a lot of growing up.

"What I said earlier, well, that came later on," Kyle continued. "By then there wasn't much left to our marriage. She wasn't a saint and neither was I."

"I remember the arguments," Sharon murmured.

"I wondered about that. They came often enough, especially near the end. The weekend we went away, we were giving it one last try. We'd brought you here to stay with your grandparents, and your mother and I went off for some time on our own. It didn't work. We argued worse there than—" He stopped, glancing at Florence and then back at Sharon. "I didn't kill her. In fact, I wasn't even driving when we had the accident. I'd hurt my hand. I couldn't drive. She was." When Florence made a strangled sound, Kyle turned to her. "I know Timothy isn't going to believe that,

but I have proof. The doctor who treated my hand in
San Antonio performed surgery to reconnect a ten-
don. He completely immobilized it, gave me a pain-
killer and sent me on my way. I'm sure there'd be a
record. Timothy can check it out. I'll write down his
name and the name of the hospital." He did so, then
handed Florence the paper. She took it without uttering a sound.

"Why did Granddad think you killed her?" Sharon
asked.

"I didn't correct the police report that said I was the
driver."

"Why not?"

"At first, I wasn't in good enough shape to care."

"Your father was almost killed, too, Sharon. Didn'
you know?" Hallie asked.

"No one talked to me about the accident. Not then,
not later." She threw her grandmother a resentful
glance.

Kyle intervened. "Your grandmother was in a lot of
pain."

"For seven years?" Sharon demanded.

"That kind of pain doesn't go away. To lose a
child...it's the worst thing that can happen to a parent."

Sharon shook her head angrily. "So everything was
just a big mistake!"

"The situation built up over the years, Sharon.
Your grandfather never liked me. He blamed me for
stealing your mother away from him. Your grand-

mother . . . just went along with him, I think, until she believed it, too."

"Why wouldn't anyone talk about her? Why? When I asked!"

Florence cleared her throat. "We didn't want you to think badly of your father, even if *we* did. We didn't think it would be good for you. So we agreed not to say anything."

"But couldn't you see how curious I was?"

"You know what that did to the cat," Florence murmured in all seriousness.

Sharon shook her head again, her hands opening and closing at her sides in unconscious mimicry of her father in an agitated state. It might have been something in the genes, Hallie thought.

"I was terrified they would tell you," Kyle confessed. He seemed to sense that he was battling for his daughter's loyalty and that his only weapon was the truth. "And if they did, how could I defend myself? I could give you my side of the story, but would you understand? Would you even listen? I'd be saying bad things about your mother. Someone you and they thought was perfect."

Florence sat forward in her chair, her face a picture of remembered pain. "We did spoil Cynthia. But we'd waited so long for a child! You can't imagine how happy we were when we found out one was on the way." She smiled tightly. "When Cynthia was born your granddad whooped and danced so much I thought the sheriff was going to put him in jail for disturbing the peace.'' She paused. ''She was like sunshine in our lives. We saw everything new again through her eyes. Then she grew up and we were so proud. We planned everything. She was going to marry Walker's boy and we'd merge the two farms....'' She looked at Kyle. ''Then it all seemed to go wrong. You came.''

''And I've been damned ever since.''

Florence held his gaze. She offered no apology.

Sharon stamped a foot in frustration. ''You can't do that, Gran! You can't plan people's lives!''

''It was more a hope than a formal plan,'' Florence defended.

''If things went wrong, then it was pretty formal! And you blamed Daddy.''

''There was more to it than that!'' Florence cried, her face once again reflecting past distress.

''What?'' Sharon took her up on her claim. ''Tell me what?''

Florence waved an ineffectual hand. ''He...he wasn't what we wanted for her. We were afraid he was just going to use her and then be off. It was a certain...attitude. He was arrogant, ambitious! And she was just an innocent young girl.''

Hallie again thought back to what Walker had said about Cynthia, and according to him that last statement was untrue. Kyle must have known it, but he didn't contradict her.

''But they fell in love!'' Sharon insisted from her vantage point of almost fourteen years.

"We knew what was best for her!" Florence retorted.

"Just like you think you do for me!"

Florence's shoulders sagged.

Sharon looked from her grandmother to her father. "You both think you know what's best for me. But maybe you don't! Maybe you should give me some credit for having a mind of my own. Hallie does. She says *I'm* the one who should decide who I'm going to live with. No one else, just me! Not you, Daddy. Not you, Gran. Not Granddad! Just me," she repeated firmly.

Hallie felt Kyle's gaze flick over her.

"And I want to think about it for a day or two," Sharon announced.

Florence's head jerked up as she realized there was a possibility her granddaughter might not go to Atlanta. "Of course you should," she said eagerly.

Sharon shook her head. "I'm not saying I've changed my mind about living with Daddy. I just want to think about it, that's all. I want to think about everything."

"It's probably for the best," Kyle said quietly.

Sharon nodded at Hallie, who nodded back.

KYLE DID Timothy's chores that evening, taking care of everything to the best of his ability. It had been years since he'd performed some of those tasks, but he found that a knowledge once implanted wasn't easily forgotten.

The house was quiet as he made his way back inside. The day had been long; everyone was exhausted. They'd spent so many hours winding up for the final leave-taking, then been denied it by Timothy's collapse.

Kyle had no idea what was going to happen next. It felt like they'd been sitting on a powder keg that blew up but all the pieces had yet to hit the ground. Whenever he remembered Sharon's face... He would gladly cut out his tongue if he could reclaim his venom-filled words. That she'd overheard what he'd said about her mother! It had been the truth, but that was no excuse. Neither was the fact that he'd thought her safely outside or that Timothy had just accused him of murder.

She had looked beyond stricken—her face so white, her eyes so shocked. It was like she'd been hit with twin shotgun blasts: her mother was a slut and her father had killed her. No wonder she wanted time to think. An adult would need time. And she was a child, whether she liked it or not. She might be starting to mature emotionally, but she still had a long way to go.

Hallie had told her to make up her own mind, to decide for herself. Hallie...

Kyle paused halfway up the stairs. He couldn't get the look in *her* eyes out of his mind, either. The suspicion, the hurt, the pain. He'd spent last night on the couch downstairs and was prepared to do it again—if that was what she wanted.

HALLIE STOOD at the window, hugging herself with her arms. She was cold, but not because of the temperature. A thoughtful replay of the past few hours was responsible for chilling her. She had learned so much, but she knew there was much more to be learned.

Kyle came into the room, shutting the door quietly behind him. He still wore his coat, the rough russet suede that so closely matched the color of his hair. As usual his presence changed the atmosphere in the room, making it come alive with an electrical charge.

His gaze swept over her. Hallie had to turn away in order to remain steady on her feet.

She felt Kyle move, take off his coat, drape it over the foot of the bed. The longer they didn't speak, the louder the silence became.

She closed her eyes, swayed, then opened them when she sensed Kyle's nearness. The pulse in her throat fluttered, her breathing became shallower. But he didn't touch her. He stood across from her with his hands stuffed in his pockets.

"I'll sleep downstairs again tonight if you like," he said after a long moment had passed.

Her shoulders lifted, fell. There was so much she wanted to say, to ask! But she couldn't make anything come out of her mouth.

He waited. Finally, removing his hands from his pockets, he started to turn away.

"Kyle!"

He pulled up short.

"Don't...don't leave," she requested. "You... I...we..." She stopped, distraught by her inability to find the right words. "Not yet!" she finally managed. "Not when there's so much—"

"What do you want to know?" he broke in, unwilling to prolong the misery.

If she could have been anywhere else, doing anything else, she would have been! The possibility was high that what she might learn in the next few minutes would only hurt her more. "Everything," she croaked.

"Your pound of flesh," he murmured.

She hadn't meant that at all! "The truth, Kyle," she corrected him. "Just the truth."

A smile that could easily have been a grimace touched his lips. "I'm surprised you're not asking for a lie detector test."

"Kyle...please."

"What first?" he murmured seriously. The time had come.

"Cynthia?" The name of the woman who had always been between them—who, even though she'd been dead for seven years, still had the power to disrupt their lives. It tasted bitter on her lips. "Tell me about Cynthia."

His face grew bleak. "You heard what I said earlier."

"Yes."

"What more is there to say?"

"Did you love her?"

"In the beginning."

"Was there more to it than what you told Sharon?"

"It was exactly as I told Sharon. The marriage just didn't work out."

"Because she was spoiled?"

"That was a lot of it."

"What else? Talk to me, Kyle. Tell me." When he didn't respond, she continued. "You said she slept with other men?"

"Men, boys, it didn't matter."

"Did you know about it at the time?"

"Yes." His jaw tightened. "It was hard not to. She didn't make a secret of it."

"Yet you tried to make the marriage work."

"For Sharon."

"What happened that last weekend, Kyle? How did you hurt your hand?"

He moved restlessly. "We were arguing in our hotel room. She... broke a window and tried to jump through it. I stopped her."

The starkness of his words caused a chill to run up Hallie's spine. He'd spoken so quietly, so unemotionally. "That's when you cut your hand?" she whispered.

"On the glass." He glanced at the thin scar that ran across the base of his knuckles. Hallie had seen it before, but she'd thought he'd gotten it, as he had so many others, while on assignment.

"She tried to kill herself?" she asked huskily.

He nodded. "It was the first time things had gotten so far out of hand. I knew she was unhappy. I knew she was becoming more unstable. But I never suspected ... Or maybe I was too angry to care. By that time the only person I was thinking of was Sharon."

"Did Florence and Timothy ever find out?"

"Not unless Cynthia called that last day to tell them, which I doubt. They'd have accused me of trying to push her if she had, so that's one fabrication they missed."

"She told them that you hit her, that you were seeing other women."

"I didn't hit her and I didn't cheat on her, either." He laughed hollowly. "I may have wanted to, but I didn't."

"You knew Cynthia told her parents lies about you?"

"I didn't know for sure, but I suspected it. I was never their favorite person, but I could feel the ice getting thicker."

Hallie hesitated. "And the accident?"

Kyle took a deep breath. "This was what I didn't want to get into," he said more to himself than to Hallie.

Hallie came closer and touched his arm. "Kyle, don't stop now. Please."

He looked at her hand and then at her. Hallie did her best to withstand the onslaught to her emotions.

"You almost guessed it," he said quietly. "We were arguing. And when the curve came ... she didn't take it. She was looking straight ahead. She had to have seen it."

Hallie's eyes widened. "You think she did it on purpose?"

The terrible question made Kyle wince. "I don't know. The car turned over, and over again. The doors flew open. We were tossed around. The seat belts were automatic and they went with the doors. We both ended up outside on the ground. I came to, looked for her, found her. Only—" he swallowed "—she wasn't... I couldn't stop the blood! I tried. I used every bit of first-aid training I'd ever learned. Direct pressure. Tourniquet. Nothing worked. Blood was coming from her ears, too. I knew how bad a sign *that* was. No one stopped. I could hear traffic on the road above, but I couldn't get to it. And no one saw us. I had to sit there, holding her as best I could, and watch as she died." He blinked and shook his head, trying to pull himself from the horrors of the past. "I didn't love her any longer. She'd killed that a long time before. But it still wasn't easy. Finally someone came, then the medical people and the police. I don't remember much from that point on. The hospital is a blur. I think I remember being taken there."

"And the police thought you were the driver," Hallie said softly, tears glittering in her eyes. Kyle had a gift for making a listener feel what he saw. It was in the timbre of his voice, in the sureness of his conviction. Although she'd never met Cynthia, she could see her lying in his arms.

"It was assumed," he said.

"And Florence and Timothy—"

"—believed it."

"And blamed you. Why did you leave Sharon with them, then? Surely, under the circumstances, someone else would have been better."

"There was no one else."

Hallie looked at him. "Your stepmother?"

Kyle ran a hand through his hair. "You mean to cover all the bases, don't you?"

"As Sharon said, all secrets do is hurt people."

"I wouldn't leave a buzzard to my stepmother's tender mercy!" Kyle almost snarled. "Certainly not Sharon. You said I lied to you, Hallie, but I didn't. If I remember correctly, you asked if there was anyone I wanted to see back at the ranch where I grew up. I told you there was no one, not even an old friend. And there isn't! Yes, I have a stepmother there and a half brother and half sister. But they aren't people I want to mix with, much less expose you to. That woman married my father when I was sixteen. She pushed her way in, had two kids and pushed me out. My father couldn't see anything wrong with what she did. He told me to stop complaining. So I left as soon as I could and I never went back. Not until I went to see him just before he died. He told me he was splitting the ranch between us. Half to her, half to his three children. I didn't want it. I'd already decided to do other things with my life, but it was what he wanted. At the funeral she accused me of worming my way back into Dad's good graces so I could steal part of the ranch away from her kids. Right then and there, I signed my part over to them. I didn't want to have anything more to do with them. Then a few years later, they came here. Wanted Florence and Timothy to get me to give them some money for back taxes they said I owed. When they found me in Houston I called a lawyer, and I haven't heard from them since. Now do you see why I don't want to visit them? Why I don't care to even think they exist?''

Hallie nodded mutely.

Kyle ran his fingers through his hair again and moved closer to the window. He looked out for a moment, then he turned around and asked, "Anything else?"

Emotion tightened Hallie's throat. Had she unconsciously saved this question for last because it was what she dreaded most?

"Only one thing," she said huskily. "What about me?"

"I don't understand."

She took a breath. "Kyle, why did you marry me?"

"I still don't..." He frowned. "This is from the other day, isn't it?" he demanded. "You still believe what Sharon said, just like you believed the Langs." He laughed bitterly.

"I just want to know where I stand, Kyle."

Hallie didn't know if she'd gone too far. He'd told her about his marriage, he'd told her about the accident—two things he'd never talked about before.

Should she have waited until tomorrow to ask about the rest? Until the day after tomorrow... or the day after that?

The words burst out of her. "I just need to know if you love me!"

Her first instinct was to slap a hand over her mouth to prevent the words from escaping. With them, she'd revealed her deepest insecurities, her secret fear. But it was too late. The words were already scattered about the room like tiny bits of her heart.

Kyle stared at her, obviously taken aback. Oh, God, she thought, if he didn't love her...

Her face crumpled as all the tension of the past few days broke, and tears—silent evidence of her pain—rolled down over her cheeks.

Kyle made a strangled sound, and the next thing Hallie knew, she was being held so tightly in his arms she could barely breathe. He murmured something to her, but she couldn't make out the words. She didn't need to understand them, though. His holding her was message enough.

That his marriage to Cynthia hadn't worked, that for years his in-laws had considered him a murderer, that she herself had doubted him, none of it seemed to matter now.

He bruised her lips, trailed fire down her throat, then tried to tear aside her blouse when it wouldn't yield. Hallie laughed shakily, but the laugh turned into a gasp of pleasure as he succeeded in removing the garment and continued to kiss her and touch her like a man long starved.

Then he lifted his head to look at her. And for Hallie, meeting his gaze was like a desperate plunge into uncharted seas. She knew she might drown, but she didn't care.

CHAPTER SIXTEEN

A BRIGHT BEAM of sunlight radiated across the hard-wood floor, onto the colorful rag rug, then to the bed and Hallie's face. Slowly she came awake, stretching like a contented cat, a sense of well-being pervading every speck of her being from her fingertips to her toes.

She reached out to the man lying next to her and adjusted the blanket so that his shoulder and the back of his neck were covered. In sleep he reminded her of the little boy he'd once been, and she gently stroked his cheek.

As she resettled on her pillow, the bright ray of light again crossed her face and she raised her hand, shielding her eyes. Then she realized its signifi-cance—it was Walker's sun! As promised, it had chased away the darkness of her despair.

Slowly her hand fell back to the bed and she smiled. No longer did she have to worry about the lack of Kyle's love or the possibility that he would reject her. He had made the opposite abundantly clear, both in actions and in words.

He'd explained that meeting her had coincided with his plans to get Sharon back; it hadn't been a part of it. In fact, in his words, it had been "damned inconvenient!" He hadn't planned on falling in love, much less during the absolutely worst time possible. He'd needed to concentrate on his custody fight...and had found that he couldn't concentrate at all. Most amazingly, he'd been unwilling to take the chance of losing Hallie. As if someone else might come along and steal her away.

Hallie hugged the thought to herself; a pleased smile was on her lips when Kyle opened his eyes and looked at her.

Hallie started to giggle. Kyle, coming awake slowly, still managed to smile.

"What's the joke?" he asked huskily.

Hallie leaned toward him and kissed him full on the lips. "Just that I love you."

"That's a joke?"

"Only on me. I do love you, Kyle. More than... everything!"

He chuckled as he gathered her in his arms. "Be careful, Mrs. McKenna. A statement like that can get you into a whole lot of trouble."

She played with a lock of his hair, suddenly becoming serious. "I won't ever doubt you again, Kyle. I'm so ashamed of the last few days. I know I hurt you."

"I'm tough. I can take it."

"But you shouldn't have to!" she exclaimed. "Everything just...built. And when I asked, you wouldn't—" She stopped, unwilling to blame him.

"All I was trying to do was get through the week with all of us left in one piece. I didn't want to delve into the past. I thought if I could just hold it all together, everything would turn out all right."

"Like an ostrich with its head in the sand."

He laughed. "I've never been compared to an ostrich before. Other, worse things, yes. But that in particular, no."

"What worse things?"

"Never mind."

Her hands curled, relaxed, on his chest. She could stay like this forever, she decided, with his hand gently rubbing her back and her cheek next to his on the pillow.

She marveled at the turn her life had taken when she met him. What would she be doing now if he hadn't come into her life? Still getting up, going to work, happy enough in her own way, but with something essential missing.

She stroked his cheek again and he smiled at her, lightly kissing her wrist.

"Kyle," she said softly, "what will happen if Sharon decides not to come with us? What will we do?"

He became very still. "I'd rather not think that way."

"I know. But if we have to."

He sighed. "I don't know. Keep coming back for visits. Try to prove to the Langs that what I said is true. Try to convince them—convince her!—that I didn't kill Cynthia."

"And what if she decides to come with us? What about the Langs?"

Kyle rolled onto his back without comment.

"They only acted the way they did because they love her," Hallie said. "Because they were afraid to lose her."

"You're asking me to say that makes everything all right." Kyle said harshly. "That they can act like that and it doesn't matter."

"No, what they did is wrong. And they're probably going to pay for it dearly for the rest of their lives. But... it was done out of love. That means something, Kyle."

He turned his head to look at her. He knew what she was referring to without her having to say it—her childhood, her years without love. "What do *you* think we should do about the Langs if she decides to come with us?"

"Forgive them."

Kyle laughed shortly. "Timothy won't like that."

Hallie thought about it and grinned. "No, he won't, will he?"

"He won't know what to do if he doesn't have me to hate."

"Maybe his blood pressure will go down."

"Now wait. You're supposing they'll go along with this."

"Florence will, and Timothy will have a hard time holding out on his own."

"You have this all worked out, don't you?"

"It's worth a try."

"If we get Sharon," he reminded her.

"Yes," Hallie said softly.

Kyle turned back on his side. "A ready-made family," he murmured.

"What?" she asked.

"A ready-made family. It's what you'll have if Sharon decides to come live with us. I never really asked if that was all right with you. I just rushed you into this whole affair."

"A family, ready-made or otherwise, is what I've wanted all my life."

"You and Sharon, you seem to be getting along better."

"I think so."

He hesitated. "What do you think she'll decide?"

Hallie said nothing. She truly didn't know.

With a sigh, Kyle gathered her into his arms again, resting his chin on the top of her head. Hallie was still, her thoughts, like his, with Sharon. After a long minute, their gazes met and held.

Hallie tenderly cupped his cheek as his hand stroked her breasts, her waist, her hip. She smiled and lifted her mouth, ready to unite them in a kiss.

As separate beings, each was prey to storms of uncertainty, buffeted this way and that by their own private doubts. But together, as a couple, they were strong. Their love could chase away any doubt, leaving them able to face whatever life had in store.

She heard him whisper her name, just as she heard her own voice whisper his. The next instant their lips met, intense with love and longing and trust.

SHARON TOOK one look at them as they came into the kitchen, and she could see that whatever problem had sprung up between them was no longer there. They were back to lingering glances, special smiles and the need to be near each other. Aspects of love—and this time she didn't mind. In fact, it was oddly reassuring.

Her grandmother was making bread again. It gave her something to do, she'd said when Sharon had asked her.

"Have you heard anything about Timothy this morning?" her father asked, sitting at the pedestal table with a cup of coffee in front of him.

"I heard from *him*," her grandmother said. "He wants to come home. Says he's fine and the doctor won't believe him."

"Have you talked to the doctor?"

"He wants to run those tests. I told Timothy to let him."

"Granddad's rung home three times so far this morning. Gran says the doctor is threatening to take the phone away."

"Sounds like he's back in form," Kyle murmured, glancing at Hallie.

"I still want him to take those tests—to be sure," Florence said.

The phone rang and Sharon ran to answer it. A minute later she was back in the room. "That was Walker," she announced. "He'd heard through the grapevine that Granddad was in the hospital and he called to see how everyone is."

Florence frowned. "I meant to ring him last night, and I forgot. Was he upset that we hadn't told him?"

"He mainly just wanted to know if we were okay. He didn't seem surprised that Daddy and I—and Hallie—hadn't left for Atlanta. I guess he heard that, too."

"I'll call him later," Florence said, more to herself than to them.

Sharon resettled herself at the table. She returned Hallie's smile with a quick one of her own. She'd been wrong about Hallie. She wasn't ridiculous, she was nice. Her attention moved to her father. He was definitely happier than he'd been yesterday, but there was still a certain tenseness in the way he held himself, in the watchfulness of his gaze.

She knew what it was, of course. He was waiting for her decision. She wiggled uncomfortably in her chair. She'd spent long hours last night tossing in her bed, thinking about everything. Her mother, her father, her grandparents, even Hallie. For Hallie had told her to get all the facts before she made her decision.

She once again looked at her new stepmother and gave another quick, almost nervous, smile. Then she cleared her throat. "I, ah, Gran, could you come over here for a minute, please?" she requested.

Her grandmother's hands stilled above the floured board, then she rinsed them and came to the table.

"I, ah, I've decided," Sharon said. "I still want to go live in Atlanta with Daddy and Hallie."

No one pressed her for reasons, for which she was grateful. She looked quickly from her father, to Hallie, to her grandmother. Then she pushed away from the table. "I'm going to tell Candy," she said.

When the screen door slammed shut behind her, she was able to draw her first easy breath of the morning.

HALLIE COVERED Kyle's hand with her own and squeezed it with mute joy. She was deeply aware that their happiness had come at Florence's expense. Kyle, too, made no joyous exclamations.

Florence had done nothing more than flinch slightly. "It's no surprise," she murmured. "I expected it. She's been determined to go live with you for the past year." She started to get up but Kyle stopped her.

"I don't look on this as a victory, Florence," he said quietly.

Habit was hard to break. "Am I supposed to believe that?" Florence snapped. But in the next breath, her animosity faltered, and she shocked them by saying, "I've thrown Cynthia's letters away. It's something I should have done years ago. I knew some of what she said was lies. She wasn't a virgin when she married you. She tried to pretend that she was to us, but I knew better. And when she accused you...it was too much like she used to do when she was a little girl. If she got into trouble, she blamed the child she was playing with. If she committed adultery, it was you, not her, who was doing it. I don't know if she was desperate to look good in our eyes, or if it just wasn't in her to admit when she'd done something wrong."

"Then why... all those years—" Kyle demanded.

"I couldn't tell Timothy that! Not about his little girl! And if you think back, just now I said I knew *some* of what she said was a lie. I figured there was plenty of blame to go around, for you, too."

"It was easier," Kyle accused her. "More convenient."

"I believed it. I believed you killed her."

"And now?" Kyle challenged.

"Now I don't know."

When Kyle seemed at a momentary loss for words, Hallie sat forward. "Florence," she said softly, "it's time to let it all go. To let the past... be the past."

"That's why I threw away the letters. Enough harm has been done. I don't want it to continue." The telephone rang again and Florence stood up. "You're welcome to stay for as long as you like," she said levelly. "And you're welcome to come back to visit." With the phone still ringing, she set her shoulders in simple dignity and left the room to answer it.

Kyle and Hallie watched her go, then they looked at each other.

"I'd have never believed it," Kyle said quietly.

Hallie could only squeeze his hand again, her throat too tight for words.

TIMOTHY CAME HOME from the hospital the next morning, which was undoubtedly a relief to the hospital staff. He and Florence caught a ride with Walker, who was only too happy to provide transportation, while Hallie, Kyle and Sharon prepared to leave for the airport.

Kyle packed their suitcases in the rental car, so that once Timothy was home, their leave-taking would be less traumatic.

Walker's pickup rolled into the driveway and stopped. Sharon, at the front window, described what was happening.

"Granddad's getting out...so's Walker and Gran...Granddad's reaching for the suitcase Gran took to him yesterday...Gran's trying to stop him... Granddad doesn't like it...Gran's fussing at him... Granddad's starting to get mad...oops! Walker's coming around...he's taking the suitcase from Granddad...Granddad's sputtering, but Walker isn't listening...now they're coming toward the house..."

The front door swung open. "I can dang well carry what I want! I haven't had a blasted operation! There's not a thing wrong with my back or any other part of me, so the doctor and his fancy tests say!" Timothy protested all the way inside.

Sharon grinned and hurried toward them. Hallie and Kyle followed more slowly. The girl ran over and hugged her grandfather's neck, kissing him on his leathery cheek.

"Welcome home, Granddad!" she said brightly.

Timothy, still disgruntled, patted her on the shoulder. "I wasn't sure you'd still be here," he grumbled.

"She wouldn't leave without saying goodbye," Florence said.

"No... well..." He spied Hallie and Kyle and his expression soured even more.

Walker interrupted any remark he might have been about to make by saying, "Now that you're home, I have to get going. My boy called last night and said he was going to stop off for a quick visit on his way to Dallas for some kind of engineering conference. He might even be there already."

"Walker," Florence admonished, "you should have told us!"

Walker's craggy face broke into a smile. "It was worth it watching Timothy try to collect all his goodies. His box of Kleenex, his plastic water pitcher—"

"I paid for it!" Timothy exclaimed.

Walker shook his head, still smiling. "I suppose you did, one way or another." He came over to shake Kyle's hand and hug Hallie. "Glad I got the chance to say goodbye properly this time," he said, his gaze noting their resumed closeness. And exclusively to Hallie, he said, "Don't get caught out in any more rainstorms."

She smiled in return. "The clouds have almost entirely disappeared."

"And the bridge ahead is in fine repair."

"Looks like it," she said, her grin widening.

"Have I missed something?" Kyle asked, a puzzled frown on his face.

Hallie giggled and Walker thumped him on the shoulder. "Not so's you'd need to worry about." He leaned closer so that only Hallie and Kyle could hear, "You've got yourself a mighty fine wife here, son. You take care to treat her right."

"I will," Kyle said, still frowning slightly.

"You, too," Walker said, wagging a finger at Hallie.

Hallie thought of Walker's missing wife and the unknown story of his marriage. Maybe one day she'd ask Florence about it. "I promise," she said solemnly, and hugged the big man once again. Then she slipped back into place at Kyle's side. There was no worry that she would ever leave *him*.

Walker had a few words with Sharon and then, with a brief wave, got back into his pickup and drove off.

Timothy set his shoulders. "A lot of mumbo jumbo," he grumbled. "Walker better be careful or he's going to get a trip to the funny farm, instead of the old folks' home."

"Seniors' center," Florence corrected.

"That's old folks, isn't it?" he retorted.

"Come sit down, Timothy," Florence urged him.

"I don't want to sit down. I've got stock to take care of."

"Kyle's been doing it for you. I told you that."

"All the more reason to check on them," he complained.

"You're supposed to rest," Florence reminded him.

Timothy waved her words away.

"We'll be going soon, Granddad," Sharon said.

He paused, looked at her, then looked at Kyle and Hallie. It was obvious that Florence had filled him in on what had happened after his collapse. It was also obvious that he wasn't mollified by Kyle's claim of innocence. But if nothing else, he now seemed to realize that his continued opposition could have no positive effect. He took his granddaughter by the shoulders, gave her a tiny shake, pulled her close for a gruff hug and a quick "You take care of yourself, little girl," then he released her and stomped outside. A measure of how disconcerted he was, was his use of the front door. In the week Hallie had been at the farm, she'd never once seen him use anything other than the kitchen door.

Kyle nudged Hallie forward. "We should go," he said quietly.

Florence seemed about to protest, but she acceded to the wisdom of a swift, clean break. She extended her arms to Sharon and the girl hurried into them. Florence held her tightly, then let her go.

"I didn't do this for your mother," she said. "Maybe I should have."

Sharon looked at her with tears brimming on her dark lashes. "I'll call, Gran. I promise."

Her grandmother patted her cheek, tears collecting in her own eyes. She seemed incapable of further speech.

After Sharon broke away and tore out the door, Hallie moved closer to the older woman. "It's all going to work out, Florence. I feel it—in here." She patted her chest.

"I hope so," Florence whispered hoarsely.

Kyle put an arm around Hallie's shoulders and drew her away.

Just as he had when they'd arrived here, Kyle walked along the path with confidence and purpose. He saw Hallie into the car before coming to claim his own place behind the steering wheel.

Muffled sniffs came from the back seat. "I didn't know it was going to be this hard," Sharon said.

Hallie could have easily echoed that sentiment. A little over a week ago she'd sat in this car with Kyle, unsuspecting of the breadth of the ordeal that lay ahead of her. The hatred, the reflected animosity, the jealousy, the suspicion, the fear, the heartache. But as with all tests of will and endurance, once survived, the combatant is the stronger for having gone through it. That was the way she felt today—stronger, and filled with far greater confidence than she'd ever had.

She reached over to cover Kyle's hand as it rested on the gearshift knob. He'd started the car, but had paused before backing out the driveway. Was he thinking along the same lines as her?

They had been through so much together this week. Not only had she endured, but so had their marriage. She knew things about Kyle now that she might never have known otherwise. And she loved him all the more.

She met his gaze—his pale green gaze—and again responded to his magnetism.

Kyle lifted his hand, bringing hers with it, until her fingers were a hair's breadth from his lips. "Have I ever told you how much I love you, Mrs. McKenna?" he murmured huskily.

"Once or twice," she said softly in return.

"Remind me to tell you on a regular basis," he ordered.

"I will," Hallie swore.

Kyle pulled his gaze from her to look at his daughter in the back seat. "Are you ready?" he said bracingly.

Sharon took a deep breath, rubbed the tears off her cheeks, and nodded vigorously.

"All right, then," Kyle said, turning back around. "Let's go!"

With that, the car moved out the drive and down the road, leaving the farmhouse and the couple who lived there to themselves.

EPILOGUE

THE TELEPHONE RANG just as Timothy came inside from doing his chores. Florence, concerned for the safety of the meal she was cooking, adjusted the burners before hurrying to answer it.

Timothy peeked under each pot lid, then helped himself to a cup of coffee, which he took to the table and started to sip.

Florence was gone for quite some time, causing Timothy to wonder if he should do something with the pots. But just as he'd gotten up, Florence came bustling back into the room, emitting little squeaks about burning dinner.

Timothy resettled himself at the table. "Who was that?" he asked.

Pot lids were discarded, spoon handles flew. "Hallie," she said.

Timothy's lips tightened. True to her promise to Florence, the woman had kept in frequent touch. "How's Sharon?" he asked.

"Just fine, Hallie says. She's off on a school trip to hear a symphony orchestra."

Timothy snorted. "Music!"

"It'll be good for her."

Timothy shook his head. In his day, school was school, not play.

"There's some more news," Florence said. "That's why Hallie didn't put off calling until Sharon could talk to us, too."

Timothy waited.

"She's going to have a baby!" Florence cried, turning away from her pots.

"Sharon?" Timothy bellowed.

"No! *Hallie!* Honestly, Timothy. Sometimes I wonder about you."

He blustered around a bit, embarrassed. "Well, it sounded like... It wasn't very clear."

Florence folded her arms over her ample bosom and shook her head. "It's been a year, Timothy. When are you going to admit that Sharon is happy? Isn't that what you want—for her to be happy?"

Timothy blustered some more.

"You know it is," Florence continued when he didn't form a coherent answer. "And she is! We can't ask for anything more than that. And Hallie and Kyle have brought her back three times, not to mention her month's visit with us in the summer. They're doing everything they can!"

"He's certainly won you over!" Timothy complained harshly.

"Hallie's won me over. He's, well, maybe we judged him too quickly, Timothy. I'm not saying he's a saint or anything. He probably wouldn't like it if I did, but he's not as bad as we thought, either. You called that doctor in San Antonio he told us about. You even went down and looked at the records at the hospital where Kyle's hand was operated on, and at the hotel where he said he broke the window. Everything was true. Maybe it *was* an accident. Maybe Cynthia *was* driving and missed the turn.''

"As I said, he's won you over.''

"Oh, Timothy…'' she moaned, and he could see she was crying.

He fiddled with his cup, tried to look anywhere but at her, then at last he got up and put an unpracticed arm around her shoulders to offer comfort.

"It's not that bad,'' he murmured awkwardly.

"But it *is!* You just won't—'' She bit her bottom lip.

"When's this baby due?'' he asked gruffly.

"Next fall. In September, I think she said.''

A moment passed. "Maybe we should have them here for Christmas.''

"Oh, Timothy,'' Florence cried softly, and she looked at him with happy tears in her eyes.

Surprising even himself, he leaned forward and kissed her cheek.

Shocked, Florence stared at him.

He performed the act again and began to enjoy the feeling it gave him. It was the first time in recent memory he had rendered her speechless.

"What would you say if I was to ask you out for an ice-cream dessert this evening?'' he proposed, a slow grin creasing his leathery cheeks.

Florence blinked. "What's happened to you?" she whispered.

"Does something have to be wrong for a fella to start feeling frisky?"

"Second childhood!" Florence murmured her thoughts out loud.

"Well?" he demanded. "What about that ice cream?"

"After we eat?"

"Of course after we eat!"

Florence shook her head in disbelief, then she started to nod energetically.

She was shocked even more when, after the meal, Timothy thanked her for the great dinner and helped her clear the table.

HARLEQUIN SUPERROMANCE®

WOMEN WHO DARE
They take chances, make changes
and follow their hearts!

Dangerous to Love
by Carol Duncan Perry

Vicki Winslow refuses to do the sensible thing—enter the
witness protection program. She's done nothing wrong and
she isn't going to cut herself off from her family. So now she's
hiding out, protected only by secrecy and her own wits—if
you don't count her eighty-seven-year-old great-aunt, her
poetry-quoting cousin, two large dogs, one rifle and a pet
skunk named Sweetpea.

Caine Alexander aims to change this situation. Not that
Caine's any knight in shining armor. *Hell, no.* A man could get
killed playing hero. Still, he's promised to protect Vicki, and if
any man can make good on such a promise, Caine's the man.
Too bad Vicki doesn't want his protection.... Because she's
stuck with it.

**Watch for *Dangerous to Love*
by Carol Duncan Perry.**

**Available in July 1995 wherever
Harlequin books are sold.**

Take 4 bestselling love stories FREE

Plus get a FREE surprise gift!

Special Limited-time Offer

Mail to Harlequin Reader Service®

3010 Walden Avenue
P.O. Box 1867
Buffalo, N.Y. 14269-1867

YES! Please send me 4 free Harlequin Superromance® novels and my fre
surprise gift. Then send me 4 brand-new novels every month, which I w
receive before they appear in bookstores. Bill me at the low price of $2.8
each plus 25¢ delivery and applicable sales tax, if any.* That's the comple
price and a savings of over 10% off the cover prices—quite a bargain!
understand that accepting the books and gift places me under no obligatic
ever to buy any books. I can always return a shipment and cancel at any tim
Even if I never buy another book from Harlequin, the 4 free books and th
surprise gift are mine to keep forever.

134 BPA ANR.

Name	(PLEASE PRINT)	
Address	Apt. No.	
City	State	Zip

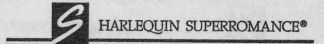

presents

Big Luke, Little Luke
by Dawn Stewardson

This July, meet the third of our Four Strong Men:

Mike Alexander was the best friend Navy pilot Luke Dakota ever had. So when Luke received a letter from Mike's wife, Caitlyn, he wasn't too concerned—until he opened it. In the letter, Caitlyn told him about Mike's death and the birth of their son, Luke. His namesake.

Drawn by a sense of responsibility to Mike, Luke arranged for a leave of absence and set off for Arizona.

Once there, his life was sent into a tailspin. He learned that Caitlyn's business was in the red, military intelligence wouldn't leave her alone and, worst of all, she was convinced that Mike's death was the result of foul play. Luke became determined to help Caitlyn fight her unseen enemies. But he soon found himself up against an enemy he couldn't conquer—himself. Because Luke Dakota was falling in love with his best friend's wife....

**Look for *Big Luke, Little Luke* in July 1995
wherever Harlequin books are sold.**

4SM-3

HARLEQUIN SUPERROMANCE®

A KISS TOO LATE
by
Ellen James

It *must* be a bad dream—but it isn't. There actually *is* a naked man sleeping in Jen Hillard's bed. Worse, it's her ex-husband. Sexy, handsome, exciting—Adam Prescott's always been able to sweep her into bed. He's just never cared enough to sweep her into his heart.

But now Jen's finally found the nerve to make a new life for herself, so how could she have let this happen? Silly question. Well, okay, so what if she's done the one thing she'd sworn she'd never do—let Adam Prescott back into her bed? She'll be damned if she'll let him back into her life. And her heart? Well, that's another matter. He's always been there.

REUNITED!
First Love...Last Love

Available in July wherever Harlequin books are sold.

REUNIT3